THE WOUNDS OF WAR

A Sequel to *Journey to Gettysburg*

Mark L. Hopkins

MARK L. HOPKINS

Copyright © 2016 Mark L. Hopkins
All rights reserved
First Edition

PAGE PUBLISHING, INC.
New York, NY

First originally published by Page Publishing, Inc. 2016

ISBN 978-1-68409-527-8 (Paperback)
ISBN 978-1-68409-528-5 (Digital)

Printed in the United States of America

CONTENTS

Prologue 7
The Wedding..11
Sharing Their Stories 21
The Farm..36
Keeping the Wolf and the Yankees from the Door 46
Gathering at the Friends Meeting House.......................55
Aunt Elizabeth 63
Putting the Community Plan to Work 72
Selling Wine in West Virginia 78
Challenges Mounting Up 90
Help from Unexpected Places...99
Daily Work on the Schendler Farm 105
The White Knights of the Camelia 108
Standing Up for the Right 116
Evil in All of Its Forms 125
An Eye for an Eye...133
Finally, Some Good News 142
Planning for a Brighter Tomorrow................................151
Family Council..159
The One Constant in Life Is Change............................163
To Politic or Not, That Is the Question 172

Resolving the Election Issue 177
A Surprise Visitor from the Deep, Dark Past 187
Making a Momentous Decision 198
Accepting the Challenge..204
The Election and Beyond 213
On to Richmond...216
The Court of Appeals Building..224
Thoughts of Home 228
Aftermath of the Tragedy..236
Author's Notes: The History Behind *The Wounds Of War*.............243
Afterword..251
About the Author 252

PREFACE

The Wounds of War began as a short follow-up story to the novel *Journey to Gettysburg*. Then it grew into a full-fledged novel standing on its own. When I did the research on *Journey*, it took me to Winchester, Virginia, and into the Quaker community just north of that small city at the northern edge of the Shenandoah Valley. It became obvious that those conservative Christian people were targets during the Civil War and mistreated following the war. They did not participate in the fighting, but instead offered their Hopewell Meeting House for a hospital and their family members as nurses and caregivers for Union and Confederate soldiers alike. Still, at the end of the war, they faced taxes ten times what had been usual before the war and the "carpetbaggers"—northerners who saw an opportunity to get rich on the misery of the defeated South—came in droves to take their farms if they couldn't pay the taxes. The question in my mind throughout the research period was, "How did they survive in the face of such overwhelming odds?" The answer to that question is found in the pages of this book.

The main characters in *Wounds of War* are the same as in *Journey*, with young Matthew Mason, the beautiful Ami Ruth, Matthew's father, Isaac, and Ami Ruth's Aunt Elizabeth playing the main roles. The setting is different in that the Civil War is over and the Reconstruction period is running full force with its heavy taxes, adjustment to the new social order now that the slaves are free, and the Ku Klux Klan attempting to intrude in every phase of life. In the midst of this comes John Murray Mason, scion of Virginia's celebrated Mason family, father to Isaac and grandfather to Matthew. What follows is a page from the history of old Virginia: fiction, yes, but based on the actual history of what happened to the people of the South and, specifically, those of Northern Virginia during those tumultuous years following the war.

A number of people have helped me write this book. These include my wife, Ruth, always a first editor in my writing, who encouraged me to stay with it until the story came alive. Editor and writing consultant Kathryn Smith cleaned up my writing style and played the role of muse. (This, while she was writing her own best-selling nonfiction book.) Each time I seemed to get bogged down, she had a question or a comment that created the needed motivation. Kathryn continually challenged me to be more descriptive and to paint pictures with words so the reader could not only see what was on the page but could also envision what was in my mind. Of major importance was the staff at the Handley Library in Winchester, Virginia, and, most specifically, Ms. Becky Ebert, a Quaker lady herself, who heads up the Archives section of the library.

I would be the first to acknowledge that Matthew Mason and his family are not real people. They are figments of my imagination. However, they are very much alive in my mind, and like good friends they continued to talk to me and suggest the twists and turns of their story in such a way that they make the typed page come alive with their thoughts, their problems, and their dedication to each other. As a treasured grandmother used to say, "That's what families do."

PROLOGUE

It was the dead of night when Matt heard a commotion up the lane by road. His wife, Ami Ruth, was already standing by the window of their bedroom. Just as he joined her, a burning cross illuminated the night. As the fire rushed up the shaft of the cross and onto the cross pieces, gun shots rang out. Matt ran back around the bed and began pulling on his pants. The gun shots outside continued and they were getting closer.

By the time Matt and Ami Ruth were down the stairs and at the front door, two-dozen horsemen had crowded into the yard. Their white costumes, complete with cut-outs for eyes, made them look like ghosts. Several of them carried torches and the terrifying thought seared through Matt's mind that they had come to burn the house.

One of the men called his name. "Matt Mason, we want you out here!"

Ami Ruth clutched his arm, her fingers digging deep to keep him beside her. "Matt, don't you dare go out there."

The voice from outside came again: "Mason, if you don't come out we are going to come in and get you. We are going to have a meeting, you and us."

Matt leaned over and kissed Ami Ruth lightly on the cheek. "I will be all right. You stay right here but be ready to get out the back door if things gets out of hand."

He stepped out on the porch. "There you are, Mr. Matt Mason. I'm sure you have heard of us. We are the White Knights of the Camellia and we protect the rights and property of white Virginians. We have heard who you have working on your farm."

"Rumor has it that you are paying them like white men." This came from another voice somewhere back in the throng of horsemen.

The first voice came back even louder, "What do you have to say for yourself?"

The image of Mr. Schendler, Ami Ruth's father, flashed into his mind. He had lost his life here on this very spot when he came out to talk with some Yankee renegades shortly after the Battle of Gettysburg. Matt had survived Gettysburg himself and he was determine that now that the war was over no one was going to take his new life away.

Matt walked down the steps and faced them there in the front yard. He refused to be intimidated by these night riders who paraded into his front yard carrying guns and torches.

Matt thought of trying to explain to the men why he had brought freed slaves to work during the harvest, but he quickly discarded that idea. He knew these men were in no mood to listen. Standing there in the silence, Matt felt very alone and vulnerable. Then he felt the presence of his Pa as he came around the corner of the porch. When he glanced over his shoulder, he saw the Henry 60 Repeating Rifle in his father's big hands and heard the rifle being cocked. Immediately there was a response from the men on horseback. Rifles were lifted and pointed at Isaac Mason.

Matt's Pa took dead aim at the leader of the group. He said, "I think this has gone far enough. My name is Isaac Mason. Matt is my son. He and I were both in Pickett's Charge at Gettysburg while most of you men were home tending your farms. We have seen guns fired in anger and the result isn't pretty."

The white-draped leader responded, "Easy now, Mr. Mason. We have you out-gunned here, twenty to one. If you push this someone is going to wind up dead."

"You are right about that," Isaac said. "I should have been dead two years ago. No one I know in my division is still alive. You do have me outgunned, that's for sure. But my gun is aimed directly at you. If any shots are fired, you can be sure my first bullet is going to bury you."

None of the White Knights replied, and the leader's horse pawed the ground nervously, as if his owner had conveyed his uneasiness.

Isaac's deep voice grew louder and he spoke with authority. "These folks are Quakers. They don't believe in violence. However, I am not a Quaker. Neither are the men we have working in the winery. If you listen closely, you will hear them coming up the lane now. Very shortly the twenty-to-one advantage you think you have will become much more even. Several of our men served in the Army of Northern Virginia and they know what to do with a rifle."

Matt heard a murmur from the group of horsemen and felt the same murmur in his mind and heart. After Gettysburg, Matt had hoped to never again be in a situation where men were dying all around him. Now, here in the heart of Shenandoah farm country, he found himself once again facing impossible odds. The wrong word could lead to a blood bath. The question haunted his mind, *Am I destined to always be in a life or death struggle?*

THE WEDDING

The bell in the Schendler Farm barn was ringing loudly on a beautiful hot day in mid-August 1865. The sky was blue, the trees in full leaf, and the front yard of the big white house was full of smiling friends. Even so, Matt Mason remembered having some of the same butterfly-in-the-stomach feelings he had two years before when he was standing in line with Trimble's Brigade at Gettysburg, looking across the open field at the blue-coated army on Cemetery Ridge. But this time it wasn't fear and anxiety that dominated his mind—it was anticipation.

Today he was standing on the porch of his adopted home just north of Winchester in Northern Virginia, looking out at all of their friends, his and Ami Ruth's. They were gathered on the lawn to help celebrate their wedding. The bell, their alarm system in troubled times, was announcing to the world that it was their wedding day.

Matt had first come to the farm in 1863, a shoeless, homeless boy following the trail of the Army of Northern Virginia. Now two years later, he had just passed his eighteenth birthday. Most who had known Matt when he was a boy said he was the image of his mother. But his hair, almost blond at birth, was now a dark brown. His body was hardened by his daily regimen on the farm, and he was a full six foot three inches tall, almost as tall as he remembered his father being when he had last seen him on the battlefield at Gettysburg. Standing on the porch above the others and next to David, Ami Ruth's older brother who was a head shorter, he was, indeed, a formidable young man.

It was David who had proposed the plan that had led to this day. He had arrived home just after the Schendler parents had died in a violent confrontation with renegade Union deserters who had come to raid the farm. It was David who decided their waiting for marriage was a good idea and that Aunt Elizabeth, the sister of Ami Ruth's mother, was the best person to come and live in the big house with Ami Ruth until both of the young people were older. Matt had been staying in a makeshift room in the barn and all his things were still there. His eighteenth birthday had seemed way too long to wait back then, but now it was all coming together, the plan, the marriage, Matt, and his beautiful bride-to-be.

All the preliminaries had been observed. Both Matt and Ami Ruth had presented their intent to be married at the Society of Friends Meeting House—he to the men's group and she to the women's. They had been questioned, examined, and pronounced ready for marriage.

Most of the men who had weighed in on his readiness for marriage were standing under the big oaks and the women who had examined Ami Ruth were sitting on quilts in the shade on this summer afternoon. Many had come earlier bringing their covered dishes to add to the wedding feast that was planned for the backyard. Matt could see the kids playing tag off in the distance, and Big Billy, his bay horse, grazing in the field up by the road.

As he waited for the wedding to begin, Matt looked beyond the people to the lane that ran up to the road. He remembered looking up that same lane two years ago when the Union deserters were coming toward him with their guns blazing, and he had nothing for protection but some bales of hay and his Henry 60 Repeating Rifle. That was the day he met all of these neighbors. Ami Ruth had run to the barn back then and rung the bell, which was the signal that they needed help. The neighbors had come to their aid by the dozens in wagons and on horseback, some running, but all carrying pitchforks, shovels, hoes, anything to use as a weapon. He knew when he saw them that these Quaker people would never use the weapons, but they served well as intimidators since the deserters didn't *know* they wouldn't use them.

Their nonviolent approach to life seemed strange to him at the time, but over the past two years, he had come to know them and to respect their ways. The Schendlers were Quakers and Ami Ruth was adamant in her parents' faith. Matt was raised by a Quaker mother and a non-Quaker, or English, father. He always felt as if he had one foot in the Quaker world and the other in the "real" world. Still, he loved Ami Ruth and had adjusted to their living pattern during the time he had lived on the farm. Each Sunday he would hitch up the buggy, slip on his black jacket and straight brim hat, and drive Ami Ruth and her Aunt Elizabeth, who lived with them, to the Society of Friends services over at the Hopewell Meeting House just a couple of miles down the road.

Matt's eyes roved over the yard full of friends and neighbors and fell on Mr. Joshua Ridgeway. He had become both a friend and mentor over the past two years. He had advised Matt on several issues related to the farm and then served as the convener when the men's group gathered to evaluate his readiness to marry Ami Ruth. He was a man who had a constant smile on his face, totally at home with himself, his family, and the relationship he had with his God.

All that had brought Matt and Ami Ruth together began when he happened onto the Schendler Farm in a heavy rainstorm in the summer of 1863. He was on a trek through Virginia looking for his Pa, who was fighting with the Army of Northern Virginia. As his mother lay dying a few weeks before, he had promised he would find Pa and tell him about her and what had happened at their little farm near Mt. Airy in North Carolina. When he finally found his Pa, the army had been headed for Gettysburg and that fateful battle that became the turning point in the war between the North and the South.

Over and over he had heard the war described as the Civil War, but Southerners saw that conflict very differently from their neighbors in the North. Every battle Matt knew of occurred on Southern soil except the one at Gettysburg. Several hundred battles in the South and one in the North. When Southerners called it the War of Northern Aggression, they had good reason.

Much had happened in the more than two years since he had returned to the Schendler Farm after surviving Gettysburg. The war had dragged on for another two years. It had been over now for four months, but everything remained unsettled for the Quaker farmers of this rural area of Virginia. Their government was gone, replaced by a military administrator and a long list of new rules and regulations that still made little sense to the local population. Homes and land had been ravaged by repeated battles.

What was not unsettled was his love for the beautiful Ami Ruth and his personal commitment to the Schendler family. This day, August 15, 1865, was a new beginning for Matt Mason, Ami Ruth, and the Schendler Farm. There was a time when he was sure this day would never come, when two years seemed an eternity.

Suddenly, the bell stopped ringing and silence fell over the yard. Matt's mind was jolted back to the present. Then David Schendler began to speak. He was a Quaker clergyman trained in the seminary in Philadelphia, and he was using the formal words that opened a Quaker wedding. Matt tried to listen, but his mind was too full of memories and of anticipation. He knew Ami Ruth would be coming down the pathway to join him very soon, and his eyes kept moving over the people on the grounds that had come to help them celebrate their wedding.

David opened his remarks by welcoming the people and reporting that he had assurance from the men's and women's groups of the Meeting House that Matt and Ami Ruth had been cleared for marriage. David's words continued, but Matt had stopped hearing them almost immediately, as he saw movement off to the right. Ami Ruth and her best friend, Mary Ann, were walking along the tree line out toward the fence. Ami Ruth was wearing her best dress, pastel blue with light-colored flowers, and she had fresh flowers in her blond hair. He had never seen her look so lovely, and a lump formed in his throat. His eyes followed their progress. Soon they were at the gate by the lane, standing behind all the guests.

"Friends," David said, "we hope you don't mind, but we have deviated a bit from our usual wedding structure. I have been in the North for several years, and they have some practices that are different from ours. One of those is the introduction of music into the proceedings. Another is the introduction of the bride into the ceremony at just this time."

David's voice stopped and Matt heard music coming from the little group that had come together for this occasion, the same group that played for the Saturday night socials that were held at one farm or another in their Quaker community. Dancing was not a part of their custom, but music to accompany a shared meal was certainly something that occurred on special occasions. At first the sound was soft, but it gained strength and then Ami Ruth and Mary Ann were walking down through the people and everyone was standing.

Ami Ruth had the look of her Dutch ancestors—tall and blond with deep blue eyes. Her hair usually hung in a braid down her back, but today it was rolled up behind her head in what some called a French roll. Her face was angular with high cheek bones and an expressive mouth that usually spoke softly but, from time to time, made her perspective known in no uncertain terms.

Matt had a flash in his mind, *Was anything ever so beautiful?* He could see her face clearly, but her beautiful blue eyes were lowered, looking at the ground. He knew her so well. He knew she was thinking, *Everyone is looking, I can't risk stumbling.*

Suddenly the tension was back. Oh my, the butterflies in his stomach. The overwhelming anticipation of something wonderful happening. In a few minutes, his life would be complete, his future would be secure, and he could be certain not only of where he would spend the rest of his life but with whom he would spend it. His Ma's face flashed into his mind and he heard her voice saying, *My cup runneth over.*

As Ami Ruth walked toward them, the music faltered, and just as she reached the steps of the porch, the little orchestra went silent. Something was happening at the back of the gathering. Several men were stepping out from under the trees and were approaching the gate to the lane. Matt could see that they were gathering around someone who had entered through the gate.

Matt caught only a glimpse of the face of the tall male figure, but he immediately knew who it was: Isaac Mason had just come through the gate! Matt's father, who had fought at Gettysburg and been captured and interned in a Yankee prison camp, had just come through the back gate. Before he had another conscious thought,

Matt was off the porch and running through the crowd of guests. He heard his own voice yelling, "Pa, Pa!" as if it was coming from outside of him. He saw his Pa turn toward the sound, and he was wearing that unmistakable smile that Matt's mother had talked about so often.

Isaac Mason was a big man, more than six-foot-five-inches tall, and with thick muscles around his shoulders and neck. Standing to his full height in the group of men by the fence, he was head and shoulders above the rest. As Matt approached his father, he noted that his Pa now had some streaks of grey in his dark hair and his weight had slipped significantly from the 260 pounds he had carried before the war. He was wearing his grey army pants and a pullover shirt, and he looked almost haggard with a full beard and hair flowing down his back.

Everyone could see the big man and knew by Matt's yelling that it was his Pa, the man he had been looking for when he first came to the Schendler Farm, the man who had spent the last two years enduring hardships they could never imagine.

At the end of the war, Matt had placed many advertisements in newspapers across the South, and into Pennsylvania and Maryland, looking for his father. Then just three weeks ago, he had received a letter. It was the first time he knew that his Pa was alive and that he was coming. Now he was here, right at this climatic moment, in the midst of his wedding. His father grabbed him in a full bear hug and lifted him off of his feet.

The smiles of the guests turned into laughter and everyone began to cheer and applaud. It was clear they were witnessing something momentous. It was like the story of the prodigal son in the Bible, only it was the father who had come home to the son and not the other way around.

Matt looked back to the porch, wanting to share his happiness with Ami Ruth, and immediately realized that the wedding had stopped right at the crucial point. Ami Ruth, Mary Ann, and David were waiting for him to resume the ceremony.

Matt and Isaac walked together, arm in arm, back through the people to the porch. Ami Ruth came down the steps and gave her hands to the man who would soon be her father-in-law. She stepped back and said, "We were worried you wouldn't make the wedding but here you are! You have made this day complete."

Matt leaned over to his Pa and said softly, "Would you join us on the porch, Pa?"

In a few seconds, five people were standing on the porch, only this time it was Mary Ann and Ami Ruth on David's left and Matt and Isaac on his right. David resumed his role as the master of ceremonies. He asked for anyone in the group who wanted to speak to please do so now. Almost immediately, Sister Ella Ridgeway, Joshua Ridgeway's wife, stood up. She had served as chairman of the women's group at the Meeting House and began to report on their examination of Ami Ruth. She was a short lady, thick by any standards, and she wore a simple grey dress with a white apron around her considerable waist.

Mrs. Ridgeway's voice was soft as she addressed the group but she spoke with authority. "I have served as the convener of the women's group several times over the years, and we have questioned many young ladies who desired to be married. It is our conclusion that Ami Ruth is very much ready to take on the duties and responsibilities of being a good wife to this young man. Her mother was getting her ready for such responsibility when she died, and her Aunt Elizabeth has done very well at completing the job. I know of no reason why she should not be cleared for marriage in the best tradition of the Society of Friends."

When Sister Ella sat down, her husband, Joshua, stood up. He was a man older than Matt's father but, despite their difference in age, had become Matt's close friend. He had been the convener of the men's group.

Joshua had an unusually deep voice, and it was firm and loud enough for the group to hear without straining. He said, "We have all come to know Matt Mason over the past two years. We came to his aid when he was standing alone to protect the Schendler Farm from the renegades. We welcomed him into our number at the Meeting House Sunday after Sunday over the past two years. We know him to be an honorable man, responsible, and capable of taking care of Ami

Ruth and a family. Our men's group cleared him for marriage with no reservation."

Several others rose to say warm words about the couple, but Matt was no longer listening. He knew he was going to say his vows when the group grew silent. He had never been good at memorizing, but he found himself saying the vows over and over in his mind, hoping not to make an embarrassing mistake, hoping to make this wedding all that Ami Ruth wanted it to be.

Matt was on his third time through the vows when David nodded at him that now was the time. He and Ami Ruth stood and he took her hands and looked into her blue eyes and smiled. Matt swallowed hard a couple of times, then he repeated the vows, letter perfect just as he had memorized them, just as Ami Ruth had written them for him.

"In the presence of God and these friends, I take thee, Ami Ruth, to be my wife, promising with Divine assistance to be unto thee a loving and faithful husband so long as we both shall live."

When he finished, he took a deep, deep breath and then listened as Ami Ruth repeated her vows. Then it was over. The hard part was over.

Isaac leaned forward and whispered into Matt's ear, "Son, do you have a ring?" Matt leaned over to whisper in his Pa's ear. "Quakers don't use rings, Pa." Brother David heard Matt's whisper and smiled at the two of them. Pa's face had just a momentary shadow of doubt, but his big smile came back quickly. When he married Matt's Ma, they couldn't afford rings, so the subject never came up. He wondered why in later years when he offered to buy her a ring that she always found other things they needed more.

Finally came the words Matt was waiting for. The young pastor looked back out to the group and said in a firm voice, loud enough for the entire company to hear, "A marriage only needs God to sanctify it. It does not need one to intercede in the process, so the role I am playing is only that of a convener. These young people, Ami Ruth and Matt, are now husband and wife. We have prepared the wedding certificate here on a table in front of the porch. It is our intent that each of you will sign it as witnesses of this marriage today."

There was a slight rustle of approval from the crowd. David stepped to the edge of the porch, smiling broadly. "Now, friends and neighbors, may I be the first to introduce you to Mr. and Mrs. Matthew Mason!"

Suddenly, there seemed to be total noisy confusion. The small music group began to play, the people were applauding and yelling, and the bell in the barn began to ring. Matt took Ami Ruth's hand, and they walked down the steps and into the throng of guests and everyone crowded around. Matt had his hand pumped by nearly everyone there, and Ami Ruth must have been kissed by all the women and at least half of the men. It seems that Quaker people were reluctant to show any physical interaction between men and women except in exceptional circumstances. Weddings fit into the exceptional category.

David's strong voice announced that the food was ready in the backyard. The noise continued as the line grew at the signing table. As each guest signed the certificate, they moved around the side of the house toward the tables lined with food.

Isaac Mason was still on the porch with David when Matt finished accepting congratulations. Father and son were wrapped in a bear hug again when Ami Ruth walked up.

"Pa," Matt said, "we thought about postponing the wedding when I heard from you but decided we didn't really know when you would make it all the way here from Mt. Airy. That is a pretty hard three-to-four week walk. We had already planned the wedding and we decided to go ahead with it as scheduled."

Ami Ruth nodded vigorously. "We believe that God decides all the important things that happen to us and your being here in time for the wedding just shows how He loves us. Your coming wasn't by chance. He wanted you to be here with us."

Isaac was struck by the soft-spoken young woman his son had just married. She seemed much older than her eighteen years, and he marveled at her beauty. He said, "Son, you have guests. You should go take care of them. Is there a place I can go to clean myself up at bit? We will talk later after everyone has gone."

"Yes, Pa, there is a sink on the back porch," Matt responded. "Take your time and come join us when you are ready."

Matt was reluctant to leave his Pa, whose dark eyes were filling with tears. He knew his Pa was thinking about his own wedding, his wife, and the life they had shared on the little farm in North Carolina. Matt knew what he was thinking because his mind was there too. Isaac Mason sat down on a rocking chair on the porch and closed his eyes.

Matt took Ami Ruth's hand and they followed the guests around the house to the feast that had been prepared for them. Some of the group Matt didn't know except by sight but most he had come to know well over the past two years from seeing them at the Meeting House. Virtually all came to help when the renegades attacked two years ago, and Matt felt a rush of warmth as he looked at their friendly faces. He had been a stranger when he first came, but today he felt like he was home. These were his friends, his people.

SHARING THEIR STORIES

～⁕～

The warmth of the gestures and voices of the people gathered around the tables in the backyard showed they were sharing much more than just a meal together. Their mutual regard and love for each other was obvious. On top of that, the food was overwhelming, as all the ladies had made a contribution in addition to what came out of the Schendler kitchen. There were meats of all kinds including pulled pork, beef steak, and strips of bacon. The homemade breads exuded an aroma that hung just above the tables, and the desserts—pies, cakes, and cookies—covered one complete table at the end of the buffet line. Several times mothers had to shoo children away from the dessert table when they were attempting to start their dinner at the wrong end of the feast.

How could such opulence be present in such a time of uncertainty? Despite the problems in the outside world, here in this group of Quaker friends and neighbors, the desire to share with each other and to be a part of every other family's life was dominant.

As the group filled their plates and began to eat, the musicians continued to play popular tunes of the time. At one point, Matt could hear a muted voice singing a tune that was known as "Bright Mohawk Valley":

> From this Valley they say you are going
> I shall miss your bright eyes and sweet smile
> for you take with you all of the sunshine
> that has brightened our pathway a while.

Come and sit by my side if you love me
Do not hasten to bid me adieu;
just remember the Bright Mohawk Valley
and the farm boy that loved you so true.

From time to time, the musicians took a brief break and filled their plates at the tables, but soon they were back to their instruments and playing again.

This was what Ami Ruth liked to call Schendler Farm hospitality. The guests lingered into the late afternoon before, one by one, the families made their way to their wagons and horses and headed up the lane to the road.

Isaac Mason approached Matt after both had helped clean up the tables in the backyard and the last of the guests had slipped away. "Son, let's go talk," he said. They rounded the house and settled into the rocking chairs on the front porch. In the dusk of the evening with the breezes beginning to move, the air felt much cooler on the skin. Matt heard David's footsteps at the door, but Ami Ruth's tactful brother retreated, deciding that it was best if father and son were left alone to share their thoughts. Matt heard the kitchen noises through the open door and knew that Aunt Elizabeth had taken charge as she always did, and Ami Ruth and Mary Ann were serving as able lieutenants for the necessary chores in the kitchen that followed a large gathering.

After a moment, Isaac spoke quietly. "Son, I have wondered for two years what happened after I left you there on the battlefield at Gettysburg. I didn't know if you survived it or became a resident of one of the mass graves that are a part of the cemetery there. When I read your notice in the Mt. Airy newspaper, I couldn't believe my good fortune. Tell me what happened."

Matt paused before responding, pulling together the memories and images of that terrible day. Finally he said, "I lay there on the ground behind the rock fence where you left me for the longest time, and I must have fallen asleep. A man with a white coat woke me up, standing over me with a lantern. He was looking for any wounded who were still on the battlefield. Before I was fully awake, he had me up and over his shoulder. He carried me across the battlefield and up the ridge to the Seminary building that had been turned into a field hospital. He put me down on a wagon there and left to go back to his search. I wasn't hurt in the battle, though I looked a mess with blood all over me. Mercifully, it was someone else's blood."

Isaac responded, "I remember seeing the blood when I was there with you on the ground. You said you weren't hurt, so I assumed you had picked it up as you marched toward the ridge."

Matt felt the evening breeze just beginning to rustle in the oak trees in the front yard and heard the tree frogs and crickets beginning to make their night noises. Even so, his mind was focused on that tragic time two years ago. He remembered every detail of that day and one of the peculiarities was that there were no sounds of birds or crickets at all in the woods along the ridge where he and several thousand others waited for the beginning of what had come to be called Pickett's Charge. He remembered that every nerve was on edge, as he was sure that any minute he might feel the sting of a musket ball.

Matt continued in a subdued voice, "Everywhere I looked there were dead and dying men. I felt very fortunate not to be one of them, and I knew I didn't belong there in the hospital, so I slipped away. Later, I found a stream where I could clean myself up. I tried to sleep that night but woke up while it was still dark. They had already begun loading the wounded into the wagons for the trip back to Williamsport, so I began checking wagon to wagon to see if you were among the wounded." He turned and searched his father's face. "Pa, it is hard to imagine today, but there were more than seven hundred wagons carrying ten to twelve wounded men in each. I climbed up and down and looked in wagons for most of the day. By then the wagons had begun to move out, and I was afraid I was missing several of them. By nightfall, I realized that I had a better chance of finding you if I came back to Williamsport and checked the wagons when they were getting ready to ford the river."

Isaac said, "The whole time I was in the camp, I tried to find some way to communicate with you, but I didn't know if you had made it. Even if there was a way to communicate I didn't know where you were."

Matt heard a low snort coming from beyond the gate in front of the house. Big Billy had heard their voices and walked up to the fence. He was making sure Matt knew he was there.

"Hold on a minute, Pa," he said, and he disappeared into the house. When he came back, he had an apple in his hand.

"Let's walk out to the fence, Pa. Big Billy is used to my coming out next to the gate with an apple, a carrot, or something for him when we sit on the porch in the evenings," Matt said. While they were walking through the soft grass, Matt continued telling his Pa what had happened following that last battle at Gettysburg.

"It took me two days to get to the river," Matt said, "and I waited another day for the wagons. It was a shock to find out that there were only about 120 wagons left when they finally arrived. The rest had broken down or been destroyed by Yankees as they were passing along their roads. You weren't in any of the ones that made it to Williamsport, so my only hope was that you had been taken prisoner and would appear on the prisoner of war lists. That didn't work either since the prisoner exchanges that had gone on the first two years of the war did not occur during the last two and the North didn't share their list. For all this time, I wasn't sure I would ever see you again."

When they arrived at the front gate, Big Billy was leaning over the fence ready for his treat. Matt held the apple for him on his open palm and the big bay horse took a bite out of it. He paused for just a few seconds and was back for the rest of the apple. When he had eaten it all, Matt reached up and scratched his handsome head between the ears.

"I found Big Billy at Williamsport. They were shooting the horses, Pa, but I was able to get there in time. He had a minié ball in him but a doctor fixed him up. He and I made our way back here where the Schendlers had offered me a place to live until the war was over. Unfortunately, Ami Ruth's parents had died at the hands of a bunch of Union renegades just before I got here, and she was the only one left."

Isaac put his hand up and asked in a shocked voice, "What happened to them, Matt?"

"A group of renegades came to the house looking for food or whatever they could steal." Matt responded. "Mr. Schendler went out on the porch to talk to them and they shot him in cold blood. Later, they killed Mrs. Schendler. Ami Ruth was hiding behind some boxes in the attic and they didn't find her. She was scared they were going to set the house on fire but they didn't."

Pa was surprised to hear him chuckle just a little before he continued. "When I arrived here, she didn't know it was me, and she sprayed the lane with minié balls. I didn't know it at the time, but she can shoot the ears off of a rabbit at a hundred paces! I had to hide in the wheat field until I could yell loud enough for her to know it was me. There is some irony looking back on all of that, in that we got married on this very porch where she was standing when she was shooting at me."

They were once again sitting in the wooden rocking chairs on the porch by the time Matt finished his story. Isaac was smiling as he thought about Ami Ruth with a Smith and Wesson shooting at intruders coming down the lane.

"Well, son, if my cursory look around this farm is an indicator, and that beautiful, soft-spoken young lady you married is as wonderful as she appears, you certainly have found yourself a great place to live," he said.

"Oh, Pa," Matt said eagerly. "The more you see, the better it will be! Ami Ruth is just special, and this farm is a wonderful place. From the house you can only see about a third of the farm. It extends back over the ridge to the south and up the next ridge. We have a winery over there and grapes are our biggest cash crop. Now that the war is over, we have just begun selling Schendler Wines in Washington, and Baltimore. When we get the new fields producing, we can sell wines up and down the eastern seaboard, both north and south."

David appeared at the door and announced that they were done in the kitchen. Pa smiled that big smile of his and said, "Matt, I think it was a wedding I happened into when I arrived earlier, and unless I am mistaken, you have a beautiful new bride who needs some attention. Let's put off our talk until tomorrow or the next day. We have plenty of time. You go see where that lovely young lady is."

Matt blushed a little, but stood up and made his way to the door. "Tomorrow," he said and went inside. David joined Isaac in the rocking chair Matt had just vacated. Their talk went on into the evening, but Matt's mind was no longer on his father. In a very short minute, he found Ami Ruth in the kitchen. Their eyes met and she knew immediately that he had come for her. Aunt Elizabeth turned toward Matt and smiled.

She said, "Where have you been? I expected you an hour ago." She then glanced over at Ami Ruth and said, "Go on, I can finish up here."

No more words were spoken as Matt and Ami Ruth mounted the stairs to their bedroom.

* * *

The next morning things were beginning to get back to normal at the big house on the Schendler Farm. Aunt Elizabeth was up at her usual time, just before the crack of dawn, and soon the smell of coffee and bacon drifted through the house. When Matt awoke, Ami Ruth was already gone, and he found her in the kitchen helping her aunt prepare the rest of the breakfast. Just briefly, their eyes met, and she gave him a shy but radiant smile. He basked in the warmth of that smile as he stepped down the back stairs and walked over to the barn.

At the bottom of the ladder that led to the loft room, Matt called out "Pa! Breakfast is almost ready!" An answer came quickly followed by his Pa's bearded face and broad smile at the top of the ladder. "You can wash up at the sink on the back porch," Matt continued. "The ladies are in the kitchen and David will be there soon. You won't believe all the smells coming from the big stove! It will remind you of home before Ma got sick."

Before Isaac could respond, Matt had retreated through the barn door and headed back to the big sink on the back porch. He knew the well water that came through the pump would be cold, and he looked forward to the feeling of the icy water on his skin. Nothing woke you up quicker. Matt had begun shaving not long before, but he didn't need to do it more than once or twice a week, and of course, he had shaved for the wedding. He smiled to himself as he thought of one of the questions that had been asked as the men's group at the Meeting House was clearing him for marriage. It came from Mr. Owens, a man he didn't know well but who held a position of respect in the group.

Mr. Owens had asked, "Matt, do you shave yet?"

Matt thought for just a few seconds before he responded, "Mr. Owens, I have been shaving for two years and haven't cut myself either time." The men had all laughed.

Mr. Owens's question was not a rude inquiry into Matt's youth. Instead, he was interested in whether Matt intended to grow the beard that was traditional among Quaker men. In truth, Matt might well grow a beard, but it would be awhile before that effort would be practical—or noticeable. After Matt's humorous response, the tensions were significantly eased and the bridegroom-to-be had answered all their questions easily. Just that short exchange had taught him something about the use of laughter to ease the tensions in a group. It was knowledge that would serve him well in the future.

Before Matt had finished with his morning ritual, his Pa was coming up the back steps. Matt paused at the door into the kitchen, looked back at his father, and heard the deep voice say, "It is so good to be here with you and this wonderful family, Matt."

In a few minutes, everyone was at the big pine table and what was before them was indeed a Schendler Farm breakfast feast. Some of the food came courtesy of the leftovers from the wedding buffet. Eggs were fixed three different ways and you could take your pick. The warm bacon glistened in a big platter in the middle of the table. There were bowls of grits with slabs of butter melting on top, and here and there around the table were small china bowls of grape and apple preserves. Cups of coffee steamed at the places of David, Isaac, Matt, and Aunt Elizabeth. Ami Ruth was not a coffee drinker, but she had her small cup of tea. Toast had been grilled in a skillet on the big stove and was still sitting there close to the heat of the oven, staying warm.

Everyone sat quietly waiting for their traditional saying of grace before meals. Aunt Elizabeth spoke, "Matt, you have been the man of this house for the last couple of years, but this morning it is official.

This may be the Schendler Farm, but it is the Mason house. I think you are the one to speak to the Lord for all of us this morning."

Matt nodded. He felt himself swallow twice and then accepted what he judged to be a personal honor for the man of the house. Saying grace was not a new thing for Matt. He had heard his Ma say the blessing at their table three times a day for his entire life. She had begun teaching him to say the prayer before meals when he was about five years old.

He began as his Ma always did, saying, "Lord, thank you for all your many blessings. Thank you for your son, Jesus, who came to earth to show us how to live." Then he began a prayer that could only have come straight from his heart. "Thank you for our many friends and neighbors who came to celebrate with us yesterday and for their support and affection during these troubled times. Thank you most especially for bringing Pa home to us and keeping him safe through four years of terrible war. And most of all, thank you for my wonderful new wife. Had you asked me what I wanted in a wife, I could not have thought of all the things she is. You have blessed me well beyond anything I deserve. Bless David and Aunt Elizabeth, who mean so much to us. Now bless this food you have provided. Keep us all in the protective palm of your hand and guide our future as you have guided our past. These things we ask in your blessed name. Amen."

There was a collective "Amen!" said around the table and hungry hands began to reach for the bowls and platters. Matt felt his Pa's eyes on him and returned his look across the table. Without any words being exchanged, he knew they were both thinking of Ma. Had the cancer not taken her, their lives would have been very different right now. For sure, wherever they were, she would always be with them.

The food disappeared quickly, and the sounds of contentment around the table were easy on the ear. There was a satisfied smile on every face.

When the dishes were scraped and placed in the sink for washing, Matt suggested to his Pa that they retreat to the front porch and continue their conversation of the night before. In a short minute, they were back in the wooden rocking chairs, looking out on the broad lawn. The sun shone down on Big Billy and the grey mare as they grazed in the front paddock. The dew on the grass had a shine to it, and father and son watched squirrels leaping in the oak trees and chattering back and forth.

Matt began. "Pa, tell me about your leg and the prison camp. What happened after you left me behind the rock wall in the middle of the battlefield?"

"It was a terrible thing, Matt," Pa responded slowly. "I shudder when I think about it. The smoke from the big guns was everywhere, and you could only see what was right in front of you. Men were falling all around me. Then there was the stone wall. Muskets seemed to be sticking out over every rock. There were three or four of us that reached that wall. I came up over it and glanced to each side. There were only a handful of us left. I saw a Yankee off to my right with his musket aimed right at me. He couldn't have been more than ten feet away. The guy next to him fell into him as he shot, and instead of hitting me in the chest or head where he was aiming, his shot caught me in the thigh about halfway up. My leg felt like it was on fire and I fell down on the ground. When I opened my eyes, there were several faces staring down at me and gun barrels pressed against my chest. My war was over." Isaac's voice had trailed off into a whisper with his last words.

"Pa, you could have been killed right there," Matt said softly. "It is almost as if you saw the minié ball coming that buried itself in your leg. I think God Almighty was looking out for you."

Pa continued as if he had not heard. "I could hear the sound of gunfire, but it was more in the distance. They got me up and half carried me over to a stand of trees about fifty yards behind the rock wall. They sat me down against a tree with about twenty of our boys. Most were wounded, some bad and some like me with minié balls stuck in their bodies and bleeding. All of us knew that the fighting was over for us. They had us and we weren't going back to the other side. The best we could hope for was a prison camp, and the worst possibility was that we wouldn't make it that far. I know you have heard that about half of all the soldiers wounded at Gettysburg died of pneumonia or infection."

"That was certainly true on our side too," Matt said. "Every wagon I looked in had men who were in a very bad way. Most of them didn't even make it back to Williamsport."

"We were there under those trees all night waiting for what would happen when daylight came," Pa continued. "The next morning some blue coats came by with some water and hard tack. By that time, none of us had eaten anything in almost two days. It was really bad grub, but we were glad to get it. We were told that wagons were coming to get us, but we would have to wait our turn. We learned that in the final count, there were more than seven thousand taken prisoner by the Yankees that third day of fighting. I knew I was in a bad fix, but I certainly was not in it alone."

Pa stopped for a few seconds, staring off into the distance as if trying to remember every detail. Matt felt the cool of a breeze and heard cicadas that had begun to talk to each other in the trees. Finally, Pa took a deep breath and continued. "The wagons arrived about midmorning, and those of us who couldn't walk were loaded into them. Those who could walk followed the wagons on foot. In many ways, I was lucky to be shot in the leg. It put me in a wagon with a doctor who had been captured with the rest of us. I never asked him how he happened to be in the midst of the fighting, but there he was, moving from one wounded man to another in that wagon.

"When the doctor got to me, he took one look at my leg and said, 'There is no exit wound so that minié ball is still in there. And it has to come out. If we don't get it out, you will get an infection in your leg, and it will take your life in about a week.' I told him to get it out, and I would do my best not to yell too loud. He opened up his coat and came out with something that looked like a pair of scissors but with pinchers on the end. He said, 'Son, I know it hurt like hell when you got shot in the leg, but getting that ball out of your leg will hurt twice as much.' He told me to bite on something, so I took a hold of a wad of cloth from the wagon cover. The wagon was rolling along and hitting bumps. His hand was shaking so much that it was hard to get the pinchers into the hole in my thigh. He tried three of four times before he got it to fit into the hole. He must have reached into my thigh three or four inches with that thing. He was right about the pain. I could feel every movement of the pinchers and every jerk of the wagon was agony."

By this point, Matt was feeling his father's pain just from the description. He grimaced and said, "Oh, Pa, I don't know how you stood it."

"I was watching the doctor's face while he was probing for that minié ball," Pa said. "His expression told me nothing. I knew if he couldn't get a hold of that ball I was not going to make it. But in the midst of what was the worst pain I ever felt, I saw him smile and in a couple of seconds, he was showing me the ball caught between the pinchers of his instrument. Then he took out a little bottle filled with colored fluid. He smiled again and said, 'This is a waste of good drinking whiskey but right now we need something to clean out that wound.' With that, he poured a splash of that liquid into the hole in my thigh and it felt like he had poured fire in there."

Pa rubbed his thigh and looked straight at Matt. "Son, I hope you never have to feel anything like that. It leaves you totally weak and fighting for consciousness. There weren't any bandages available, so he told me to tear off the tail of my shirt and cover the wound with that. He said he would come back and look at it again after he cared for some of the other fellows. It was late in the day when he made his way back to look at the wound. He said it seemed to be doing all right, but the crucial time was about two days away. Then we would know if I was going to get fever in the leg or not. I was one of the lucky ones. It did not get infected and for that I probably had the drinking whiskey to thank."

Matt laughed softly, and Pa looked over at him and smiled. He said, "I know what your Ma would have said to the drinking whiskey treatment. She would have called it the Devil's cure."

Pa shifted in the rocker, unconsciously stroking the place where he had been injured. Every word of his story seemed measured now. "We were in that wagon for the better part of three days. We ended up in a prisoner of war camp called Point Lookout just below St. Mary's City, Maryland. I was there along with about two thousand others. In some ways it was a miserable place with not enough room for everyone and nothing to do day after day. We kept up with the war through the rumor mill. The Yankee guards were always pleased to tell us about Union victories. You should have heard them cheer when Atlanta fell. They didn't tell us about any Southern victories though we imagined there were some. I didn't find out until they released us about four months ago that there wasn't much for the South to cheer about over the last two years of the war."

"We watched the war from here, Pa," Matt said. "It seemed every week or two the two armies were coming together somewhere around Winchester. In the end, they said there were four major battles fought in Winchester and about eighty more scrimmages between smaller groups in the region. We saw gangs of deserters pass our way over and over. We did what we needed to do to protect the farm, but none of us have had much sleep over the past two years."

Isaac leaned forward in his chair for a few moments before continuing. "When I was released, I hitched a ride on a boat down to Norfolk. From there, I walked across the North Carolina border and made my way west to Mt. Airy. It took me about two weeks to walk it, and I was beholding to several along the way who took me in and gave me food and water. I was only eating about one meal a day, and it was meager rations at that. But that was what I had become used to at Point Lookout. I don't remember being hungry, but I do remember being constantly tired. I knew that our farm was gone from our conversations when we were together before Gettysburg. Your Ma was gone too, and I had no idea if you had made it through that nightmare in the field below Cemetery Ridge. It was as if everything I had known before the war had been destroyed." He turned bleak eyes on Matt. "Son, I never want to feel that alone again as long as I live."

"I've had some of the same feelings, Pa," Matt said. "I didn't know where you were or if you were dead or alive. Ma and the farm were gone. Pa, Ma was in great pain before the good Lord took her. She struggled with it as long as she could, but by the end, she wasn't herself anymore. She told me you wanted us to burn the farm rather than let the vultures take it, so when Ma was gone, I torched the place. I didn't take anything out of it except what I could carry on the mule."

Matt hesitated again, wondering if he should tell about the journey north or if enough had been said. He decided not to focus more on the tragedy of Ma's death and the little farm. If he needed to tell about the journey north, he could do it later.

"By the grace of God, I had this wonderful Schendler family to be with and a full day of work to do every day while the war was going on all around us," he said. "And, Pa, I don't want either of us to ever be alone again."

"When I arrived at our farm, it was just as you told me when you found me on the banks of the Potomac before we went on to Gettysburg," Pa said. "The farm was nothing but black ashes and your Ma's grave was up the hillside from the house. You remember the Martin family, the one you gave the cow to before you left looking for me?"

Matt nodded.

"I stayed with them for about a month, helping Mr. Martin with the heavy farm work. It was nothing but blind luck that I saw your notice. I went into town one Saturday afternoon with Mr. Martin and was standing outside of the general store, which is next to the newspaper office. They had posted all the notices of people looking for those lost in the war on the bulletin board outside their office. I would never have bought a newspaper so their posting it was, really, an act of God. I couldn't believe my eyes when I saw your notice about me. I must have made quite a sight dancing around the sidewalk in front of the newspaper office!"

"I would like to have been there to see that, Pa," Matt said, chuckling a little.

"The editor came outside to see what the ruckus was and I told him. He took me back inside and handed me a sheet of paper and a pen to write you a letter. He didn't even ask me for money for a stamp. He told me he would write the story of our making a connection on his bulletin board outside the newspaper office for the next week's newspaper. The editor said there had been way too much bad news printed in the newspaper. It was time we had something good to share with the people. I didn't see the article. As you know, the Martin farm was north of Mt. Airy, and I didn't go back through town the next day when I headed into Virginia.

"Son," Pa said. "It was a long walk to get here, but I have never been so happy to be anyplace as I am to be here with you. After the last two years, this is a Godsend. I hope it is okay if I stay with you for a while until I figure out what to do with the rest of my life."

The words burst from Matt's mouth. "Pa, I don't want to ever be separated from you again!" he declared. "There is enough here for us to do forever and never get it all done. Tomorrow I will take you on a tour and you will see for yourself. For now, I have some chores to do, but this should be a rest day for you. I'll bring you another cup of coffee, and you can enjoy the front porch for a bit."

Pa responded, "Son, that would be wonderful. I can't tell you the last time I had real coffee. The Martins were brewing theirs from acorns. But I would hate to dip into your stock, it has to be low."

"Don't worry about it, Pa," Matt responded. "This is a special day and having a second cup of coffee is just what the doctor ordered."

Matt was gone for just a minute, and when he returned, he handed his Pa the fresh cup of coffee. Then he disappeared back into the house. Just as the screen door closed, Isaac heard the clip-clop of a horse coming around the porch to the front of the house. It was David, Ami Ruth's brother. He stopped the horse in front of the steps and dismounted. In a few seconds, he was sitting in the second rocking chair next to Isaac on the porch.

David said, "Isaac, I am very pleased you are here and that Matt has someone else to depend on. I would love to stay, but I have responsibilities in Philadelphia with the Society of Friends. So I am saying a fond farewell to you all."

"I'm sorry to see you go, David," Isaac responded. "I think there is enough farm here to keep all of us busy, but I understand that you have a higher calling."

"I'm not sure there is anything higher in my priorities than this family, but I do need to go back and take care of my responsibilities in Philadelphia," David said. "I spent the last twenty minutes with Ami Ruth and Aunt Elizabeth and said my good-byes to Matt earlier in the morning. Leaving here is very hard, but I think she and Matt are at a good place in their lives, and together, they can handle whatever is necessary here. I do think having you here is good for everyone. I hope you will stay. I know that both Ami Ruth and Matt want you to. I grew up here and have some bias but sincerely believe this is a great place to live. I'm sure you will find it so as well if you can stay long enough to give it a chance."

"I am not making any promises right now," Isaac said, "as I am still recovering from my ordeal of the last two years, but this is a great place to get my feet back under me and get ready for the rest of my life."

"Well, sir," said David, "I will say my final good-bye and wish you well." David shook Isaac's hand, walked down the steps, and mounted his horse. He paused for just a minute to take one last look at the house and barn, then nodded to Isaac, turned the horse, and headed out the gate and up the lane to the road. In a moment, he was out of sight down the road to the east.

THE FARM

It was just an hour after daybreak the next morning when Matt and Isaac left the breakfast table. Matt had been up earlier and had Big Billy and the grey mare saddled and ready for the tour of the farm. Matt had brought the smaller grey horse home with him from the war along with Big Billy, the big bay he had found after the Battle of Brandy Station.

Matt suggested, "Pa, you ride Big Billy. He is stronger and will hardly know you are on him."

Pa looked at the big horse and issued a low whistle. He said, "Matt, that is some horse. He was hard to get a look at last night in the dark, but he is a fine animal. I can see why you are so proud of him. Tell me again where you got him?"

Matt responded eagerly. "I was camping out at the battle site of Brandy Station where the Union cavalry had surprised JEB Stuart's unit and run off several of their horses," he said. "You had always told me that a tame horse or mule would come back to where he was used to being fed, so I stayed overnight there, hoping there would still be a horse or two around that had been run off during the battle. About dusk, a white horse and this big bay came back to the stream for a drink. I put a rope around Big Billy's neck and he has been my horse ever since. That is, except for the army taking him at Potomac. It was a miracle that I found him when I got back to Williamsport. They were shooting the horses. They couldn't get them across the pontoon bridge they had built over the Potomac, and they wouldn't leave them for the Yankees. I arrived just in time to stop the shooting and rescue Big Billy. He had been shot in the flank, but one of the doctors at the tent hospital fixed him up."

"How about the grey mare?" Pa asked.

"I came on her by accident," Matt said, scratching the smaller horse between the ears. "I was looking for a place to ford the Potomac River and came onto a clearing where the mare was grazing. She was saddled and had a Henry 60 Repeating Rifle in the sheath on the saddle. I found her Yankee rider in the grass. He had run into a low hanging branch and was dead from the blow. I had been walking up to that time because of Big Billy's injury, but from that time on, I had two horses and a repeating rifle. It would have taken me two to three weeks to get back to Winchester on foot, but finding the grey mare helped us make it back here in less than a week."

As they started their riding tour, it was obvious that Big Billy was at least a full hand taller at the shoulder than the grey mare. With Isaac on his back, they were, indeed, a formidable pair traveling down the back lane toward the south ridge.

Matt pointed out the wheat field and the vegetable patch that supplied most of the food for the dinner table by way of the Schendler kitchen.

"Pa, when I first came here, they sold the vegetables in Winchester along with the wheat. That was before the war and before any of the grape juice in the wine casks had matured into wine," Matt said.

Pa stopped Big Billy at the edge of the vineyard on the south ridge and asked, "How does all this work, Matt? You know well what we were attempting to grow on our farm. I have had no experience with wine. How do you make it?"

Matt was pleased to tell him what he had learned on the Schendler Farm. He said, "Grapes are a good crop for the hillsides. We seem to have the right soil for them, and evidently, the growing area needs to be well drained. For that reason, the only place where we have planted grapes on flat land is by the lane in front of the house. And, as I understand it from Ami Ruth, that was a mistake her father made before he had any experience growing grapes. Evidently, the water stays on the roots too long on the flat land. So we have a good crop for the hillsides. It takes a few years to get the vine stock up producing grapes. Then once you have the grapes, you can press them and store the juice in barrels. It takes the grape juice a few years to age into really good wine. So you have to make a real sacrifice of land to reach the point of productivity for a winery."

Matt continued, "When I arrived here, we had about ten acres planted in grape stock. We now have almost sixty acres planted. One acre can produce between two and ten tons of grapes depending on the soil and the weather conditions. When everything we have planted is producing, we hope we will hit about two tons per acre. At peak production, we should harvest more than 120 tons of grapes each fall. One ton of grapes will produce one barrel of wine. One barrel of wine will sell on the open market at about seventy dollars per barrel. So if all comes out as I calculate it, at capacity a couple of years from now we should be able to generate between eight and ten thousand dollars a year from the winery. Right now, we aren't doing a fraction of that, but that is where I have been aiming. And of course, creating wine from grapes is a labor intensive business and people have to be paid, so the cost of producing that barrel of wine is pretty high."

Isaac thought for a minute. "That is an ambitious plan, Matt. So the goal is to keep everything else together—the animals, vegetables, and wheat—and to focus on the wine as the cash crop."

"That's it," Matt nodded. "Then we can decide what we are going to do with the rest of the land Mr. Schendler bought. As I said earlier, we are not even using 40 percent of the land we have available."

"Matt," Pa said, "your Ma was always against drinking any kind of alcoholic drinks. How is it that this Quaker family is growing grapes to make wine?"

"I asked Mr. Schendler that same question and he told me that there was some discussion of it at the Meeting House," Matt replied. "He said he happened in on a gathering of the leadership and overheard them talking about his first vineyard effort by the lane in front of the house. He decided to join the group uninvited and let them say what they had to say to him directly. Evidently, some thought a Quaker should not be planning to sell wine. He told me he let everyone have their say and then responded to them. He told them to look up the second chapter of the Gospel of John and see who turned water into wine at the wedding in Cana. Mr. Schendler said he never heard another word about it after that."

Isaac laughed his big laugh. He said, "I was never much for drinking anything alcoholic but that wasn't because I was taught there was something wrong with it. I didn't drink when your Ma and I got married, and for sure, I was smart enough not to drink while I was married to her. That would have been near suicide." He laughed again and Matt joined in.

Father and son walked their horses over to the top of the ridge and stopped to look at the valley and across to the ridge on the other side.

Matt said, "The grapes you are looking at planted down this ridge were put in the ground by Mr. Schendler almost a decade ago. The winery has had ten years in production but only seven years when wine could be sold. From the crest of this ridge you can see much of what I have been working on the past two years."

He heard his father's appreciative low whistle again. "My gracious, Matt," he said. "You have been working overtime on this valley." From their vantage point on the ridge, they could see the root stock planted off down the south side of the ridge, along the East Ridge, and in the distance. Across the valley, the vineyard stretched along the ridge on the other side.

"Pa," Matt said, "you are looking at the winery there in the valley. It was a large, open span building when I came. We've built an addition that doubled the size of the original building. Virtually everything we do on the farm is homemade," Matt continued. "We have a small saw mill back at the edge of the woods and the addition to the winery building was constructed with lumber from our own trees. We are fortunate to have a crew of five who know how to make things from scratch and can also guide the produce from vine to wine. We don't see them often up at the big house, but they are generally on the job by sunup and don't head home until it is approaching dark. All live not far down the road."

"I am amazed, Matt," Pa said. "The whole Southland is struggling for labor, and you not only have a permanent crew of five—these men are skilled!"

"Pa," Matt responded. "We pay them well too, about fifteen dollars a month, greenbacks, except for Jesse. He is our foreman, and we pay him twenty-two dollars a month. That is better than they can get anywhere else in the valley."

Matt continued, "Today, the grapes that supply our winery are double what we had just two years ago. Almost everything we have planted are called Norton grapes after a man who developed them in this region about eighty years ago. Some over in the county east of us are trying to adapt a grape grown in France for use here in this area, but no one has yet had the new variety in the ground long enough to know if it will work for us. See that patch with the fence around it on the East Ridge? That is our effort at developing the new variety. We are still about a year away before that effort can be called productive.

"If you wonder where the root stock comes from, we generate our own. Each grape has seeds and we strain the juice to get the seeds out. On the other side of the winery, we have a hot house where we plant the seeds. It takes some care, but by the time we get through the winter after the seeds are planted, we generally have sprouts strong enough to be planted. They begin to produce grapes in their third season. If we were trying to plant several varieties of grape, it wouldn't work so well, but for now, we are concentrating on Norton grapes. Experience tells us they grow well here in our region."

Pa stopped Matt's explanation with a new question. "Matt, do you have enough men on site to harvest the grapes?" he asked.

"Pa, you have hit on the primary problem we are facing today and that is a lack of labor," Matt admitted. "Before we had so many acres in the vineyards it wasn't a major problem, but today, finding workers to put into the field to cut the grapes and then to handle the processing in the winery is a major worry. I'm not sure there are enough men in the entire area who would be available to cut the grapes and move them through the wine-making process. Before the war, we had lots of labor available in the region. Today, there are just not enough healthy men who don't have their own farm responsibilities. I am not sure what I am going to do, but I only have about six weeks to solve that problem. The grapes will begin coming ripe in late September, and we will have only about a month to harvest them before they will be spoiled."

Matt and Pa rode down into the valley near the winery. They tied the horses onto the hitching post, and Matt led the way into the building. Coming in from the bright light outside, it took just a minute to get used to the dark in the winery. As they stood there with their eyes getting adjusted, both immediately smelled the heavy aroma of grapes and fermenting wine. Matt suddenly remembered the tour Mr. Schendler took him on the first time he had visited the farm. Just inside the door, the wooden framework they called the bleachers began to rise from the floor. This was the framework where the wine casks were stored side by side. Each had code words on the outside so one could know at a glance when the wine was stored, when it would be ready for the market, and what kind of wood had been used to make the casks.

"Pa, we use several different kinds of woods in the barrels and the kind of wood affects the taste of the wine," Matt explained. "Virtually all the wine casks are made of oak but other woods were used originally. They didn't work as well, so we are focused just on oak now. The old winery building was almost filled with wine casks, and it was obvious we needed more space." They walked through the doors into the addition and found two men building new wine casks. Isaac looked around the facility as Matt stopped to talk to the two men.

When Matt was finished with his conversation, Pa motioned toward the wall just behind them. He asked, "Matt, what is behind the double doors in the wall of the old building that was covered over when the new facility was added?"

Matt looked solemn. "Ami Ruth says that this farm was a station on the Underground Railroad and dozens, even hundreds, of slaves came through here on their way north to freedom over the last several years," he said. "She said that they would arrive late at night in the barn up close to the house and would be moved by covered wagon down the back lane and over the ridge to the back of the winery. The wagon drove through those double doors and the people were housed in two big rooms under the old winery. Once they were inside the barn, they were never seen outside again until they were ready to move on north. The next way station was a Quaker farm over the north ridge toward the West Virginia border. Ami Ruth said she wasn't sure where they went after that stop. But the goal was always to get across the Potomac and into Pennsylvania. There they were able to stop for a while with one or another of the Quaker families from the area between Gettysburg and Lancaster."

Pa let that sink in for a few seconds and then asked, "Matt, how did the slaves know this farm was a station on their route?"

"There were signals that were used on the different farms. Each farm had its own signal and, from time to time, the signal was changed. Sometimes there was a quilt hanging on the line in front of the barn, and sometimes some other signal was used," Matt responded.

"Your friends certainly took their lives in their hands helping slaves run away from their owners," Pa said admiringly.

"Pa, these are really good people and they live their faith every day," Matt said earnestly. "They don't believe in slavery just as they don't believe in war and killing. When it all began, Ami Ruth said that her father went to a meeting at the Hopewell Friends Meeting House one night and came home telling what was about to happen. She said they were told to keep extra food on hand for visitors all the time, though they might never actually see them. A knock on the backdoor would tell him they were in the barn, and he would move them across the ridge to the winery before daylight. As you can see in this valley, you have to be on the ridge, well inside the property line, before you can see anything going on here. That is why the Underground Railroad leadership chose the Schendler Farm to be a part of their organization. Mr. Schendler knew there could be big trouble if they were found out, but thought it was worth the risk because of the God-given role the family was to play. Once he committed to using his farm as a way station, Mr. Schendler developed the plan to use the barrier of the ridge and the hiding place under the winery to take care of the visitors."

Pa said seriously, "Matt, I would like to think we would have done the same thing on our farm in North Carolina if the opportunity had presented itself. Still, it took some real guts on the part of Mr. and Mrs. Schendler to risk everything for strangers, no matter how right it seemed at the time. So the runaway slaves passed through here but none ever worked here at the Schendler Farm?"

"You are right, Pa," Matt said. "Quakers don't hold with slavery and see everyone as equal before the Lord. They would not have reached out to free slaves, but they certainly would have provided hospitality to any wayfaring stranger, just as they did for me when I happened to arrive here in the middle of the night when I was looking for you."

"So let me see if I have this straight, Matt," Pa said. "Most of the farm productivity today is in the vegetable patch along with the pigs and cattle I saw earlier. These are used as support for the farm, the family, and the workers. The primary cash crop is the three fields of grapes up on the sides of the ridges. The future plan is to use the winery to produce four or five times as much wine, to store it until it ages, and then to sell it in the cities up and down the eastern seaboard. Do I have it right?"

"You do have it right, Pa, as far as it goes," Matt said. "We have more than a thousand acres here that have been in the Schendler family for more than a hundred years. According to Ami Ruth, the first family came here in the 1720s with a land grant from the British. I saw that land grant document once. It has the name of the British governor, Lord Fairfax, on it. A few years ago, Mr. Schendler added an additional four hundred acres from the farm just to our west. So altogether, we have fourteen hundred acres but less than six hundred are in production.

"More than half of the farm has never been in production and isn't now, even with the additional land dedicated to the vineyards. We have access to water with a stream that runs along both sides of the north ridge. Most of the remaining land is woodland, though there is a beautiful meadow just across the north ridge that would be great for raising cattle or, down the line, planting something productive. We have deer on the land for hunting and even a bear from time to time. It is a great property with lots of potential."

Isaac whistled in appreciation. "It makes our farm in North Carolina seem very small by comparison. I can see why you are so enthusiastic about the possibilities of this farm and its future."

Matt continued, "Most of the farmers in this region grow tobacco. Mr. Schendler told me that he tried tobacco but the dry leaves caused his eyes to water and made him sneeze. He decided not to persist with that crop. Still, it is a possibility, especially in the field right in front of the house that has a high water table. It is in wheat and grapes now, but like I said, the grapes really aren't productive there. The wheat is a usable crop, but tobacco is a much better cash crop. Pa, did you ever consider growing tobacco on our farm?"

Pa smiled. "No, Son. Tobacco was never in my plans. On the farm where I was raised near Lexington, Virginia, we grew tobacco. But evidently I had the same affliction Mr. Schendler did. Every time we began to dry the tobacco leaves to get it ready for the sale barn, I would get the red eye and my nose would start running. The longer we worked around tobacco, the sicker I got. I always said that if I ever had my own farm, for sure, I would never raise tobacco. Even if I wanted to, your Ma would have pitched a fit."

Matt smiled, "So you were never a smoker like so many of the farmers I know?"

Isaac grinned. "Even sitting around the fire when we were camped out, I could never stay in the group for long if several were smoking. I tried it. I thought that if I smoked I would get over it. That didn't happen."

Pa hesitated a moment and then said, "Son, you mentioned my staying on here for at least awhile. What did you have in mind? You obviously have some important things planned. How can I be of help to you?"

"Pa, I want you to stay here with us forever!" Matt said. "You can stake out any section of the farm you want for your efforts. I know you will have some good ideas I haven't thought of yet. I know too that if I could make this into a wonderful farm, we can do even better together. Knowing you, your mind is already at work with what we could do to improve things and make the farm more productive."

"Matt, let me think about it for a bit," Pa said. "We will talk again tomorrow or the next day. Let's go back to the house now. It is time for me to have a rest, and I am sure you have things to do that have stacked up while you were planning the wedding celebration."

KEEPING THE WOLF AND THE YANKEES FROM THE DOOR

Running a farm is a full-time job and the next few days passed quickly. Each day seemed a slightly different version of the last with breakfast and dinner together as a family at the beginning and closing of each day. During his time at the Schendler Farm, Matt had grown used to retreating to the barn each evening and coming up the back steps into the kitchen each morning. Now that he was married, it was a joy to break that habit. Matt and Ami Ruth retreated up the stairs each evening and memories of their nights together found their way into his crowded mind many times each day. With Matt's father on the scene with him each day and Ami Ruth with him each evening, he could not imagine a more fulfilling life.

It was late in August, just a couple of weeks after the wedding, when Matt heard horses' hooves on the lane while he was still at the breakfast table. He hurried through the house and was standing on the porch when several men, some dressed in Yankee military uniforms, arrived on horseback in the front yard.

One of the uniformed men spoke. "Are you Matt Mason?"

"Yes, sir, I am," he responded.

"Are you the owner of this farm?" he asked

Matt thought for a second before he answered. He noted the distinct Yankee accent in the leader of the group and his mental guard was immediately up. "I am not the owner of it, but I am responsible for it. The farm belongs to my wife's family, the Schendlers. Why do you ask?"

The man who had spoken lifted his leg over the back of the horse and dismounted. As he approached the porch, Matt walked down the steps to meet him. Their hands met in a tacit hand shake. By then, Isaac had appeared on the porch behind him, and Ami Ruth was standing just inside the door listening.

The man continued. "Mr. Mason, my name is Darrell Richardson. I am the adjutant in charge of this region under the military governor, General John Schofield. My job is to make sure that everyone in the area knows their responsibility for paying taxes and to see that the taxes are paid. Your farm has been assessed and you owe one thousand dollars. As of today, you are notified of your responsibility and you have ninety days to pay."

By the time he finished speaking, Isaac had joined Matt at the bottom of the steps, and Matt felt the security of his presence in the face of this startling news. "Mr. Richardson, this is my father, Isaac Mason. He has recently come to this area and is staying with us."

Mr. Richardson nodded curtly at Isaac. Isaac nodded back at him but didn't say anything.

Matt continued. "I hope you don't find my question inappropriate, but can you tell me how the assessment was made on this farm?"

"Certainly," Richardson responded. "The assessment is based on the number of acres you own. According to the land grant in the assessor's office in Winchester, you own a thousand acres, and so your obligation, as I said, is one thousand dollars payable by the end of November."

"Is there any allowance for the fact that this farm utilizes less than half of the acreage it owns?" Matt asked.

The man smiled indulgently. "That, sir, is not my concern. You own a thousand acres and you have the potential to utilize all of it or not. The fact that you don't is an oversight I am sure you will remedy. We are aware that this farm has not paid any property tax since 1860. If the taxes are not paid, the farm will be forfeited and sold for back taxes. That may seem a little harsh, but we are treating you no differently from any other farmer in this region. We anticipate your payment at my office in Winchester by the end of November. Your payment will just be one of many that are due then. Most of the farmers in this area are getting a visit from us this week."

With that comment, Mr. Richardson nodded curtly, turned on his heel, and walked back to the horse. He slid his foot into the stirrup and lifted himself onto the saddle. He turned his horse toward the double gates at the edge of the front yard and, followed by the other men, began a slow trot up the lane to the road. Matt and Isaac stood silently, watching until the horsemen were up the lane and off of Schendler property.

Too stunned to speak, Matt walked slowly up on the porch with Isaac, and Ami Ruth pushed open the screen door and joined them. She was crying. Matt took her in his arms and fought to hold back the tears that were just at the edge of his eyes. His mind was moving rapidly, *Where on earth would we get one thousand dollars? It might as well have been a million!*

Isaac was the first to speak. "Do you have a reserve fund for taxes? Mr. Schendler must have been paying taxes in previous years."

Ami Ruth wiped her eyes on her pale blue handkerchief and hesitated just a few seconds as she blew her nose. "Before the war, I heard my father talking with mother, saying that getting the one hundred dollars together for his end-of-the-year taxes was a chore every year. I remember him saying that when the wine was mature, it would all be much easier. That man is right. We haven't paid any taxes that I know of since the beginning of the war. No one could get crops to market, and for the last year or so, most of what we might have taken to the market was stolen by deserters or confiscated by the military of one group or another. What we did sell to the Southern military was paid for in greyback dollars, which are worthless now. We had some money in the bank in Winchester, but all the banks in Virginia are closed now, and there isn't much hope of getting back any of the money we had deposited there—not in the near future, if ever."

She began to cry again, and Matt and Isaac exchanged a worried look over her bowed head. Next, Aunt Elizabeth's soft voice came from just inside the door. "Let's let this settle on us for a while before we panic," she said. "Others will have the same problem, and there may be somewhere, someone we can appeal to. Let's don't talk about it now. Tonight after supper is time enough. In the meantime, let's give it some thought, take inventory of our assets, and see if we can think through what is to be done."

Her practical suggestion was followed by all four. None of them said another word about the taxes, but thoughts about the problem were on all their minds as the day wore on. Work around a farm is never done, and the day was filled with seeing to the needs of the animals and the winery.

About midafternoon, a lone horseman trotted down the lane. It was their friend Mr. Joshua Ridgeway from over on the far side of the Loop road that encircled the Quaker farms north of Winchester. Matt was in the barn and, hearing the horse's hooves, went out to meet him. Mr. Ridgeway did not dismount and his usual big smile was notably absent.

"Matt, were you visited by the government men today?" Mr. Ridgeway asked bluntly.

Matt responded, "Yes, sir, they were here before we finished breakfast this morning."

"Several of the elders have asked for a community meeting tonight at the Meeting House to talk about this tax situation," Mr. Ridgeway said. "We plan to meet about an hour before sunset. Can you make it?"

"Yes, sir. We will be there. Will any womenfolk be a part of that meeting? Aunt Elizabeth and Ami Ruth will want to be there too," Matt responded.

"I think we need everyone who can come," Mr. Ridgeway said. "We have a crisis on our hands, and some of our people will find it simply impossible to raise the funds. We need everyone's best ideas for dealing with this situation."

"Mr. Ridgeway, my father is here with us now. He isn't a part of the Society of Friends but he probably has more experience dealing with Yankees than all the rest of us put together. Is he welcome at the meeting as well?" Matt asked.

"Certainly, Matt, feel free to invite your father. I'm sure there will be no objections. I'll see you in a bit." Mr. Ridgeway turned up the lane, and Matt watched him as he reached the road and guided his horse into a faster trot toward the Mansfield Farm.

Matt didn't have much heart for the work of the farm over the next several hours. His mind was on the tax problem and the prospect of raising one thousand dollars when there was no crop to sell and no one with any money to buy a crop even if he had anything to take to market.

Shortly after lunch, Matt and Isaac rode down to the winery. Neither had much to say as they rode together across the ridge and down to the big building where the wine was silently aging in casks. Most were still a year or two away from being mature enough to sell at the price they needed for each barrel. Matt was intent on figuring out what their ready inventory was and the financial potential of those assets and any others he could find.

Suddenly, Isaac posed a question. "Matt," he asked, "if you have no money, how have you been paying the five men you have working in the winery?"

"These men have been working for the Schendlers for several years," Matt responded. "Mr. Schendler paid them in Confederate dollars, and I continued that practice until the money became worthless at the end of the war. Over the past three or four months, we have been giving them food for their tables and promising to make up the wages when the banks and money situation straighten out. In truth, there is very little work in the area where a man can earn a working wage. So they trust us to make the situation right when we can begin getting our crops and the wine to market."

Isaac stopped Matt at the door of the winery with another question. "Matt, tell me more about this Quaker community that we are a part of here in the Loop so I will know a little something about them before the meeting tonight. And why is it called the Loop?"

Matt was grateful to have his mind taken off the tax problem. "Pa, the Quakers in this area came here from Pennsylvania in the early 1700s," he said. "There were about a hundred families who were offered a land grant of 100,000 acres in this region by the

British governor for the Virginia territory. The land grant is roughly a circle. On a map, you can put a tack in the location of the White Hall Store that is about two miles west of us and draw a circle around it to encompass the area in the land grant. Each family received 1,000 acres. Remember how the adjutant talked about our having 1,000 acres here? Well, as I told you a couple of days ago, we actually have around 1,400 acres because of Mr. Schendler's purchase of additional land a few years before the war."

Matt hesitated for a few seconds as they entered the winery, letting his eyes adjust to the darker interior. They could hear the sounds of men working and the aroma of grapes fermenting dominated the air.

The thought of an even bigger tax bill was a sobering one, and his mind was jolted back to the immediate problem. "Eventually they will catch up with that purchase, and we will owe $1,400 and not $1,000. When Mr. Schendler made the purchase, the vineyard was being planted across the ridge, and he could envision taking all the ridge land and planting it in grapes for making wine. Anyway, Pa, the road that goes around the original land grant is called the Loop Road and the land in the grant is referred to as the Loop. Many of the families in the original group that migrated here over a hundred years ago are still here living in the Loop."

Isaac nodded thoughtfully. "Aren't we far enough north of Winchester that some of the Loop is actually in West Virginia?"

"That is true," Matt said. "About half of the Loop is north of the border."

"And West Virginia pulled away from Virginia in the early days of the war because they did not want to separate from the Union," Isaac said.

"Yes," Matt agreed. "They were Union territory all through the war and have been officially since about 1862."

Isaac thought for a moment then said, "If there were a hundred families in the original Loop, can we assume that a number of the families who live at the bottom of the Loop here in Virginia have close friends and relatives that live north of the border in West Virginia?"

Matt was beginning to see where his Pa was headed. If they could think like a community, they might have a ready solution for at least a part of their problem. It was likely that the families North of the border were not in the sort of jeopardy of those who lived south of the border. It was also likely that there was a market within their own Society of Friends community for any products they could pull together for that market.

"I think you have the beginnings of a really good idea, Pa," Matt said, his face brightening a bit. "The Hopewell Meeting House was the only one in this area for almost a hundred years, and everyone attended meetings there for many years. Now the West Virginia Quakers have their own Meeting House north of the border, but most of our people know those folks from past relationships. And, just as you said, many are related either as families that came here together or by marriage."

"Matt, Winchester is the largest city in Virginia that is here in the Shenandoah Valley, but Charles Town and Martinsburg are both just north of the West Virginia border with Pittsburgh up in Pennsylvania being only a couple of days on a wagon farther north," Isaac said. "Do our other Friends north of the border trade north, or do they come back across the border to Winchester?"

"I don't know the answer to that," Matt replied, "but some folks at the meeting tonight may know. Let's bring it up."

The men walked into the winery together feeling somewhat better. A plan was forming.

* * *

While Matt and Isaac were at the winery, Aunt Elizabeth and Ami Ruth were having much the same discussion, though it focused primarily on what they had on hand to sell to raise money for the taxes. As was generally true, Aunt Elizabeth was not only a fountain of information on preparing food, she knew the value of virtually everything that grew on a farm.

"I have never seen prices like these in my lifetime," said Aunt Elizabeth. "The war has made things out of the reach of normal folks. To make matters worse, the fighting in this area kept the farmers from being able to plant their crops in the spring for the past two years, and even when the war was over in April, they had no seeds and no money to buy seeds. In most years, it isn't unusual to have some difficulty keeping food on the table in the winter, but this year, many of our neighbors are having trouble putting food on the table in the summer."

"Several at the wedding commented about the food," Ami Ruth said. "We are lucky that my folks believed a farm should stand on its own and be self-sustaining. Otherwise we would be in the same boat as some of our neighbors."

Aunt Elizabeth continued. "We have been lucky with our vegetable patch and having pigs and milk cows on this farm. So many of the farms in the Loop raise just a specialty crop, such as tobacco. Well, you can't eat tobacco. You have to sell it to generate the money you need for other things, and no one has money to buy anything. Of course, the Ridgeways raise mostly wheat, the Poteates have apple orchards, and others specialize in beef cattle, vegetable crops, dairy and beef cattle."

Ami Ruth nodded. "That was why when we had such a big banquet at the wedding, the table offerings were absolutely filled to overflowing. Everyone brought only what they specialized in and then shared in each other's bounty," she said. "Unfortunately, unlike our farm, most would have difficulty standing alone without trading with others or buying necessities at the store.

Looking back, my father could have made more money with tobacco or beef cattle, but he focused on variety, making this farm independent in a way most envy now. We are lucky he did."

Aunt Elizabeth agreed but continued in a somber tone. "To make matters worse, this is a year of the empty shelves in stores, and that is true at the White Hall Store and in Winchester as well. Some things that are needed simply are not available and staples are expensive. Even flour is selling for a dollar a sack and coffee for a dollar and a half a pound! No one I know has ever seen prices like that in northern Virginia. The prices in the stores tell me that we will be buying nothing. If we can't raise it on our farm, it will not find its way to our table. We need to think creatively about how to meet our own needs while we generate something to sell. Three months isn't a very long time to raise one thousand dollars, and we will all have to find a way to do our part."

Through all of this, Ami Ruth listened to every word. She knew the wisdom of her aunt's comments, though she wasn't sure how they could play a major role in raising the tax money. One thousand dollars was more money than Ami Ruth had ever seen at one time. It seemed an impossible amount to raise in three years, let alone in three months. Still, she had faith in Matt and his Pa. She had faith in Aunt Elizabeth. And for sure, she had faith in God, though she sometimes wondered where He was when everything seemed such a mess.

GATHERING AT THE FRIENDS MEETING HOUSE

Late in the afternoon, Matt hitched up the horses to a wagon, and the entire family headed up the lane to the road and the short ride to the Hopewell Friends Meeting House. Isaac had questioned Matt about his presence at the meeting since he wasn't a member of the group, but Matt had assured him that he and anyone else was welcome to come and participate at the meeting. "You don't need to be a Quaker to have good ideas about what to do to raise the tax money," he said.

When they arrived at the Meeting House, the discussion was already underway inside. Some voices sounded reasonable and moderate, while others were raised with emotion. Matt and Ami Ruth, Isaac and Aunt Elizabeth came through the open door in the back of the sanctuary. The benches were made of wood with straight backs, and they were set up in neat rows down both sides of the hall with an aisle down the middle. Matt and Isaac sat down on the back row in the men's section while Ami Ruth and Aunt Elizabeth walked over to the women's pews.

The Meeting House had been in the Loop for more than a hundred years. It had burned once early in its history, and the wooden walls had been replaced by flat rocks and cement. The interior might burn again sometime but not the walls. Still, there were black stains up the walls on both sides where candles had been used for light in earlier years. Most meetings today were held in the daylight hours, and light was supplied by the windows that were high up on the walls on both sides. The building had been used as a hospital first by the South and then the North during the war, and the building showed the wear and tear of hard use, including more black stains from the oil lanterns that had supplied light for round-the-clock nursing.

The room was nearly full with fathers and sons on one side and mothers and daughters on the other. The first voice Matt could identify belonged to Richard Beeson, senior member of one of the oldest families in the region. Mr. Beeson was a lean man with a hawk nose and a face weathered from working outside. He spoke loudly so everyone could hear. "The banks have closed with all our money," he said angrily. "Does anyone know if they are going to open again? Is the government going to do anything about that?"

Mr. Joshua Ridgeway, who was serving as the convener of the meeting, responded to Mr. Beeson in measured words. "I don't think we can count on any help either from the banks or from the government. The banks were dealing in greyback dollars, and with the defeat of the South, those dollars are worthless. The government in place now is not our government. This is a Yankee military government appointed by Congress in Washington. It appears that their sole job is to tax the South for enough money to pay for the cost of the war in the North."

Several voices rose at once in response. The loudest one belonged to Benjamin Thomburg, a portly man with a beard that circled his face from ear to ear. His family lived on the other side of the Loop. "How do they expect us to pay taxes when we don't have access to our money in the banks, and there is no market where we could sell our crops if we had crops to sell? The Yankees have us by the throat and they are enjoying squeezing us!"

Again, several voices rose to support what Mr. Thomburg had said. One man said ominously, "And this may be just the first squeeze."

There was a short silence as this alarming thought sunk in. The next voice heard was George Robinson's. He was different from most of the others who filled the little Meeting House as he was from north of the border in West Virginia, a Union state. They had used greenback money throughout the war and did not have the tax burden that had been levied on most in the room. He was at the meeting out of concern for his relatives and friends who were caught up in this dilemma. Mr. Robinson was known as one of the major religious leaders of the Quaker community. He was wearing his usual Sunday go-to-meeting black jacket and his straight brim hat was sitting in his lap.

Mr. Robinson said quietly, "We need someone to appeal to. We Quakers did not fight in this war. We did all we could to maintain our neutrality. We even made over our Meeting House into a hospital to take care of the Yankee wounded. Many of them were nursed back to health in our homes. Our women served as their nurses. Much of what would have been marketable crops were taken by the Yankee army to support their war effort. We aren't the enemy. and yet our people are shoved into the same bucket as everyone else south of the border. I recognize that those of us who live above the border are in a much different situation than those in the lower Loop, but we are a community and what affects you affects us. Surely there is an appeals process on these terrible taxes." He looked around the room. "Does anyone know?"

Mr. Ridgeway quickly responded, "That is a very good question and we will put together a committee to search out the answer before we leave here today. Are there some other thoughts from among us?"

The next voice came from the side of the building where the women sat. It was Mrs. John Poteate, a small, frail lady of advanced years. Many had called upon her when it was time for babies to be born as she was a gifted midwife even at her age. Most of the women would put their trust in her above many of the doctors available to serve the Quaker community.

She spoke softly, but everyone strained to listen. "Whatever may come from a committee appealing to some group in Winchester or in Washington, we can't count on help from outside. Our history is that wherever Quakers are, they are set apart from the English around them. That was true in England, in Pennsylvania where many of our relatives live, and it is certainly true here. Whatever we plan to do with an appeal to the local military leadership, we had better plan right now to comply with their outrageous tax demands. We should not expect help from anyone outside our Friends community. If we count on anyone but ourselves, we may be sorely disappointed and we all may lose our farms."

Several voices rose in support of her comments, dire though they were. Mr. Ridgeway asked that others who had thoughts to share, please hold them for now. He said, "I want to set aside the next few minutes for a time of quiet prayer." Immediately, heads bowed in all the pews and the room grew silent.

After what seemed like an eternity, Mr. Ridgeway spoke again. "Are there other thoughts that should be shared?"

The next voice was a surprise to the Masons sitting on the back row. It belonged to Aunt Elizabeth, who stood up in the midst of the women's pews. "Many of you know me because I have been on your farms and have worked with your womenfolk," she said, turning to gaze around the room. "You have done a good job laying out the extent of the problem we are trying to solve. I want to steer us in another direction for a few minutes. Most of us have generated the food we serve on our tables from our own fields and livestock. You have only to look around at our people to know that we generally eat pretty well."

Aunt Elizabeth's little joke served to lighten the mood, and there was soft chuckling here and there. She continued. "Most of our farms specialize in something such as wheat, as the Ridgeways do. Others have apple orchards that produce each fall, like the Poteate family. The Schendler Farm is known for a variety of different products, and we are moving toward focusing on vineyards and wine making as a cash crop. The point is that we all have excess food and other products that we could trade from farm to farm to make up for something others don't have."

There was a murmur of approval, and Aunt Elizabeth went on. "Bartering has been in place since the beginning of time. Quakers have always been masters of the barter system. We have only to take stock of what we have and to set aside what we don't need for ourselves to be shared with others who do not have enough."

Several of the women voiced positive responses to what Aunt Elizabeth had said. One suggested, "Why don't we create our own store just for bartering?"

Aunt Elizabeth smiled broadly. "A wonderful idea! Creating a store here in the Meeting House once each week would go a long way toward seeing that stomachs stay full around the Loop. Let's do it." She gracefully resumed her seat, and Ami Ruth squeezed her hand.

Mr. Ridgeway took charge again. "Okay, ladies, how about Miss Elizabeth, Mrs. Poteate, and Mrs. Ridgeway take charge of the Meeting House store and let's see what we can put together that will be best for everyone."

A deep voice came from the back of the men's section. It belonged to Thomas Moon, one of the younger men in the group. He was a short, thicker-built man with a thin beard. His family had come to the Loop about twenty years ago. His father had passed away just last spring, and now Thomas Moon was the head of the household, with a mother and two sisters to take care of. Their farm was one of the smaller ones, about five hundred acres, which meant his tax obligation was less than the others.

He asked, "Do we have enough to sell now if we put everything we have together? What if we brought two or three wagons to one place and everyone came together with whatever they had to sell, and we packed all our goods in the wagons and sent them up to Martinsburg or Charles Town, kind of like a farmer's market? Would that make enough of a dent in our tax obligation to make it worthwhile? Perhaps we could do that every week for the next couple of months to earn whatever we could before the taxes are due."

Mr. Ridgeway said, "It is encouraging to feel the spirit of cooperation beginning to catch on! Looking at this problem as an individual, it is difficult to see how any of us can generate enough money to handle this situation, but together, and with God's help, we are beginning to get some new ideas on how to pay those taxes.

He held up a blank sheet of paper. "Let's take a poll and see how much money we need to raise to meet the tax obligation of just the group gathered here tonight. Then we will begin to see the extent of the problem we have as a group. When we leave the building, I would appreciate one person from each family coming up and signing this paper and telling us your farm's assessment, and the extent of your obligation.

Then we will ask for a small committee to put together a plan to be shared with the group when we come together a week from now here at the Meeting House."

To the surprise of many in the group, they heard a new voice. It was Isaac Mason, speaking from the back of the men's section. "Mr. Ridgeway, if I may, could I talk with the group for a few minutes?" he asked. Mr. Ridgeway nodded, and Isaac Mason strode down the middle aisle to the front of the room. Many recognized the tall, imposing man from the wedding. Others who had not attended the wedding had heard about the big man who had come to live with the family on the Schendler Farm.

He spoke softly at first. "Most of you don't know me. I am Isaac Mason, father of Matt Mason whom you have adopted as one of your own here in the Loop over the past two years. I have been off to war since it all began almost five years ago now. I was with Stonewall Jackson for a while here in the Shenandoah Valley, and then with General Lee until the last shot was fired at Gettysburg. I spent the last two years at a prisoner of war camp in Maryland. It is only by the grace of God that I am here with Matt, Ami Ruth, and Miss Elizabeth. No one that I know of from my division is still alive."

Several people murmured in response, and one could be heard clearly throughout the building. "Fighting is not our way, but we respect your dedication to a cause," a man said.

Isaac continued. "I know fighting and war is not your way. It is certainly not my way anymore either. I have had my fill of it. I lost a lot in that terrible war: my farm, my wife, five years of my life, and I almost lost my son. The best thing I can say is that I learned a lot along the way. I would appreciate taking a few minutes to share some of what I have learned.

"First, it is natural for us to refer to the Northerners as 'Yankees.' Those blue uniforms just draw venom out of us and the word 'Yankee' means something very bad to us when we say it. However, if I learned nothing else in prison under several dozen Yankee guards,

I learned that they don't like that name either. They don't see themselves as 'Yankees.' They are from Maine, Pennsylvania, New York, Minnesota, Vermont, Rhode Island, and so on. Each has a state they identify with in the North, but there is no state called 'Yankee.' When we say that word, they hear us say 'enemy.' They realize that we do not judge them as individuals or potential friends. We have to stop using that word."

Isaac's voice was rising now, and he spoke with growing passion. "We need to utilize every advantage we have to handle this crisis. Mr. Robinson is different from the rest of us. As a resident of a Union state, he is an example of an asset many in our group have. He has people he is concerned about who live south of the border. We need to use Mr. Robinson's knowledge and influence north of the border to urge our friends and relatives there to help us with this almost insurmountable problem. We need to have a meeting with the northern Loop folks as soon as we can put it together. Only then will we know about the possibilities of help from that quarter. Thank you for listening." With that final word, Isaac made his way back through the center aisle to the back of the Meeting House, nodding to a few of the men as he passed them on the way back to his seat.

Mr. Thomburg was already on his feet and coming down the aisle. "What Mr. Mason says makes a lot of sense," he said in his booming voice. "We have to stop thinking of those north of the Mason-Dixon Line as enemies. As Quakers, we were not a part of this war. We have no enemies except for the Devil who rears his ugly head way too often among us. This is a time for us to pull together as never before. I applaud the ladies' effort to create a barter store. I am very much for holding a meeting in the Northern Loop so those folks can understand the problems we are facing and can, perhaps, find some way to help us. And most assuredly, I applaud the efforts of Mr. Ridgeway and the rest of our leadership to bring us together so we can see these impossible individual problems as ones that can be solved if we work together. God Himself may well have created this challenge to pull us together and remind us that He is still in charge and we, as His children, are responsible to Him for those less fortunate around us."

Mr. Ridgeway rose beside him. "Amen!" he said. "We will let Mr. Thomburg's comments be our benediction. And we will set another meeting on the same day next week to report on our progress. In the meantime, could I see Mrs. Ridgeway, Mr. Robinson, and Mr. Isaac Mason for just a few minutes outside on the porch when we finish with signing the tax obligation document? So, until we meet again we will say "Amen" to this gathering, the first of many we will hold until this crisis is behind us."

They were hardly in the wagon on the way home when Isaac spoke to Aunt Elizabeth. "Those were some very important words you shared with the group," he said. "Before you spoke, almost everyone was caught up in the tragic consequences of the situation. I sensed despair on every side. After you shared your thoughts with them, folks began to see what we could do together, how we can weather this storm if we stick together as a group, as a people. Your words showed confidence that we could make it through this crisis. It was as if God was using you as his instrument to help pull the group together tonight. Everyone was impressed."

Aunt Elizabeth did not respond to his words, but had someone been watching closely, they would have seen a warm smile passing between her and Isaac Mason. She sat quietly, obviously preoccupied with the enormous job that had to be done and her part in finding a solution that was workable for the Schendler Farm and also for the Quaker community.

AUNT ELIZABETH

Aunt Elizabeth was up before anyone else the next day, as was her habit. She carried a candle with her as she stopped in front of a mirror and quickly looked at herself before she continued downstairs. She was tall and thin with long blond hair that she kept in a knot on the back of her head. Quakers were mostly Dutch and English, and they were big people. Many of the Quaker women her age were already growing thick from child bearing, with their skin weathered from working outside in the sun. Elizabeth had worked for many of the families but mostly inside with kitchen duties and taking care of the house or women recovering from childbirth.

Her face was a creamy white accented with a quick pink-lipped smile. Her dominant feature was hard to miss. She had eyes that were a deep blue, and combined with her blond, almost-white hair, she seemed to have stepped right out of one of the paintings of Dutch girls that hung on the walls of many of the Quaker homes.

She had never married, but it wasn't as if she didn't have opportunities. There were several who had courted her in her younger years, and there were many good memories associated with those times. Still, she had aging parents who needed care, and after her sister married and moved to the Schendler Farm, it was all up to her. She had not thought of marriage for many years, and now that she was in her late thirties, she was resolved that God intended her to live out her life in service to other families.

As she stood for a few seconds in front of the mirror, tucking a loose strand of hair into her bun, Elizabeth recalled Isaac's warm words in the wagon last night on the way back from the Meeting House. She had never met anyone quite like Isaac. She had learned to love and respect Matthew over the past two years, and Isaac seemed to be a model of what her niece's new husband would become a decade or two down the road. He was a larger-than-life man with a smile that created a tingle in the back of her neck and left her wanting to see him again.

Suddenly, a feeling she had almost forgotten came flooding over her, leaving her a bit weak in the knees. Elizabeth shook her head as if to clear it of such fantasies, reached for the rail and headed down the stairs. There were fires to start in the stove and water to bring in for coffee and tea. The light of a new day was slipping in through the back windows.

Elizabeth's mind had not stopped working since the meeting the previous night. She had found it hard to sleep and spent most of the night lying in her bed staring into the darkness with the comments at the Meeting House running through her agile mind. During the past two years at the Schneider Farm, she had served as a teacher and supporter for Ami Ruth who had needed an older adult to fill the gap left by her beloved parents. Now Elizabeth was feeling a greater challenge than just the Schendler Farm and her immediate family. The idea for the barter store was a good one, but there was more, much more that could be done. However, her first and most important challenge was right here at home.

Elizabeth looked at the problem of saving the farm through the eyes of a veteran homemaker. She knew many places where they could economize and other places where they could generate income to help raise the tax money to save the farm. She and Ami Ruth could not deal with the big issues, but they could see that everything they needed for day-to-day living would either be generated on the farm or could be bartered with others in their community. It would require looking at each of the assets they had and figuring how to maximize the value of each.

When Ami Ruth arrived in the kitchen that morning, Elizabeth began to outline her plan. She was talking and working on breakfast at the same time. "First," she said, "we are going to take inventory of everything we have that is either needed for supporting the family or can be bartered or sold."

THE WOUNDS OF WAR

When the menfolk were gone from the breakfast table and the dishes taken care of, Aunt Elizabeth and Ami Ruth walked out to the storage room in the barn. Among the stores there, they found a large sealed barrel that took their combined efforts to get the lid off. The pungent aroma of coffee beans filled the air, and they found it was two-thirds full. Elizabeth knew that coffee beans were expensive and would certainly be valuable in the marketplace. Their supply in the house was running low and coffee was one of the items she had assumed they would have to learn to do without.

The barrel of coffee beans was a major surprise. She did not know they were there in the storehouse and had been buying coffee at the White Hall Store. Her mother had always said, "Don't look a gift horse in the mouth." Until now she wasn't exactly sure what that saying meant. However, the barrel that was nearly full of coffee beans was certainly a gift, and she wasn't going to question where it came from, even though she wondered. They bagged about ten pounds for their own use and filled several five-pound containers using the wheat scale to set the weights. Coffee could be bartered with neighbors for things they might not have available for the family.

Later, Elizabeth asked Matt if he had bought the coffee beans and he told her he had not. She decided they must have been stored there from two years before by Mr. Schendler. Coffee beans would spoil in about a month if stored in open air but, sealed air tight in a wooden barrel, they might last indefinitely. More than once, Elizabeth wondered where her brother-in-law had bought the coffee beans and what he would have used for money while the war was going on all around them.

When they finished with the rest of their inventory, they found that they had five bushels of shell corn, two of Irish potatoes and four of sweet potatoes, eight chickens, six of them laying hens, various baskets of squash, beans and okra, and a tin of baking powder. One of the things they did not have that would be needed was salt. Normally, they would buy it at the White Hall Store or in Winchester, but Aunt Elizabeth absolutely ruled out buying anything.

She explained to Ami Ruth how they would get salt for cooking. "We will dig up the smokehouse floor and boil and strain the dirt under it. We will boil it down and strain it again and again until all the dirt is gone. When the water is steamed away, all that will be left is the salt left in the ground from hog slaughters of previous years."

Ami Ruth had never heard of such a thing, but as the days passed and the work progressed, it happened just as Aunt Elizabeth said it would.

Later that day, Aunt Elizabeth took Ami Ruth out to the pig pen. They had a sow, a boar, and six piglets. She opened the gate of the pen, and with the handle of a broom, she persuaded the piglets out of the pen and toward the ridge at the back of the last corral. When she got to the edge of the ridge, she yelled loud enough to scare them up the ridge, and then turned back to Ami Ruth with a satisfied smile.

She said, "These little pigs are perfectly capable of foraging for themselves up on the ridge. We will put some food out for them from time to time here at the edge of the ridge, which will keep them coming back down to the farm. When we want them, we can easily round them up. In the meantime, if we get folks coming by in the dead of night who want to take what we have, the pigs will not be easy pickings. The boar and the sow easily weigh 400 pounds each, and the piglets will be spread out up on the ridge. It is not likely any of them will be lost to night riders."

Ami Ruth asked the obvious question, "What about the other animals?"

"The cows and the old mule will set up a howl if anyone enters the barn," Aunt Elizabeth said. "We should be able to hear them up in the big house. The horses will be inside with the noise makers and both of them are spirited enough to make getting them outside more difficult than a night rider might want to risk. Anyway, the cows and mule are our alarm system for anything inside the barn that may be in jeopardy. And of course, Mr. Mason is still sleeping in the room off of the loft. Any movement downstairs should alert him that there is trouble. He isn't Quaker, and I think he has Matt's Henry 60 rifle."

As the week passed, Ami Ruth found herself getting up earlier and earlier, almost matching Aunt Elizabeth's schedule. She would walk down to the kitchen in her robe and sit in a chair next to the stove and slowly drink a cup of hot tea while she listened to Aunt Elizabeth outline the plans for the day. By the time she rose from her warm chair and retreated to get dressed, she was usually tired from anticipating all they were going to do in the hours ahead. Usually by then Matt was stirring, and they would talk a bit before they dressed and came back down the stairs to meet the rest of the family at the breakfast table. Talk around the table was always related to the taxes and where the money would come from. In fact, the only talk at the table that didn't seem to be related to the tax obligation was the prayer at the beginning of the meal, which had been and would always be a part of their family tradition. It was their acknowledgment that God was always present in their home and in their lives.

The weekly visit to the White Hall Store and the bimonthly visit to the markets in Winchester became a thing of the past. They needed to make it on what they could produce on the farm and to act as if there was no outside world to lean on. They were farmers and they were Quakers. They needed only to have the land to live off of, and only the neighbors and their needs would intrude on their self-sufficiency. If the neighbors needed help and the Schendler Farm had it to give, they had only to ask. As for Aunt Elizabeth, Ami Ruth, and the Schendler Farm, they were not asking for help from anyone. They intended to live like the pioneers their parents had been and to be standing upright on their own feet when the crisis was behind them. In their minds, the crisis was serious but temporary. They would weather it and all would be back to normal by spring. They would see to it. God would see to it.

Each night, when Elizabeth found herself in bed staring into the darkness, her mind would wander back to the events of the day, to Isaac Mason and his growing presence in the family, to the things that needed to be done tomorrow and later in the week, and sometimes, it would wander back to the barrel of coffee beans in the barn. Where did Mr. Schendler get them and where did the money come from that he could spend for such a treasure? She kept the books for the household products, what was bought, where it was bought, and how much each item cost. Those coffee beans were off the books. There was no record of such a purchase in the past. She did not know where or when he purchased them. Where the money came from was a puzzle she would have to think about.

Ami Ruth became used to Aunt Elizabeth's early morning conversations. Actually, they weren't really conversations. Aunt Elizabeth talked and Ami Ruth listened. The words that stood out in her mind were plow, plant, cut, can, feed, and kill. With that last word in mind, one of the milestones came when Aunt Elizabeth coaxed her young charge to hold a struggling chicken down on the chopping block and cleave off its head with a hatchet. Another time when Aunt Elizabeth caught a chicken she had designated for supper without having a hatchet in her hand, she held the chicken by its head and twirled it around and around until the head came off in her hand. The headless chicken flopped around the yard until it lay in a bloody pile ready for the hot water that would help get the feathers off. Ami Ruth preferred the hatchet method, but the twirling chicken technique was not lost on her. She filed it away for future reference.

The early morning conversations and the daily work schedule were not enjoyable daily fare, but each was a learning experience that, in retrospect, Ami Ruth understood and valued. None of the lessons taught by Aunt Elizabeth were lost on Ami Ruth. She knew that each one was going to make her more ready to shoulder the burden of the farm and family down the road. Despite the fact that she felt tired all the time, she relished the learning experiences.

"Aunt Elizabeth," Ami Ruth asked one morning. "How have you learned so many things that I never heard from my mother?"

Aunt Elizabeth shrugged her slim shoulders. "Oh, I just learned them in the usual way. Because I never married, I made my way by working for several Quaker families in the area, mostly aging folks who needed a younger hand. A lot of it was grandmother knowledge I picked up from the older women who would answer my questions and teach me in return for helping them with the usual farm chores. I learned early that being attentive when older folks were talking was the way to learn things. Some of it I just puzzled out on my own."

Ami Ruth was not through with her questions. "You seem to know everything about the farm animals as well as planting and getting the crops in and yet you worked most of the time in the house with the women."

Aunt Elizabeth responded, "Well, if you kept your ears open at supper time, you could learn a load of things you never thought about. For instance, everything on a farm has a time and place. That includes killing hogs, making sauerkraut, putting up blackberry preserves, everything. You plant corn when the dogwood blooms die and drop off. With wheat, you plant after the last spring frost and cut it when it turns golden like an early fall sunset. Hogs are killed in the time of an early moon. If we do it at any other time, the meat will not have enough lard in it to lather up the pan and the cooked meat will not be right for eating," she explained.

One day, early in the fall, they were walking to the barn when more than two dozen chicks began swarming around them in the yard. Ami Ruth remembered that Aunt Elizabeth had said a month ago that they could kill one of the roosters for supper, but they needed to leave the eggs from the laying hens in the nest for about three weeks so they could hatch. That way they would have chicken all winter for the table. Here was the evidence that Aunt Elizabeth did, in fact, know exactly what she was talking about. Here was supper for many evenings through the winter. Before long, they would be back to having eggs for breakfast again.

Another day, Aunt Elizabeth suggested to her that she ask Matt if one of the winery workers could help out for an afternoon. They needed to find some honey from one or another of the bee hives up on the ridge. They knew the hives had to be there, otherwise where would the bees in the vineyard be coming from? She told Ami Ruth to instruct the man to find one or more honey bees that were buzzing around the vineyard in the late afternoon and follow them as they retreated up the ridge to their hive. Once the hive was found, he could come and report where it was. Aunt Elizabeth promised to show Ami Ruth how to get the honey without getting stung.

The report took them to an old dead tree up on the ridge. The bees looked like formidable adversaries to Ami Ruth, but Elizabeth built a fire around the trunk of the tree and put green leaves on it so it would smoke. They walked home with enough honey and comb material to cover their needs for several months, and the bees didn't even seem to mind. The bonus was that they had enough honey stored to sell. Sugar was a rare delicacy that cost money at the store, but you didn't need sugar if you had honey.

What they did need from the store were glass jars, the kind people in the North had been using for several years now, but the fighting along the Mason-Dixon Line had kept glass jars from arriving in the South. Aunt Elizabeth had heard from friends in West Virginia that the new glass jars were far superior to anything they had used for canning purposes before. The store at White Hall could get the jars, but the overriding question was, what would the store need that the Schendler Farm had a supply of that could be bartered?

Elizabeth and Ami Ruth hitched up a wagon the next day to find out. It was a short ride, just two miles up the road into the center of the Loop. When they arrived at the store, they found the shopkeeper, Mr. Mueller, standing behind the counter as usual. He was a rotund man with a Quaker beard, one that fit around his face with no mustache, and he was wearing a stained apron that had long ago been white. Aunt Elizabeth thought it odd that Mr. Mueller wore a Quaker beard since he was not a Quaker. Still, he seemed to be a likable man who knew almost everyone in the Loop. He had been running his store for many years and, in past times, had always been a very valuable member of their community.

When they entered the store it was obvious that the shelves were nearly empty. Any problems that affected the Quaker community were going to affect the store that supplied most of the Quaker farms in the Loop, and both supply and demand at the store were significantly down.

Aunt Elizabeth approached the counter, smiled at the shopkeeper, and asked, "Mr. Mueller, what do you need from the farms to supply your store?"

Mr. Mueller responded quickly, "We need anything and everything. My shelves are almost bare. Most people have stopped trading here because they have no money to spend. I haven't been able to convince anyone that we can trade and we can barter. As time passes, money will again be used, but not for the next few months while we are going through this adjustment time with the military government."

Aunt Elizabeth told Mr. Mueller what she needed. "We plan to can more than ever before this fall, and I need some of those new jars that our neighbors to the north can buy in Martinsburg or Charles Town. Can you supply them?"

The shopkeeper thought for a moment and responded, "Yes, Miss Elizabeth, we can get most anything you need if you will assure me that you will buy them when they arrive."

"Sir," she responded, "I don't have any money, but I do have some products from our farm that may be of use to you as resale items. How about coffee beans?"

Mr. Mueller smiled broadly and rubbed his hands together. "You are right on target there. Everyone wants coffee, but I don't have any and have no prospect of getting any. Do you have some you could let me have?"

Ami Ruth could see Aunt Elizabeth stifling a smile. She knew she had a deal in the making; it was up to her to make it as good a deal as she could. "Well, sir," she said, "how many glass jars and lids will you give me for five pounds of coffee beans?"

Mr. Mueller was obviously surprised by her offer. In a few minutes a deal was struck and the two ladies were back on the wagon and on the way home. He promised that they would have five jars for five pounds of coffee, twelve jars for ten pounds, and thirty jars for twenty pounds. No wonder Aunt Elizabeth was smiling! She could envision canning thirty jars of grape jelly to go with several jars of honey and selling them at an outdoor market in Charles Town where there were no vineyards. She was already calculating how much they could charge.

As they rode home, Aunt Elizabeth was thinking, *This was easy, maybe even fun.* Ami Ruth was thinking, *There will certainly be lots of work that will go into canning all that grape jelly!*

PUTTING THE COMMUNITY PLAN TO WORK

The Meeting House leadership had called their second meeting exactly a week after the first and followed that with a regular meeting every two weeks. The primary tasks they had agreed to in their first meeting were to create a meeting with the Northern Loop Quaker group—the ones in West Virginia—to share their problem and see if they could expect help. In addition, they were to find a place to appeal the heavy taxes placed on each of their farms and to make a case for exempting the Quaker farms from such a burden. Their case with the military leadership was that their Quaker community had remained neutral during the war. Why should they be taxed for a war in which they were not involved?

The women put together their barter store and that proved a very successful venture. Coming to the Meeting House once a week with a wagon half full of their farms' specialties allowed them to go home with a variety of different commodities that made purchasing items at the store unnecessary. Their once-a-week effort soon became part of the basic living plan of the women of the Quaker community, and it served to bring the ladies closer together as a group as well. When they were together, there was a never-ending patter of conversation about how to economize and how to keep their families stable amid the rising tension felt by their men.

The men had much to report to the group at the second meeting. The Quakers from north of the West Virginia border were going to be an asset as the days and weeks passed. They had offered to transport goods for sale and even to buy what was offered from their friends and relatives in the southern half of the Loop.

After two trips to the military adjutant's office in Winchester, the Quaker committee was finally given a date when they could appeal the taxes levied against their farms. When they made the request at the office for their appeal, it created a flurry of activity. It seemed that the office had never thought there might be an appeal of the assessments, so no process was in place. The Quakers were given a hearing date in early September. Now it was going to be necessary to put their appeal in writing and choose a spokesman to represent them at the hearing. Several were willing to make the trip for moral support, but the hastily created appeals process would allow only one presenter.

In the meantime, Matt had been thinking through the issue of assets on the Schendler Farm. Almost everything he could think of that would generate money required more manpower than he had available. Before this crisis, it had been their practice to pay each man a half-dollar a day and the noon meal for his labor in the winery and on other assignments. Those five men were sorely needed there to finish making the barrels for the wine and to get ready for the grape harvest.

One asset he had that would not cost money was Big Billy. Mr. Schendler had told Matt that such a fine stallion could generate new money for the farm. Matt wasn't sure he liked thinking of Big Billy as a part of the farm's crops. But if Mr. Schendler was right, and he thought he just might be, offering Big Billy as a stud horse to interested breeders might generate some additional income without adding additional costs. He resolved to put an advertisement in the newspapers in both Winchester and Charles Town as soon as he could get something ready to publish.

Early the next week, Matt sent one of the men to the newspapers in each of the closest towns. They advertised Big Billy's services for thirty-five dollars, a large sum for most to pay but not more than Big Billy was worth. For purposes of the advertisement he changed Big Billy's name to King William. He didn't care for the name, but

Ami Ruth suggested that adding a bit more class to the advertisement might generate more customers.

Matt also wanted to see if they could harvest some venison from the white deer herd living on the back side of the north ridge. Two of the men who worked for the winery had sons who were in their midteen years. A conversation with the men indicated that their sons would like to exercise their hunting skills on behalf of the farm. Matt offered them ten cents a day for their efforts, and the men countered asking for a flank of meat from each kill if the boys were successful. Getting enough money together to pay the boys would be accomplished by trading the meat at the barter store or selling it to Mr. Mueller at the White Hall Store. So a deal was struck, and the farm now had two hunters who would limit their work to the backside of the ridge.

Matt counted twelve wine casks that had been stored for one to three years and most of it was ready for the market. Virtually everything else Matt was planning was a "stay even" type of effort: any money that was to be generated would have to come from the sale of the wine. Isaac and Matt discussed where to sell the wine and decided to take it north of the border to Charles Town, and perhaps, Martinsburg in West Virginia. Both were in former Union territory, and if there was money available anywhere in the region it most likely would be there. And for sure, any purchases would be in Union dollars. It was most likely that taverns or merchants south of the border would not have the ready cash available to buy wine.

Charles Town was only about ten miles away, and there was only the Opequan Creek to cross between the farm and Charles Town, so one man could transport the wine. Isaac volunteered for the task, and told Matt if he was unsuccessful at Charles Town, it was not much farther up the road to Martinsburg and he could try there.

Matt's primary concern, other than keeping all the functioning parts of the farm running, was to find workers willing to help get the grapes into the winery and to help the experienced hands there get the juice pressed and into the fermentation barrels. That was necessary for the future of the farm but would not be of much help solving the tax situation for this year. In fact, paying the workers for bringing in this year's crop would be a drain that would require them to generate well more than the anticipated $1,400 assessment. It would take at least five field hands about thirty days to get the grapes in and another two weeks to process the grapes.

A quick calculation in Matt's mind told him that labor for the six crucial weeks would cost a minimum of just over $150. That meant they needed to generate about $1,650 in order to pay the men on the farm and the tax man at the end of November. Matt wasn't sure that was possible, but he was determined to try.

By the end of the next week, the third week in September, Isaac had the wine loaded on the strongest of the wagons. He had twelve casks, about 720 gallons of wine. The weight of the wine required that they use four horses and their biggest and strongest wagon to haul the wine. They did not have four horses available, so they borrowed two from the Murdock Farm down the road. Matt was rethinking his plan to send only Isaac to sell the wine. One cask of wine weighed almost 360 pounds, and normally it would take at least three men to lift it down off of the wagon. Isaac suggested that he take the two boys who had contracted for hunting deer on the trip to help with the lifting. Both were farm boys and used to hard work. He could take the boys along without upsetting any of the ongoing work on the farm or in the winery, so Matt agreed that was the best idea.

Matt watched the big wagon roll up the back ridge from the winery toward the West Virginia border. Jesse, one of the long-time hands at the winery, was standing close to Matt watching the wagon carrying his son, the other boy, and Isaac cross the ridge.

He said to Matt, "I saw Mr. Schendler head up that same road with a loaded wagon three times in the last year before the war took him and his missus. Each time he was by himself. I wondered then how he would get the wine casks off of the wagon, but each time he came back with an empty wagon."

Matt turned to Jesse and said, "Jess, do you know where he sold the wine?"

Jess shook his head. "No sir, I don't. The first time he went, he was obviously worried because he didn't know where he was going or even how much to charge for the barrels. The second time he went, he seemed to know exactly where he was going. Evidently, there are wine drinkers up north who are willing to pay for the privilege of drinking Schendler wine."

Matt now had another puzzle to unravel. His father-in-law had sold wine north of the border in West Virginia, or perhaps, in southern Pennsylvania. He emptied the wagon three times in the last year before the renegades came. He had found a market for the wine and, evidently, went back a second and third time with great success. It gave Matt hope but it also left him wondering.

Over the next week while Isaac was gone, Matt rode Big Billy into Winchester looking for workers for the grape harvest three different times. Having no success, he traveled up to Charles Town hoping to have better luck. He thought he might find Isaac there selling wine, but since he didn't see him, he assumed he had moved on to Martinsburg. When Matt came home from Charles Town, he was as emotionally low as he had been since his Ma died. He wondered what he was going to do to get the grapes out of the field and into the winery for processing. He wondered how they were going to generate more than $1,600 in just two months. He wondered where they would move if he couldn't find a way to solve this problem.

That night he and Ami Ruth sat up late talking. They moved their small couch—what some called a love seat—over by the front window in their bedroom where they could sit together in the dark and feel the evening breezes moving through the big oak trees in front of the house. Matt wasn't sure what to tell Ami Ruth other than to let her know he was worried. It turned out that his pronouncement of their dilemma was not news to her.

"Matt," she said, squeezing his hand, "I have known how worried you are for several weeks now. You are working so hard to make everything come out right for us. I can't help but believe that it will. God doesn't give us more than we can bear, and our farm has more assets that most around here."

"But the problem is labor for the vineyard," Matt said. "There just aren't enough able-bodied men in the area to cut the grapes and get them into the winery for processing. Before the war and even while the war was going on, we could find men who needed to work, who could leave their own farms for periods of time and pitch in to help us clear the field. And back then, we had only the small acreage in the front of the big house to worry with. Everything else we could handle ourselves mostly because the stress came at different times of the year. With one major cash crop, it all comes due at one time, and if you don't get it in, it spoils in about a month. If we don't find the labor and get the crop in between now and six weeks from now, we have to wait until next year to make a crop."

"I have a proposal for both of us," she said. "Let's go to bed tonight and sleep on it. Isaac may be back tomorrow and the three of us can talk it through."

Matt and Ami Ruth started to move their quiet conversation to the bed when they heard a voice through the window. They both listened intently. It was Isaac's voice, carried on the breeze. Then they heard another voice, softer and hard to distinguish. Ami Ruth looked at Matt and smiled.

She said, "It's Aunt Elizabeth, Matt. Your father and Aunt Elizabeth are on the porch in the big rockers talking. He must have come back after we went upstairs and found her still in the kitchen."

When they climbed into bed under their patchwork quilt, Pa was still on Matt's mind. His Pa and Aunt Elizabeth! That would take some getting used to. However, there was no mistaking the smile on Ami Ruth's face.

SELLING WINE IN WEST VIRGINIA

Seeing his Pa at breakfast with a big smile on his face gave Matt a much-needed emotional lift. Isaac was back and, most importantly, with an empty wagon. Further, he was in an obvious good mood. As they forked up their eggs, Matt and Ami Ruth watched Isaac and Aunt Elizabeth closely for any signs of their growing attachment, but they couldn't detect evidence of anything different between them.

When breakfast was over, Isaac suggested to Matt that they all go to the porch so he could tell them about the trip to West Virginia. A short minute later, they were gathered around the rockers on the front porch. It was a fitting place for a major family discussion. They were in the place where Matt had first arrived at the Schendler Farm, where he and Ami Ruth had been married, and where Isaac had arrived in the middle of their wedding. And the view in the distance included the lane up to the road where Big Billy and the grey mare were grazing.

Matt was sure his anxiety was showing. When he couldn't wait any longer, he blurted out, "Pa, how did it go?"

Isaac reached behind him and handed Matt a brown leather pouch that had been on a strap around his waist. With a wide grin, he said, "Matt, it went better than we could have hoped. The proof is in the pouch."

Matt opened the brass clasp on the pouch and reached inside. He felt three small bundles and pulled one out. It was a stack of twenty dollar bills, Union money.

He started to count the greenbacks in the stack, but Pa's voice broke in. "Matt, there are twenty bills in each stack, a total of twelve hundred dollars," he said. "More important, I know where to get the rest of the money we need for the taxes!"

Matt's wide eyes broke away from the stacks of money in his lap. His Pa's expansive face was showing the biggest smile he had ever seen. Matt said, "Pa, I don't understand. How did you do this? This is more money than I have ever seen at one time!"

"Well, Son, your sainted Ma used to say that 'God works in mysterious ways, his wonders to perform.' In this case, your father-in-law, on one of his trips to sell wine in West Virginia, put in place an arrangement that will be of great benefit to us down the road. That is, if we can solve some of our labor problems for the grape harvest."

Matt began to laugh out loud and Isaac joined him with his deep baritone voice. Ami Ruth was on her feet and had Aunt Elizabeth in a full body hug. Both ladies were moving their feet as if they were dancing though, of course, they weren't. Quaker ladies don't dance. But if they did, this would certainly have been the time.

Matt got up and went around the chair and reached for Ami Ruth. In a second, Matt had her feet off of the floor and was swinging her in a circle. She could see Isaac laughing over Matt's shoulder as she spun around.

When all had calmed down, they were all looking at Isaac waiting for his story about the trip to West Virginia to sell their wagon load of wine.

"I was in Charles Town for two days without selling anything," Isaac began. "I went from door to door, from store to tavern, and even set up on the roadside with a sign offering to sell our wine. I had no luck. Several men stopped and asked for free samples, but I realized after the third request that they were not serious shoppers.

"So I headed up the road toward Martinsburg," he continued. "That was a long twelve miles, and after my experience in Charles Town, I was not optimistic. I stopped at the south edge of Martinsburg and the boys and I spent the night there. The next morning I left the wagon with the boys and went into the town just like I had in

Charles Town. The result was much the same. Every stop was a disappointment. By midafternoon, I went back to the wagon. From a distance I could see that there were two horses tied up in the shade and a couple of men were talking to our boys."

Matt could sense from his Pa's voice that the story was about to get interesting. He leaned forward in his chair, riveting his eyes on his father's face.

"When I approached the two men, one of them reached out his hand to me and introduced himself as Robert Thornton," Pa said. "He told me he had heard that we were in the community selling Schendler wine, and he came to find us. He then told me a story that was three years old, about Mr. Schendler coming to Martinsburg in 1862 and twice in 1863. Mr. Thornton said that he had bought all of Mr. Schendler's wine the first time he came and contracted with him for all he had to sell into the future. He said he emptied his wagon at Thornton Enterprises all three times when he came with wine to sell. He said he kept looking for him to come again but, until now, had not seen anyone from Schendler Farm."

Matt looked at Ami Ruth, "Did you have any idea your father had made an arrangement to sell wine to this man in Martinsburg?"

Ami Ruth shook her head. "No, and I don't think mother ever knew either. Each time he came back from West Virginia, he had an empty wagon. But he never said where he sold the wine nor for how much."

Isaac continued, "I told Mr. Thornton what had happened to Mr. Schendler back in '63 and gave him a quick update on your marriage and the new situation south of the border in Virginia. Mr. Thornton indicated that he was still interested in buying Schendler wines. So I asked him how much wine he would like to buy. I held my breath as he answered. He said he still wanted to buy all that I could bring him."

Isaac sat back and let that sink in for a few seconds. He was smiling that big grin of his as he continued, "I asked him what he had paid Mr. Schendler for the first load of wine and he told me they had agreed on one hundred dollars a barrel. I asked him if that price was still all right with him and he said it was. The one catch was that I had to deliver it to his place of business before I got paid."

"Oh, Matt," Ami Ruth broke in, "Do we have enough for the taxes now?"

"Pa brought us $1,200 and that is a good start but we still will need at least another $600 to pay the tax and the workers, that is if we can find any to help harvest the grapes," Matt replied.

He turned to his father. "Pa, we won't have any more wine to sell until next fall, and we are still about $600 short. I'm not sure what we can do to make up the difference."

"I have an idea that may be worth pursuing, Matt, and it involves a new arrangement with Mr. Thornton," Pa said. "There are three things that have been on my mind on the trip home after I left Thornton Enterprises in Martinsburg.

"First, I looked inside of Thornton's warehouse. It is a big building with lots of room. He has wine casks stored there, not only ours but others as well. Evidently, he is a big-time distributor. Is it possible that we could sell him barrels of wine that have not yet matured at a reduced cost that he could keep in his storage area for a year or two and make an even bigger profit on it down the road? If so, we have more than forty barrels stored in the winery that could be transported to Martinsburg and sold for enough money to handle our problem. We could probably meet our immediate need with about twelve barrels sold at half price. It would short us a bit down the road, but it would solve the current problem. We would worry about the shortage problem when we come to it."

Isaac let that sink in before he added the next thing that was on his mind. "I couldn't stop thinking about the fact that Thornton is bottling wine, our wine and others, and selling it under his own label. I saw shelves full of glass bottles, bottles like I have never seen before. I asked a worker where they came from, and he told me they were shipped from a glass bottle maker in Buffalo, New York. If Thornton can bottle wine, so can we. If he is making a profit from buying barrels of wine from a variety of sources and putting them in smaller containers to be sold from store shelves and in taverns, we can do it from here just as well. It may not be something we can afford to do this year in the midst of this crisis, but looking forward two or three years, we can add a bottling process and begin to sell our own label. If we can do that, we can make ten times as much money as we are able to generate now."

Matt, Ami Ruth, and Aunt Elizabeth were all nodding and smiling, nearly breathless with the prospect of having their financial problem solved and a whole new enterprise for their future.

Isaac was obviously enjoying the reaction of his family and could hardly wait to share his third idea. He continued, "The last thing that was on my mind had to do with Ami Ruth's father taking his wine up over the back road into West Virginia and selling it in Martinsburg. Correct me if I'm wrong, Matt, but wasn't selling products in Union country illegal during the war?"

Matt thought for a minute and nodded, "We were pretty limited with where we could sell anything. We had the White Hall Store down the road and the marketplace in Winchester that were available to us. We only had the farm products to sell and there was no effort on our part to sell any of the wine anywhere at first. Last spring, I took a wagon load of six barrels into the suburbs of Washington. Half of it sold right away and then a couple of businessmen from Baltimore showed up and bought the rest of it. I think they must have been doing what Mr. Thornton was doing. They gave me their address and told me they would buy whatever I had available. However, most of the wine we had stored was just not mature enough to sell, though some was approaching the minimum time for taking it to market."

"That is about what I thought," Isaac responded. "So Mr. Schendler was selling wine in West Virginia to people in a Union state. Unlike Matt in the Virginia suburbs of Washington, he was selling his wine for Union greenbacks. If a wagon load of wine can bring $1,200 in Martinsburg in greenbacks, where would Mr. Schendler have spent that money back here across the border in the South? Could anyone legally accept Union dollars for payment here in Virginia while the war was going on?"

The four of them looked at each other, and they began shaking their heads. "No," Ami Ruth responded. "Greenbacks were not accepted anywhere in Virginia, though there was a bit of black market enterprise going on from time to time."

"That leads me to a most important question," Isaac said. "If Mr. Schendler sold wine for greenbacks in West Virginia but couldn't buy anything with it here in Virginia, where are those greenbacks?"

Isaac let that question soak in for a few moments before he continued. "Ami Ruth, do you remember ever hearing your folks talking about using greenbacks for purchases? Did you ever hear a discussion between the two of them about hiding money where the renegades who were moving up and down these back roads could not find it? The obvious question on my mind is, what happened to the money?"

There was silence in the group for several seconds before Ami Ruth spoke. "My parents never talked about money around me. I don't remember ever hearing them mention greenbacks or Confederate greybacks for that matter. There might have been some money hidden, but I really don't know. When we needed money for something, a new wagon, a horse, or a side of beef, my Pa always came up with what was needed, and we brought it home. No one ever talked about money."

Aunt Elizabeth had been totally silent throughout the discussion. Now she spoke. "I was never here for any length of time before my sister and Mr. Schendler were killed. I never heard any discussion about money. And in fact, my sister never talked about money at all, though she never seemed to want for anything."

Aunt Elizabeth paused thoughtfully before continuing, "There is one thing though. Since I have been here and have been responsible for keeping the books on the household purchases, there are several questions that have come up for which I have no answers. For instance, Ami Ruth and I took inventory in the storehouse the other day and found that big barrel of coffee beans. It was sealed tight and a sealed barrel would preserve the beans for months and even years. However, a barrel of coffee beans, whether it was during wartime or today, might cost as much as two hundred dollars. There is no record of it being purchased, and for that matter, Ami Ruth and I didn't know it was there. It is a legitimate question to ask where the barrel of coffee beans came from and how they were paid for."

"So it is logical to assume that there is some money hidden somewhere here on the Schendler Farm," Isaac said. "I did not know your folks, Ami Ruth. Where would they hide something that was very valuable to them?"

Such a prospect had never occurred to Ami Ruth. "I really don't know. Do you think it is here in the house somewhere?" she asked.

Isaac responded, "I have an advantage on the three of you since I have been thinking about this all the way from Martinsburg. The money could be anywhere, but trying to think as a conservative man like Mr. Schendler would, I doubt it would have been hidden in the big house or in the barn. Farms have been burned down all up and down the valley. Every time an army marched through something was being burned down, and that seemed an every-week event around Winchester. I don't think Mr. Schendler would run the risk of having it where it might be burned with the house or barn. That leaves burying it on the grounds, the gardens, or perhaps in the winery."

Ami Ruth nodded. "If he hid it in the winery, we would never have known about it in the big house. I'm not sure I could even show anyone around the winery. Except for meals which we served to the workers on the tables upstairs, I've only been inside three or four times, and Matt knows much more about that operation than I do."

Isaac said, "Let's allow this treasure hunt thought to settle a bit, but everyone keep thinking about it and in your spare time look in all the secret places you can think of. In the meantime, Matt and I need to go back up to Martinsburg and talk to Mr. Thornton about the possibility of purchasing some additional wine from us."

* * *

Matt and Isaac let a couple of days pass in order to catch up on the normal day-to-day work on the farm. Then they saddled up Big Billy and the grey mare and got themselves ready for a couple of days on the road. Just before they were ready to mount their horses, Ami Ruth appeared with a letter.

"Matt, could you post this in Martinsburg when you go through?" she asked.

Down the road a bit, Matt took the letter out and looked at the address. It was written to someone named Tybee who lived in Gettysburg, Pennsylvania. When they rode through Martinsburg late that afternoon, Matt dropped off the letter at the post office. They decided to stop at the boarding house across the street from the post office for a light supper.

The letter was not on his mind when they camped on the outskirts of Martinsburg that night. The next morning, they would arrive at Thornton Enterprises and, with some luck, would soon solve the rest of their tax money problems.

Matt and Isaac arrived at Mr. Thornton's place of business at around eight thirty in the morning and waited a bit for the wine distributor to arrive. While they waited, they accepted the offer of one of the men to show them around their facilities. There was an office in the front with a large wooden storage building just behind, similar to the one on the Schendler Farm but much larger. When they entered that big building, the smell of fermenting grape juice filled their nostrils. Walking through the building, Matt noted the wine casks with "Schendler" painted on the ends stored among the other barrels. There were products other than wine as well, but Matt couldn't make out what was in the other barrels.

The back building was what Isaac wanted Matt to see. It was the bottling building. When they walked in, the smell of fermented grapes was even stronger than in the first building. There was a table full of bottles and a framework above the table with casks of wine sitting on the framework. Each cask had a tube running down from it, and the workers below were filling the bottles with wine. Matt looked closely to see if any of the casks had "Schendler" stamped on the side, but apparently it was not their wine going into the bottles. However, it wasn't hard to imagine that it would not be long until the wine Isaac had sold to Mr. Thornton would be in those bottles and headed out to the market under a different label.

By the time they were back to the office, Mr. Thornton was seated at his imposing wooden desk. He rose from his big leather chair and greeted them graciously when they came in. Mr. Thornton was a big man, perhaps more than three hundred pounds, and his office was spacious. He wore a flannel shirt that hung out of his pants and his shoes were, obviously, those of a man who liked to work on the ground. The desk was off to the left and there were four chairs around a small table just to the right.

"Mr. Thornton, I want you to meet my son, Matthew Mason," Isaac said. "He is the manager of the Schendler Farm and the one who sent me to Martinsburg last week where I met you."

Mr. Thornton stepped out from behind the desk and took Matt's hand in a firm grip. "I'm pleased to know you, Matthew. Your father and I had a good discussion about you and the farm when we met earlier. I'm sure you and I are going to develop a good relationship too. Let's sit down where we can be comfortable."

Mr. Thornton took a seat in one of the chairs around the small table, a place obviously set up for discussion with visitors, and Matt and Isaac joined him. "Would either of you like some coffee or something cold to drink?" he asked. Both Isaac and Matt indicated that coffee wasn't necessary, but Matt noted that Mr. Thornton was treating them with some deference and that he was, obviously, a man who liked to observe the customs of hospitality for which the South was famous.

"So what can I do for you today, Mr. Mason?" he asked.

Matt was not sure where to start but thought it best to review some of the history between Mr. Thornton and his father-in-law. "My Pa told me about your arrangement with Mr. Schendler that began three years ago, Mr. Thornton. None of us on the farm knew of this arrangement, and I didn't even come on the scene until the summer of '63. Mr. Schendler's daughter and I were married just a few weeks ago, and so now the responsibility for the future of the farm and any new arrangements fall on my shoulders."

Mr. Thornton's chair creaked as he leaned forward. "I was very sorry to hear of the passing of Mr. Schendler," he said softly. "He was a fine man and one I looked forward to having a long and productive relationship with. Please give my condolences to your wife and the rest of the family. I'm sure you will step into his shoes very well."

"Thank you, sir," Matt said sincerely. "Mr. Thornton, you indicated to Mr. Schendler and to my Pa that you would buy all the wine we could bring you. Is that still something you want to do?"

Mr. Thornton smiled and responded, "Matt, I have a storehouse that isn't half full and customers from Philadelphia to Pittsburgh who can't get enough of our product. They keep us on the road day and night making deliveries. Given a fair price, I will buy whatever you have to sell and be pleased to have it. We can make a new contract, work under the old agreement, or just shake hands and agree as gentlemen to honor our word. It's your choice."

"Well, I am sure your word is good, and I do have a proposal for you that is a little different than you are used to, at least for the next year or so," Matt said. "I have a storehouse about half the size of yours that is almost full of wine that is aging. It isn't ready for the market yet, but I have the need to sell some of it now. I note from our earlier tour that you have room for storage in your warehouse. I could make several barrels of wine available to you at a good price, but you would need to store them until they are ready to bottle, which will be in one to two years."

Mr. Thornton leaned forward in his chair and smiled, obviously interested in the prospect of having wine at a "good price." He responded, "Matt, when you talk of price, what are you thinking? I have paid you $100 a barrel for mature wine ready for the market. What would you charge me for wine that is not yet ready and must be stored?"

Matt swallowed twice and thought to himself, *This is where we succeed or fail. This is where we solve our problem or we have to come up with some other options.* "Mr. Thornton, I could let you have six barrels of wine that will mature next fall for $75 a barrel and six barrels that will mature in two years for $50 a barrel. The total for the twelve barrels would be $750."

Mr. Thornton thought for a few seconds and responded, "Matt, I don't like to store wine. I like to move it to the market and have never bought wine that had to be stored before it was ready for bottling. What you are suggesting would be something very new for us. However, I was pleased with my arrangement with Mr. Schendler and want to have a long-term relationship with you as well. In the interest of that good relationship, how about all twelve barrels for $500 and I will make that deal with you right now."

The $500 offered by Mr. Thornton would just about wipe out the financial crisis. Matt was tempted to say yes, but something told him that the deal Mr. Thornton was offering was not the best deal that could be struck.

Matt responded, "Mr. Thornton, you are obviously a fine businessman. I know you have already calculated in your mind that if we store the wine until it is ready and sell it to you at $100 a barrel your profit will be well below what you can make off of it if we bring it now and you store it. It is really a 'bird-in-the-hand' when it is already in your warehouse. In our warehouse you run the risk that someone will come along with a better financial deal for us, and you will be left with less wine than you can sell. My price is solid. Seven hundred and fifty dollars for twelve barrels of wine is a very fair price.

"And, Mr. Thornton, there is one more thing an additional arrangement I would like," Matt added.

"What is that?" asked Mr. Thornton.

"I have two men devoted to making barrels for the wine, and I would like to ease the burden on them. With that in mind, I would like to buy back the empty barrels with 'Schendler' stamped on the side. So when we bring you twelve barrels of wine we would like to take home twelve empty barrels. For that concession I am willing to pay you five dollars a barrel or sixty dollars for the twelve empty barrels."

Mr. Thornton was smiling. "Young man," Mr. Thornton said, "you are going to make a fine business man. I am pleased to have you as a supplier and will take your deal and be glad to have it. When can you get the wine to me?"

* * *

Matt and Isaac were well down the road south of Martinsburg before either of them spoke about the transaction.

THE WOUNDS OF WAR

Isaac said, "Matt, I was never more proud of you than I was the moment you responded to Mr. Thornton's counteroffer. I knew the $500 he was offering would have solved our immediate problem and anyone would have been tempted to take it. You stuck to your guns and he blinked first. That was a fine negotiation."

"I wasn't sure, Pa," Matt said. "He could have backed away and left us with nothing. It was a risk. I'm pleased we have the immediate problem solved, but I still have butterflies in my stomach. What if I had lost it?"

"The point is," Isaac said, "you didn't lose it. You won it. There were two good business men at the table today. Both of you got what you wanted and both left feeling good. The best business deal is one where everyone wins. That is what happened today. Both of you won. Now all we have to do is to deliver another twelve barrels of wine to Mr. Thornton, and we have the necessary money to meet all of our obligations, the taxes, and the wages for our workers."

"That is the next thing," Matt said. "I have looked in all the places I can find for labor to help get the grape crop in, but I have had no luck. The back-up plan is for all of us to get our cutting knives and go to the vineyard starting about two weeks from now. I think if we bring the five men, the two boys, and the two of us, we will have about half of what we need to get the crop in. That will not make it a total loss, but it will certainly slow down our future plans. Perhaps one of the best things about our deal with Mr. Thornton is that we will still have about a dozen and a half barrels of mature wine for the market next year, even after we provide what we have promised to him. That will keep us in business until we can solve the field labor issues."

"And if we could find Mr. Schendler's missing money, that would certainly cure most of our ills," said Isaac.

CHALLENGES MOUNTING UP

Late September found the Mason family, along with the other Quaker families of the southern Loop, back at the Hopewell Friends Meeting House sharing their issues and problems with each other. The presentation of their petition for relief from the taxes had taken place the week before, and that was the first report given to the group.

Mr. Ridgeway continued to play the role of convener for the group. When he took his place at the front of the Meeting House, the room went totally quiet. Just as had been the case when they last met, the Meeting House was full. Matt and Isaac sat on the back row of the men's section, and Ami Ruth and Aunt Elizabeth were seated about midway up in the women's section. Mr. Ridgeway approached the group in his usual business-like way, getting right to the point.

He said, "Our committee of three, Mr. Poteate, Mr. Robinson, and myself, made our presentation before the adjutant's office in Winchester last week. Rumors move quickly in our small community, so I know that most of you have heard of the outcome. In truth, there was no outcome, just another layer of administration to appeal to. They promised to take our petition to the military governor in Richmond. They were not sure when we would get word back but maybe next month, sometime in early to mid-October."

Mr. Moon spoke from the floor in his deep voice, "I heard that he didn't give us much hope of a successful petition. Is that true?"

"It is," Mr. Ridgeway responded. "The adjutant said the tax was placed on farms and businesses by the US Congress, and it was likely that our petition would have to go all the way to the floor of Congress before we might get relief from paying what has been assessed. He told us he had read the law that was passed, and there did not seem to be any flexibility once the land had been evaluated and assessed."

The elderly Mrs. John Poteate spoke next in her frail voice. She said, "It is as I said when we met in August. It is not likely that appealing the tax will have any success. We are in the South. The Union is making an effort to recoup the cost of the war at our expense. We may get word back next month, or we may have another delay in getting the answer we want. However, in any give and take with the government, Quakers have never fared well. We need to be ready to pay the tax or to forfeit our farms. There does not seem to be any middle ground on this issue."

"Thank you, Mrs. Poteate," Mr. Ridgeway said. "We will keep you apprised of any results of the petition process. We do have some other things to report that hold more promise for us. Mr. Robinson is with us again from north of the border. Can you share your thoughts with us, Mr. Robinson?"

Mr. Robinson, a tall man of middle age with a gaunt frame, made his way to the front of the Meeting House. "The meeting with the north Loop families turned out very well. It was a well-attended meeting, and there were many offers of help," he said. "I think you folks can bring any crops or almost anything you have to sell up north, and we will either take them to market for you or we will buy everything you bring. Mr. Moon brought the first wagon load last week and took home almost eighty dollars. That is progress."

Mr. Moon responded from his seat against the wall, "Yes, I took the wagon to the North Loop Meeting House, and everything we had put together to sell was gone within a couple of hours. I think we can go back every week until the end of November, and perhaps we can bring home as much as one hundred dollars a trip. That is about eight hundred dollars we will have generated."

"Well, that isn't enough," Mr. Beeson responded. "When we listed the needs of our group at the end of the meeting last month, the total exceeded thirty thousand dollars. Obviously, we can't generate the entire amount with this effort. I know that every bit counts, but each family is going to have to be responsible for meeting their own obligation and any of us who have more than we need are going to have to share with others who can't come up with the necessary tax money."

Aunt Elizabeth's voice was the next one heard. She said, "On a positive note, the barter store is proving to be a big success. We are finding much to share and trade goods are moving at a brisk pace. With the exception of salt, sugar, and coffee, most of us will not have to buy anything at all at the store until we get through this crisis."

Matt and the rest of the family had all breathed a sigh of relief knowing they had the money to pay the taxes in hand. But there was shared anguish on the faces of almost everyone in the room as they realized that some of their friends had little chance of meeting the challenge of raising the tax money and might lose their homes and livelihood.

On the way home in the wagon, the conversation focused on the immediate problems they were going to have on the Schendler Farm.

Matt said, "Pa's last delivery trip to Thornton Enterprises in Martinsburg brought back the money needed to pay both back and future wages to the workers, and we now have enough money for the taxes whether the final figure is $1,000 or the $1,400 that may be assessed when they catch up with Mr. Schendler's additional land purchase. The farm is safe. That was the first problem we had to solve, and we are going to be okay there."

Ami Ruth asked, "What about finding enough labor to cut the grapes?"

"That is the major problem we have for the next three to six weeks," Matt admitted. "We have to find enough labor to help cut the grapes and to help with the beginning of the wine-making process. I think some of the grapes will be ready to cut by the beginning of next week. I am going to make one more trip into Charles Town to see if I can find an additional ten men for harvesting. If I don't find what we need, we will take the five men from the winery and Pa and I. We will begin to harvest the grapes. Within a couple of days, we would need at least three of the men back in the winery to begin processing them. That will leave us running behind in the fields. Without some help, there is no way we can cut all the grapes. I hate to let them go to waste, but without additional hands we can't make a full crop."

Aunt Elizabeth responded, "Matt, is there the possibility that some of the young people from the other farms could help? We now have the money to pay them and several of the families close by have older children who might be able to give us several days in the field."

"That is a fine idea," Matt agreed. "Give some thought to which families have children, and I will see if I can attract them. They will probably need to be at least eleven or so before they can stand the stress of the work and the sun. But if there are enough of them we could use them in half-day shifts. Thank you, Aunt Elizabeth."

Isaac turned the wagon into the lane in front of the house, and as they drew closer in the fading light, Matt saw that there was a horse tied up to the gate in front of the house.

"Does anyone know whose horse that is?" Matt asked. As they came closer to the gate, he saw that the horse had a rope halter but no saddle. This was strange, indeed. "Is anyone expecting company?"

There was no response from the group, but just as they came through the gate, two black faces emerged from around the edge of the porch. Isaac drew up the horse and stopped the wagon.

Ami Ruth's voice rang out from the back of the wagon. "Tybee, you came!" Then she was down from the wagon and running to meet the smiling face of Tybee, a young black man about eighteen years of age. Before Matt could get down off of the wagon, it was obvious from their smiles that Tybee and Ami Ruth were friends who had not seen each other for a very long time.

Matt approached the pair just as the second visitor came into the group. She was a smaller version of Ami Ruth except for the fact that she had a very dark complexion and black hair in braids around her head. Both of the young people had bare feet, and it was obvious they had been traveling for some distance.

Matt's eyes asked the question without saying a word. Ami Ruth began to explain.

"A few weeks back, I wrote a letter to Tybee," she said. "Matt, you carried it to the post office for me on one of your trips north. Tybee and several others came through here one night on the Underground Railroad route and stopped over with us. The weather was so bad that they stayed three days and nights in the basement hiding place in the winery before moving on. Mother and I provided their food while they were there, and Tybee, who was about sixteen at the time, became my friend. I didn't know if the letter would reach him, but I did know where the Underground Railroad was taking him. My father told me the destination in Gettysburg and that most of the runaway slaves were dispersed from there. He said he wasn't supposed to know any of the stops except the one just north of us, but someone guiding the group had told him. Anyway, I thought that if anyone knew where Tybee's group was now, it would be the people at the final stop in Gettysburg."

Matt took Ami Ruth's hand and led her away from the group. He said, "So, wife-of-mine, what are they doing here?"

Ami Ruth laughed, "Why, they are a part of our field labor force. I thought that since we helped them get free they might be able to come back and help us with the harvest. In the letter I asked Tybee if he could run the Underground Railroad in reverse and bring us some workers for the grape harvest. I didn't know if the letter would reach him. I didn't know if he was free to come and help. I didn't know if he could bring anyone with him. What I did know was that if all the pieces in this puzzle fit together, it would go a long way toward solving our labor problem, at least for this fall."

"So let me get this straight, Ami Ruth, you conjured this up in your mind and didn't say a word to me about it?" Matt asked.

"I almost told you several times, Matt," she responded. "But I thought there was only a small chance it would all fit together, and I didn't want you to get your hopes up for something that probably wouldn't happen."

By this point, everyone but Matt had been introduced to the newcomers. Ami Ruth took Matt's hand and led him to the porch steps where everyone had gathered.

Ami Ruth smiled at Tybee and said, "Tybee, this is my husband, Matt Mason. Matt, this is Tybee." Matt put out his hand to the young man who was almost as tall as he was.

Tybee took the hand and glanced toward the young woman he had brought with him. He said, "This be Seabrook, my wife. And we has a last name. We's Harts, Tybee and Seabrook Hart."

"Oh, Tybee, you are married? How wonderful!" she exclaimed.

Aunt Elizabeth broke into the conversation with a question, "So we will be six for supper?"

"Oh, yes," Ami Ruth responded. "We will have them to supper as long as they are here. Let's get them to the back porch where they can wash up from their trip. We will figure out accommodations over supper."

Matt looked at Isaac and said, "Pa, you have been in the room in the barn loft long enough. Let's move you into the house and let Tybee and Seabrook have the privacy of that loft room."

Isaac smiled at the thought and responded, "I'm pleased to move to make room for our new friends, though I have certainly enjoyed the privacy of that space above the animals. The one exception to that is when the mule decides to announce his presence which he seems to do every other morning." Everyone laughed.

Matt looked over at Ami Ruth and said, "So it's settled then. Pa will move into the house and Tybee and Seabrook will take the room in the barn loft."

Ami Ruth nodded. With that exchange, Aunt Elizabeth and Ami Ruth walked through the house into the kitchen while Matt showed the new guests the back porch.

Aunt Elizabeth asked, "Shall we eat in the dining room on the bigger table? The one we have been using in the kitchen seats four comfortably but not six."

Ami Ruth responded, "Oh, this one will do fine. It is more comfortable here and easier than carrying all the food into the dining room. This table will seat six. We just have to open it up. Stand at the far end and I will show you some Schendler Farm magic."

Aunt Elizabeth went to the opposite end of the table, and following Ami Ruth's direction, the two ladies took hold of the sides of the table and pulled it apart at the joint in the middle. As they pulled, a hidden leaf for the table materialized from underneath. It lifted up to table level as if by magic and fit exactly between the two larger sections of the table. When they pushed the two ends back together, they had a table that would accommodate six people comfortably.

"I've been here for two years and didn't know that table had such an apparatus," Aunt Elizabeth said. "I've never seen anything like that, Ami Ruth, where did you get it?"

"My father made it," she responded. "He was a wizard with wood. He could make almost anything. I remember watching him work on this table. Actually, he was working on two tables at the same time. This one he finished, and it has served as our kitchen table ever since. I don't know where the other one is. He may not have finished it since I don't remember ever seeing it again."

Before long, they were all seated at the table. It was a typical Schendler supper with all kinds of food, not the more limited fare they had become used to while they were worrying about the tax money. They had two full chickens as well as three different kinds of vegetables with milk, coffee, and tea to drink. Aunt Elizabeth had made some biscuits which were sitting at the edge of the stove keeping warm, and it was their aroma that filled the room. Ami Ruth watched Tybee with amusement as he tried virtually everything on the table. It was obvious that he had never seen so much food at one time. He was determined not to let anything go to waste.

Supper conversation revolved around the two visitors. Ami Ruth had many questions for them, and they were pleased to respond in between mouthfuls of food. Tybee and Seabrook had passed through the Schendler Farm and moved on to two other locations before arriving in Gettysburg. From there, a family from near Lebanon came and took them farther north. They had been living on the farm of that family for the past two years.

Aunt Elizabeth was curious about their names. "Where did you get the names of Tybee and Seabrook?" She asked. Ami Ruth smiled because she knew the answer to that question. She had asked it two years earlier and was surprised at the answer.

Tybee responded, "Our master on the farm in Georgia, the one we was runnin' away from when we done got here, he gived them to us. He had him a farm in Hart County, Georgia, but he come from the coast. He done named each of us after an island on the coast. So I be Tybee, she be Seabrook, and three others who be here in a day or two, they named Simon, Sapelo, and Jekyll. When we done went to the court house in Lebanon to register as free people of Pennsylvania, they tole us we had to have a last name. We done talk about it for a bit and said we goin' to use Hart as our last name. That because we all from Georgia, named after islands, and we were raised up in Hart County. We know'd we be free, but we don't never want to forget where we come from. Our chilren and our chilren's chilren need to remember that we was slaves and now we be free."

Seabrook added in a very low whisper, "Thank God Amighty."

"Yes," said Tybee, "Thank God Amighty. But thank you too and your folks. I don't never forget Mr. Schendler and the kindness he done show. I weren't sure we would make it 'til he sat with us one night and tole us about Jesus. He say we could put our faith in something bigger and stronger than we was, and Jesus would carry us through. He done seem so sure of what he be saying to us. His words was so strong that he done make us believe it. It done turn out that he be right. We done make it to Gettysburg. We done make it to Lebanon. And now we be back with you to say thank you the best way we can."

Matt asked the question that was on everyone's mind. "Tybee, you mentioned others coming. Can you tell us when?"

"We espect that Simon, Sapelo, and Jekyll be along in a few days. They be at a neighbor farm, and they had a couple of days work to do afore they come. All three 'membered you folks, and most specially, Mr. Schendler. I done ask them to bring some others along with them if they could. I done figure that we might be all that could come, but five is better than none. I be hoping several others come with them."

"We will be happy to have any help we can get," Matt said sincerely. "I hope there are others. We need about ten workers for the field. If the number is five, we will make do the best we can."

The next morning when Tybee and Seabrook woke up out in the barn loft, they were surprised and pleased to find two stacks of clothing on the floor outside of their room. The host and hostess had raided their drawers to find suitable clothes for them to wear. Ami Ruth also came up with combs, wash cloths, and towels for the two visitors. It was her intent that they would be treated like visiting family, and as such, they needed all the comforts of home.

HELP FROM
UNEXPECTED PLACES

It was two days later when a wagon pulled by an old mule came down the road behind the winery with five men and a young woman on board. Three of the men, Simon, Sapelo, and Jekyll, who had passed through the Schendler Farm on the Underground Railroad, were pleased to show the others where they stayed when they came through two years earlier. There was a happy reunion with Ami Ruth who had come to know all of them from the days when she had served their meals.

The workforce on the Schendler Farm now numbered thirteen, including the five men who were regulars at the winery. Matt had talked to his permanent workers and asked about the possibility of older children working the fields with them. Between the group of five families, there were four who were old enough, and Matt arranged with the men to bring their young people for half a day's cutting of grapes in the field through to the end of the harvest. Adding the young people, this increased their number in the field enough, so Matt was sure they could handle the harvest.

Finding places for all of them to live over the next month to six weeks was the first task for the group. The two rooms that Mr. Schendler had built under the winery were large and could accommodate as many as eight sleeping in a room. Each of the rooms had a large table for serving food, and there were several chairs stacked against the wall.

It was still warm into the night, so there was some concern for keeping the area cool enough for comfort. The big door, wide enough for a wagon and a team of horses to come through, was designed to stay open in the summer but could be closed when the weather got cold. It was more than twelve feet across, and when it was open it swung back against the south wall of the entry and was hooked there to a large rectangular board that was anchored into the hard clay wall to hold it open.

At the back of the two rooms, there was a shaft dug through the upper ceiling that connected with the floor of the first level of the winery. On the surface of the room above, it was pretty well hidden, but it served well both as a channel to help air circulation and, also, an escape route. From the ground level, there was a ladder that went up through the shaft should escape be necessary. When it was built, it was not anticipated that the underground lodging would be discovered by slave hunters, but if it was, they might need a backdoor. Of course, here in the fall of 1865, all slaves were free and there weren't any slave hunters. So what had been very necessary two years earlier was just a luxury now.

Under Aunt Elizabeth's supervision, the group of newcomers set about cleaning the two rooms under the winery. Feather mattresses were hauled out and hung over a makeshift line to be beaten until the dust no longer came out. Two of the boys carried buckets of water and rags to wash the chairs and tables, and corn brooms swept the dust off the rough wood floors.

It was decided that Tybee and Seabrook would continue to stay in the loft bedroom in the barn, and Sparrow, the girl who had come in the wagon with the young men, would occupy one of the rooms in the basement of the winery. The young men would stay as a group in the second one.

Food preparation would continue in the big house kitchen and be transported down to the winery for the workers. Sparrow, who had come with the intention of working in the field, was instead drafted to help Aunt Elizabeth, Ami Ruth, and Seabrook in the kitchen. Shopping at the barter store in the Meeting House took on new urgency. Now Aunt Elizabeth and Ami Ruth were feeding ten additional people, and they were cleaning out the store of vegetables and meat almost every time it opened. There also were several trips to the White Hall Store each week as the two ladies tried to stay ahead of the food necessities. With the cash from the wine sale, they could now afford to buy some of the commodities needed to feed a hungry workforce.

Matt gathered the group on Saturday evening to talk about the work plan for the next week. It was already early October, and Norton grapes usually needed to be harvested from mid-September to the end of October.

Matt said, "I'm no expert on grapes, but I am learning every day. Several varieties of grapes could be harvested as early as mid-August, but we are lucky that we have Norton grapes, the variety that is native to Northern Virginia. They mature a bit later than many other varieties, which has given us time to get our field hands settled and plan the work in the vineyards."

"There were now more than sixty acres of grapes on the ridges toward the south edge of the farm clustered around the winery," Matt told the group. "We will start on the north ridge because the grapes planted there had the benefit of having been in full sun longer than the other locations and are becoming ripe earlier. It may take us a week to cut the grapes on that ridge by hand and transport them to the winery. By then, I will have assessed the next focus of the harvest. We may move to the east ridge or, perhaps, to the ones in front of the house. We shall see when the time comes."

Matt and the group walked out to the edge of the north ridge, and he asked Jesse to demonstrate the proper way to cut the grapes.

Even with his experience, Jesse was a bit self-conscious to be put in front of the group but took on the task anyway. "First, the knives are very sharp, so be careful. When you cut the grapes, you put your hand under the cluster and lift them gently. The stem is cut just above the cluster. Be careful not to drop it. If the cluster is dropped, it will bruise the delicate grapes and bruised grapes affect the taste of the wine. Each of you will have a basket that is carried by a strap over your shoulder. Place the cluster of grapes carefully in the baskets. When you have a full basket, carry it to the wagon and place the clusters of grapes carefully in the crates where they can be transported to the winery. Be careful not to place clusters of grapes on top of other clusters. Again, the concern is bruising. We want all the grapes we cut to be usable."

Matt injected a thought into the instruction. "We want this process to move as quickly as possible but don't be in such a hurry that the grapes are bruised. We are better off to leave some grapes on the vine rather than to injure the ones we have cut."

Matt concluded the instruction with a thought that related to Sunday. "We do not work on Sunday on the Schendler Farm. Several of us will be going to the Society of Friends Meeting House for services in the morning. Any of you who want to go along are invited to join us. The wagon will leave the big house promptly at eight o'clock. We should be back around noon and will prepare the midday meal at that time. We should be eating by early afternoon."

"Breakfast will be at 6:00 a.m. on Monday, and we should be in the field cutting grapes by 6:45 or so," Matt added.

Sunday was a day of rest on the Schendler Farm, as was their custom. About midafternoon, Matt and Ami Ruth saddled up Big Billy and the grey mare and went for a ride together. Because of the tension of the tax problem, selling the wine, and welcoming the new visitors to the farm, Matt and Ami Ruth had spent little alone time with each other. The conversation was light and easy flowing as they rode down toward the ridge that hid the winery.

"We have lots of work to do before we get the wine up for the year," said Matt. "But everything is going as well as I could have expected. You and Aunt Elizabeth have picked up the extra burden of the meals for the new people and everyone seems pleased with how that is going."

"Aunt Elizabeth is a marvel, Matt, she really is," said Ami Ruth. "She can prepare a menu for a meal in her head. She looks at the leftovers and remembers what we have in the store house and knows exactly what we need to do next. I'm not sure I will ever be able to do that, even when I am as old as she is."

Matt smiled. "Serving meals for almost twenty people a day would be a trial for anyone. You and Aunt Elizabeth seem to have it well in hand."

"Don't forget Seabrook," said Ami Ruth. "She has been well-trained to the kitchen. She came to work in the fields with the men, which is where they were using her on the farm in Pennsylvania, but she knows how to do almost everything in the kitchen. I'm sure she must have worked in the kitchen on the farm in Georgia when she was growing up."

When Matt and Ami Ruth entered the valley with the winery, Matt guided Big Billy to the back road up the ridge to the north. Ami Ruth followed, wondering where Matt was headed. In a few minutes they were at the top of the north ridge and Matt stopped for a minute. Looking back toward the winery and the vineyards that stretched along the hillsides, he said, "There is much to be proud of here, Ami Ruth. I think your folks would be pleased."

Matt turned Big Billy off of the road into a narrow path that ran along the ridge, and Ami Ruth followed a few steps behind. The horses moved easily along the top of the ridge for a distance until they were at a place where they could see both the top of the winery and the big house and barn in the distance. Matt stopped and dismounted, leaving Big Billy with his reins hanging down. He walked over to Ami Ruth and reached up for her. She slid down into his arms, and they walked a few steps to the edge of the ridge where they could see almost the entire farm stretching out before them.

"I've never been up here before, Matt," Ami Ruth said.

"I've only been here a few times," he responded. "Sometimes when I need to think, this is a secluded place where you can see it all and still be totally by yourself." Matt leaned down and kissed Ami Ruth lightly on the lips. He said, "I want you to know that I have never been happier or more content than I am right now. I still miss your folks, but having Pa at home with us, having the work of the farm going as planned, having found a way to meet the challenges of the taxes, the expansion of the vineyards, and just everything. Most of all, I am pleased to be married to you and to be your husband."

Ami Ruth smiled. "You keep it well hidden, Matt Mason, but you are just a big mush-melon. These are words I only hear late at night when I can feel your warmth in bed. You don't say them often, but I am glad to hear them whenever they come. You should know that I feel the same way. It is like my life just started when you happened onto our farm. Life seemed totally suspended for two years until we were married. Now everything is complete."

"Well, not everything," Matt said. "I am looking ahead until we have some new additions to our household."

"Well, I've been thinking about that too, Matt," she said. "Do you think we could ask Tybee and Seabrook to stay with us after we get through this harvest season? Is there enough work for them to do here?"

Matt smiled. "Oh, I think there will always be more than we can get done, and I think there will be enough money to take care of us and them too. Those are not the additions I had on my mind. Can you visualize little Matts and Ami Ruths running around the farm?"

Ami Ruth blushed. "I thought that might be where you were headed and hoped I could steer you back to thinking about the farm. God decides when little ones come, and I am content to let those decisions be his rather than ours. If they come, they come. I will be thankful for them. Knowing you and how well things are going, I think they will come, and it won't be very long."

Matt guided them back toward the horses. In a moment, they were headed back down the path toward the back road. Later, when they rode up to the house, they noticed that Aunt Elizabeth and Isaac were on the porch in the big rocking chairs.

Both Ami Ruth and Matt were thinking that this was the way Sunday afternoons were meant to be spent.

DAILY WORK ON THE SCHENDLER FARM

Several times over the next couple of weeks, Matt smiled at Ami Ruth's question, asking if there was enough work to do on the farm so they could invite Tybee and Seabrook to stay with them permanently. Everywhere he looked, there was work to do. And they had more people to do the work than they had just a few weeks ago, which now required more supervision and direction for their young workers. Matt and Isaac were kept on the run from the winery to the vineyards and up to the big house. It was fun and exciting, but every night when Matt lay down in bed, he was asleep almost before his head hit the pillow.

The two young men he had hired to hunt deer on the other side of the north ridge were beginning to be productive. The primary work they were hired for had been postponed while they helped Isaac transport the wine to Martinsburg. But twice in the last week, they had carried deer into the slaughter house. In each case, they were able to bring Aunt Elizabeth enough venison to trade at the barter store, and each of the boys had taken home a hind quarter for their families. Hiring the boys had proven to be a good decision, and they were paying for themselves with deer meat.

Big Billy was also becoming a new source of money. It had been a month since Matt had put ads in the newspapers in Charles Town and Winchester, advertising the big bay horse's availability as a stud. Twice over the past two weeks, a stranger had shown up in their front yard with a mare in tow. Matt told the man to give him two days and then to come back to pick her up.

Matt took each of the visiting mares and led them to the corral where Big Billy stayed most nights. When he brought Big Billy into the corral late in the day, the big horse seemed to know what was expected. Matt left the two horses together overnight before removing the mare from the corral the next morning. Late in the second day, he took the mare back to the corral, and Big Billy had company for a second night. Matt made a guarantee to those bringing the mares that if they were not in foal within six weeks, they could bring the mare back for a second try at no cost. He did not anticipate any of them needing to come back.

Matt was charging thirty-five dollars per visit, and Big Billy seemed to be enjoying his new responsibility. Matt figured if there was enough business for Big Billy, he could accept as many as two visits a week, which would make another three hundred dollars each month. The big bay horse didn't seem to mind being called King William while visitors were on the farm, but to Matt he would always be Big Billy.

The grape harvest was rolling along right on schedule. The first week the workers spent on the north ridge, and the second they focused on the vineyard in front of the house. Matt noticed several times that riders stopped on the road and watched the workers cutting grapes and loading them on the wagon for transport to the winery. He had more than a little pride that things were moving along so efficiently and that very soon the harvest would be in. He anticipated adding as many as twenty to thirty new wine casks to the storage area in the winery. That was money they could count on in future years.

In the meantime, Matt and Isaac talked about the possibility of building a structure to be used as a bottling facility at the winery. It would be necessary if they were to create their own wine label. Those thoughts for the future were exciting to Matt, and he could visualize how the various areas of the farm could develop. Always there was the thought in the back of his mind that despite all the big plans for the winery, the farm must be self-sufficient. A part of the springtime had to be devoted to replanting the garden and restocking the animals that provided the food and trade goods for the farm.

THE WOUNDS OF WAR

Each week Aunt Elizabeth and Ami Ruth filled the wagon with whatever they could spare and drove it over to the Meeting House. Always, they came home with more than they took. The Schendler Farm was one of the few that had hired workers in the field, and feeding more than twenty people each day took all the effort the three women and Sparrow could muster and all the trade goods they could carry in their wagon.

Aunt Elizabeth had taken on the responsibility of keeping the financial books for the farm two years earlier when she first came to stay with Ami Ruth. In recent weeks, Ami Ruth had begun to learn that responsibility. Aunt Elizabeth said her young charge was a natural businesswoman and understood immediately how the farm's outcomes and its expenses had to come together. Aunt Elizabeth was pleased that Ami Ruth seemed to be learning every day and was beginning to take charge of the various necessities of running the farm.

In his mind, Matt had envisioned Seabrook working in the house with Aunt Elizabeth and Ami Ruth when the harvest was finished. As the days passed, the family was more and more aware that she was with child, and the baby would be born in the early spring. Considering her condition, it was necessary to modify her responsibilities in the house. Aunt Elizabeth set up a schedule so that Seabrook would have some rest time in the middle of each day.

Matt was looking for an area where Tybee could be in charge. He remembered his Ma talking about how slavery tore down the spirit of a person who was subjected to it. He knew that several in his work crew had grown up as slaves, and he was determined that each of his people would have some pride of ownership and something to do on their own that would give them a feeling of accomplishment. Even as he thought about these things, he was aware that others had very different ideas about men and their various stations in life. Matt had been told that slavery was mentioned many times in the Bible. He asked Aunt Elizabeth about it in one of their late night conversations. She told Matt that slavery was, indeed, mentioned many times, but there was no place in the scriptures where Jesus was quoted as saying that slavery was a good thing either for the slave or the master.

THE WHITE KNIGHTS OF THE CAMELIA

It was the dead of night when Matt heard a commotion up the lane by the road. When he sat up in bed, Ami Ruth was already standing by the window looking outside. Just as he joined her, a fire started up by the lane just at the edge of the road. They both gasped; it was a burning cross! As the fire rushed up the shaft of the cross and onto the cross pieces, gunshots rang out. Matt ran around the bed to the chair and began pulling on his pants, while Ami Ruth slipped into her dressing gown. The gunshots outside continued, and they were getting closer.

By the time they were down the stairs and at the front door, the yard was filled with more than two dozen horsemen dressed in white costumes that resembled bed sheets with cutouts for the eyes. Several of the men were carrying torches, and Matt had the horrifying thought that they had come to burn the house. He thought about his Henry 60 Repeating Rifle but knew his Pa had it in the barn. He stayed just inside the front door with Ami Ruth at his side.

One of the men called his name. "Matt Mason, we want you out here."

Ami Ruth whispered, "Matt, don't you dare go out there!"

The voice from outside came again. "Mason, if you don't come out, we are going to come in and get you. We are going to have a meeting, you and us."

Matt leaned over and kissed Ami Ruth lightly on the cheek. "I will be all right. You stay right here, but be ready to run out the backdoor if things get out of hand."

He stepped out on the porch, and the booming voice said, "There you are, Mr. Matt Mason. I'm sure you have heard of us. We are the White Knights of the Camelia, and we protect the rights and property of white Virginians. We know who you have working on your farm."

Another voice shouted out, "Rumor has it that you are paying them like white men!"

The first voice demanded, "What do you have to say for yourself?"

Matt thought for a few seconds about his vulnerability here in the front yard, unarmed, with twenty masked men carrying guns and torches, and he did not want to inflame the situation with defiance. Neither did he want to appear to be too meek and mild either. The image of Mr. Schendler flashed into his mind. Ami Ruth's father had gone out on the porch to talk to the Yankee renegades and had been shot right on his own porch. But he wouldn't have been shy about responding either.

Matt's response was measured but loud enough for everyone to hear. "I do have several young men and women from Pennsylvania here helping us with the grape harvest. They have been here about a week now and will be here until the end of October."

A third horseman yelled from the back of the group, "We want them gone! They don't belong here, and they are taking work from our people who could do the job for a decent wage!"

Matt said, "I looked in Winchester, Charles Town, and Martinsburg for help, even put advertisements in the newspapers, but nothing worked. I feel fortunate to have these people who have come to help me. As I said, they will be here until the end of October when we have all the grapes in the winery."

The first voice shouted back, "We will give you until the end of the week to finish with them and send them back north where they came from. If they are still here, we will be back and you won't like the result."

Matt took just a few seconds to consider his next response. He decided on a direct approach to the leaders of this white-draped group of malcontents.

"Mr. Mueller," Matt asked, "why do you come to see me in the dead of night with a mask over your face? Do you think I don't know who you are? We have been trading with you at the store for years. That is also true for you, Mr. Moore, and you, Mr. Wilson. Do you think I don't know who you are because you are covered in bed sheets? No one else in the community has an Appaloosa horse like yours, Mr. Wilson. And, Mr. Moore, I would know your voice anywhere."

At that point, Matt felt the presence of his Pa as he came around the corner of the porch. When he glanced over at him, he saw the Henry 60 Repeating Rifle at his side and he heard the rifle being cocked. Immediately, there was response from the men on horseback. Rifles were lifted and pointed at Isaac Mason.

Isaac pointed his rifle at Mr. Mueller, the leader of the group. He said, "I think this confrontation has gone on long enough. My name is Isaac Mason. Matt is my son. He and I were both in Pickett's Charge at Gettysburg while most of you men were home tending your farms. We have seen guns fired in anger and the result isn't pretty."

Mr. Mueller said, "Easy now, Mr. Mason. We have you outgunned here twenty to one. If you push this, someone is going to be dead."

"You are right about that," Isaac said. "I should have been dead two years ago. No one I know in my division is still alive. You do have me outgunned, that is for sure. But my gun is aimed directly at you. If any shots are fired, you can be sure my first bullet is going to bury you."

Isaac's voice grew louder and he spoke with authority. "These folks are Quakers. They don't believe in violence. However, I am not a Quaker. Neither are the men we have working in the winery. If you listen closely, you will hear them coming up the lane now. Very shortly, the twenty-to-one advantage you think you have will become much more even. Several of our men served in the Army of Northern Virginia, and they know what to do with a rifle."

Matt heard a murmur from the group of horsemen. Their leader spoke again. "We have delivered the message we came to deliver. We are leaving now."

"I have one more question for you, Mr. Mueller," said Isaac. "I know a bit about the organization of the Ku Kluxers in other places in the country. You don't have the guts to show your faces, and you only ride at night so you can act innocent in the light of day. You have a Grand Wizard who doesn't have the guts to join any of your night rides. He is nothing but a clothing store clerk making a profit on white sheets."

"What!" Mr. Mueller exploded.

"It's easy to figure," Isaac said. "Only a clothing store clerk could get you to pay five dollars for a fifty-cent sheet."

That was the last word from either Isaac or Mr. Mueller. The group turned their horses and headed up the lane to the road. One by one, their torches hit the ground and were quickly extinguished. Up by the road, the cross they had set on fire had already burned itself out.

Matt turned to his Pa and said, "I was really glad to see you come around the porch, Pa. I wasn't sure what I was going to say next."

Ami Ruth ran quickly to his side, and then Tybee and Seabrook come out on the porch.

Ami Ruth was noticeably shaken. Her voice trembled when she said, "What will we do, Matt?"

Matt answered quickly, "Nothing. We will continue with our work as if this visit didn't take place. However, we will put out sentries each night. We will devise a warning system to protect ourselves. None of those hoodlums will act by themselves. Cowards come in groups and late at night. We are not going to react to threats by cowards. If we ever do react to such threats, someone will be trying to intimidate us every time we turn around." Matt smiled inwardly at his own comments. He had heard his Pa say those very words years ago on their small farm in North Carolina.

Tybee touched Matt's arm. "I be worried about you, friend. We don't want to be no trouble for you. We can be out of here and head north as soon as you say."

"No, Tybee," Matt responded. "Ami Ruth and I want you and Seabrook to stay with us permanently if you think you can be happy here. We need the rest of your group to stay with us until we get the harvest in and the wine making process started."

"You want us to stay with you?" asked Seabrook.

"Yes," Matt said. "We have come to appreciate you and believe you can fit in well with life here on the Schendler Farm. We want you to be a part of our family. We have talked about it, and we hope you will stay."

Tybee looked at Seabrook but neither of them said anything about the prospect of staying permanently on the Schendler Farm.

Matt noticed that his Pa had gone around the porch and disappeared into the dark. Aunt Elizabeth came out of the door and walked to the edge of the porch. She followed Isaac with her eyes as he went off toward the barn. Matt gave Ami Ruth a light hug then followed after his Pa.

When he caught up with Isaac, he was putting the Henry rifle into the holder that he kept by the back barn door. His face was obviously flushed under his full beard, and Matt could hear his breathing as he approached the door.

"Hold up, Pa. Can we talk for a few minutes?"

The two men, father and son, sat down on the hay bales along the wall.

"I was never so glad to see anyone as I was when you came around the edge of the porch. I was feeling pretty naked out there without a gun or anything for protection," Matt said.

"Son, I thought you handled yourself pretty well under the circumstances," Isaac said. "You didn't let them get the upper hand. Your position was right, and they heard it in the tone of your voice. I don't think they came to take any real action, just to see if they could intimidate you. Obviously, from our stance, we weren't intimidated. I came and brought the Henry because they know this to be a Quaker house, and they did not expect any resistance. I thought they needed to know that there were some folks at this farm with fighting experience, and we were not going to back down from a fight if one was necessary. I don't think they will be back."

"Thanks, Pa," Matt said. Then after a few seconds, he added, "Still, I think it makes sense for us to put out a couple of sentries each night. We have seventeen men on site now during the day, including us, and twelve are with us through the night. We can take turns standing watch out at the edge of the road. There isn't much other way to get to the farm other than to come in through the front gate and down the lane."

"It's a good idea, Son," Pa said. "The sentries can carry the Henry. We'll take a little time tomorrow and be sure everyone knows how to use it. It might even make good sense to buy a couple of additional repeating rifles to use for our protection."

"I'm not sure, Pa," said Matt. "Ami Ruth may not be happy with our planning to shoot people on the Schendler Farm. Let's don't do anything until I find the right time to talk to her."

"Okay, Son, just let me know," said Pa. "Surely she can see what we are up against with these masked hoodlums running around at night. We need to protect the big house, the barn, the winery, and above all, we need to look after the people we have taken in here. They are all under our protection now."

Later that night when they had settled back into bed, Ami Ruth said quietly, "Matt, I was scared to death. We have lived with tragedy and crisis here on the farm for most of the past five years. We have lost our crops, our animals, and have struggled to get by. My parents are buried out by the big tree in the corner of the front yard. Tonight, I had a vision of your grave there too. It was almost too much to bear."

"There was reason to be afraid," Matt said. "Anytime armed men come onto our land, we can be sure they are not here for good reasons. However, backing away from them and letting them have their way is not the approach we need to take. They need to know that they can't come here on our land and intimidate us. They can't dictate to us their immoral values. This is Schendler land, and Schendler values will be observed here. We value the lives of every creature God made, including our guests from the North. We value a peaceful lifestyle for everyone, including our neighbors and ourselves, a life with 'malice toward none,' as President Lincoln said in his speech at Gettysburg."

"Matt, what would you have done if they had attempted to set fire to the porch, or if they had fired their weapons?" she asked.

"I would probably have moved as quickly as I could to get to you inside the door and to get both of us out the backdoor to safety," Matt replied. "The house is important but not nearly as much as you, Pa, Aunt Elizabeth, and our visitors."

Matt thought for a minute and then continued. "Had they moved toward the house or shot at me, I'm pretty sure my Pa would have emptied the Henry at them and he is a crack shot. I am certain we would have several dead night riders in our front yard right now."

"Matt, it is all just too horrible to think about," she said with a shudder. "I'm not sure I will ever sleep at night again. If I had lost you, my world would have come to an end too."

"Ami Ruth, we have to face whatever problems God gives us," Matt said. "We will all go to see our Maker in due time. And we will not go sooner or later because of the challenges we face. As you have said so often, God decides such things and not us. What I do know is that we cannot let ourselves be afraid of what may come. When my Ma and I studied Shakespeare, I learned that 'a coward dies a thousand deaths, a brave man dies but once.' I believe that is a true statement. We will always know that those cowards are more afraid than we are. We will defend ourselves when it is necessary."

"With guns, Matt?" she asked.

"As much as it pains me to say it, Ami Ruth, the answer to that question is yes. I don't like it, and I don't want to use guns here on the farm or anywhere else, but if it comes down to whether or not I am going to protect you from men like those, the answer is a resounding yes!"

Ami Ruth was quiet while she thought about what Matt had said. As time passed, she fell asleep in his arms. When she awoke, light was streaming in through the windows, and she could hear noises downstairs in the kitchen. Another day was dawning, and each day had its own challenges. Memories, however, fade slowly, and everyone on the Schendler Farm carried the vision of the white-clad night riders that day and every day that followed.

The White Knights of the Camelia—what a curious and romantic name for a bunch of night-riding thugs.

STANDING UP FOR THE RIGHT

News spreads quickly in a closed communities like the Loop. Within a week, virtually everyone had heard of the night riders at the Schendler Farm. Most had already heard of the field workers from Pennsylvania, so having the White Knights come for a visit was not a surprise. They had done worse at other places over near Berryville. However, it was the confrontation and the outcome that people were talking about.

No one expected to hear of rifles drawn at a Quaker house and having two men facing down twenty armed night riders became the major topic of conversation in the Loop. That was especially true because of Isaac Mason's size and his Henry 60 Repeating Rifle. By the time the rumors made the rounds, Isaac was approaching seven feet tall, and there was an army of rifle-bearing soldiers backing him up from the trees and the shadows of the big house.

Things did not get back to normal at the Schendler Farm for many weeks. Sentries were posted every night and additional guns were purchased. Until now, the Henry 60 was the most advanced rifle yet invented in the country, but Isaac went rifle shopping and came home with two Winchester 66 rifles that were a step up in quality and fire power. Only one of the new field hands had ever handled a rifle before, so Isaac selected several of the hands for target practice following work each day for the first week after the late night confrontation.

It was now approaching the middle of October, and two more meetings had been held at the Hopewell Meeting House. The petition for tax leniency had been rejected at the Military Governor's Office in Richmond. The written explanation expressed sympathy but said that there was no provision in the law passed by Congress for exception, and it didn't make any difference that the Quaker community had not participated in the war. They lived in one of the states that seceded from the Union and that was enough to include them in the new taxes.

With only six weeks to go before the taxes were due, it was obvious that some of the people at the Loop farms had raised the money but many had not. There was anxiety that was approaching panic on their faces. It was one worry to not have a crop to sell and quite another to anticipate having to move from your land and your home without any means of support.

Joshua Ridgeway, taking charge as usual, announced to the congregants in his deep voice, "We will create a new committee that will assess who continues to be in difficulty with the tax situation and how much each will be short. I would like Mr. Beeson, Mr. Poteate, and Mr. Moon to serve on this committee. When we finish today, I would like one member of each family to report their current situation to the committee so we can determine the needs of the total group."

When the discussion opened again, it was Benjamin Thomson who took the floor. "I'm sure all of us have heard of the confrontation that occurred over at the Schendler Farm," said the portly farmer. "I understand that a Quaker family depended on guns rather than God's strength to ward off the intruders. I want to express my disappointment in the Masons that they felt they needed to meet force with force. It isn't our way, and it will never be our way. We stayed out of the war because we did not want to be a part of the killing. Have we changed our minds or our commitment to God?"

Before he was finished speaking, Matt was on his feet and headed down the center aisle to the front of the room. He had taken only a few steps when he heard Aunt Elizabeth's voice, and he stood stock-still. Matt had heard Elizabeth speak forcefully only a few times, but he knew she was fully capable of standing toe to toe with any of the men.

This time her voice sounded like steel wrapped in velvet. "I can speak to this situation better than any other," she said. "I was an eye witness to exactly what happened. I know the rumors have been running ever since the night riders showed up at our house demanding that we send the workers we had hired from Pennsylvania back north. One of the reasons we are in a better position than most of the families in this room is because Mr. Schendler had the foresight to begin to plant a vineyard more than a decade ago. There were some in this room who objected to his raising grapes to make wine for sale on the open market. Many of us were here when he met that challenge by asking the group who it was that changed the water into wine at the wedding in Cana two thousand years ago. It is because we have the vineyards and the winery that we can weather this storm better than most. It is because we have the vineyard that we can buy much of what is brought each week to the barter store. So far no one has taken anything home that they brought to sell because the Schendler Farm has workers in the field that we have to feed. Our farm and our grape crop are helping everyone through this crisis."

Voices were raised around the room, mostly female, adding their support to Aunt Elizabeth's comments.

"We did not seek out that confrontation," she continued. "It came to us, and it came in the middle of the night dressed in white sheets, carrying guns and torches to burn our house down. The men who came did not care that Matthew Mason had looked everywhere for workers to help us with the harvest. They didn't care that, finally, God had supplied those field hands. They didn't care that we were doing the best we could to help all our neighbors through this crisis. They didn't care that no one on the Schendler Farm had ever turned away a friend or stranger in need. Matt Mason was the one they called out into the front yard to be threatened. He came to the Schendler Farm himself as a stranger needing a meal and a roof over his head. Then he came back to us and most of you were a part of helping him save the farm when the renegades came to steal what little we had left and to burn our house and barn. I believe that God sent him to us, and I believe that God does not make mistakes."

THE WOUNDS OF WAR

Voices again were raised around the room, and this time there were many male voices mixed in with the female. Several said "Amen" loud enough for the entire room to hear.

"I was never so proud of anyone as when Matt Mason walked out into that yard to face that gang of hoodlums armed to the teeth with their guns and their torches," Aunt Elizabeth continued. "He did not carry a gun. He took nothing with which to defend himself. He had only right on his side and the support of God to confront evil as the Bible has taught us to do. I want you all to know that despite what you may have heard in the rumor mill, no Quaker carried a gun into that conflict situation. All of us were scared like they must have been scared in Jerusalem when the Assyrians came to lay waste to their city, like Shadrack, Meshach, and Abednego were afraid when the Babylonians came to kidnap them and take them back to Babylon. We were all scared, but that didn't keep Matt Mason from walking out in front of them and facing down the evil, facing down the cowards."

Mr. Ridgeway reclaimed the floor just long enough to ask the question on everyone's mind, "Tell us about Isaac Mason. Did he violate our Quaker principles?"

"Good questions!" she responded. "I want you to know about Isaac Mason. Despite the rumors, he isn't seven feet tall." A few chuckles broke out, releasing some of the tension in the room. "He might have looked seven feet tall in front of the big house with a Henry 60 Repeating Rifle in his hands standing next to his son. But remember, Isaac Mason is not a Quaker. He is a farmer. He is a loyal Southerner. He is a soldier. Most of all, he is a father. He was totally in his element when he came around the porch to stand next to his son to face down the Ku Klux trash who threatened our home."

She paused and surveyed the room, seeming to look into every eye. "I want everyone to know that not a shot was fired. Guns were raised on both sides, but no shots were fired and no blood was shed. When you stand in judgment of what happened on the Schendler Farm that night, ask yourself how you would feel in such a confrontation. Ask yourself what you would do in such a circumstance. Believe me, you would be thankful to have two of God's soldiers standing side by side to fend off the evil that those white-sheeted hoodlums brought to our house. It was like young David standing up to the giant, Goliath, with nothing in his hands but a slingshot and the power of God."

There was a big response from the crowd. Several began to applaud and many were standing, ready to speak out in support of Aunt Elizabeth. Mr. Ridgeway reasserted himself at the front of the group, put his hand in the air asking for quiet, and the group settled down to hear the last of Aunt Elizabeth's comments.

"Now one last word," Aunt Elizabeth said. "I feel very strongly that God was in our front yard that night. God put us in position to face down the evil that rides among us doing no one any good. Because God was there and His will was done, others in our number may not have to face the crisis of life and death that we faced as a family that night."

Again, a chorus of "Amens" were heard across the room. Aunt Elizabeth took three quick steps up the aisle and sat down next to Ami Ruth. Immediately she felt her niece's hand on hers and a soft voice in her ear. "God bless you, Aunt Elizabeth," she said. "No one could have said it better."

* * *

A few days later, Aunt Elizabeth and Ami Ruth drove a wagon over to the White Hall Store and carried in the four five-pound bags of coffee that had been promised. Mr. Mueller was clearly delighted and showed Aunt Elizabeth two large boxes full of the jars she had asked for in trade for the coffee. As she was leaving, Mr. Mueller asked her if she had other needs he could meet from his store.

He would not soon forget Aunt Elizabeth's response. She said, "Mr. Mueller, it is likely that the two of us will never exchange another word following this visit, let alone any farm goods. I will get any additional jars I need and any other items we can't produce at the general store in Winchester. I am only here because when I make a promise, I keep it. I gave my word to trade the coffee for the jars, and so I am here.

"You brought your thugs and their guns into our front yard and attempted to intimidate us," she said, her voice rising. "You threatened Matthew Mason and his father and our entire family with harm unless we broke our word to our farm workers and sent them home. You are not a man we will do business with again. You are not a man we will associate with again. Considering the way you turned tail and ran when things didn't go your way, I am not sure you are a man at all."

Aunt Elizabeth turned and walked out the door, leaving Mr. Mueller standing there in the middle of his store with his jaw hanging and totally speechless.

However, Ami Ruth remained in the doorway. She took a few steps toward Mr. Mueller and was surprised to see him cower from her. Her voice was low and measured. "Mr. Mueller, you know that I am Matt Mason's wife. He was the man you called out of our house in the middle of the night, the man you threatened with your guns. He didn't back away from your gang of cutthroats. You advertise yourselves as a Christian army. You aren't. More likely you are the Devil's spawn."

Her voice gathered force and her blue eyes flashed. "Matt stood up to you like a soldier in God's army. He didn't need a gun. My father never needed a gun to face off with evil. My husband doesn't either. You would be well advised when you see me or any of mine walking down the street in Winchester to turn and go the other way. Isaac Mason gave you a warning when you were in our yard dressed in your bed sheet. Let me add to it. All the people who live at the Schendler Farm are not Quaker. We now have three repeating rifles on site. I will never shoot one of them, and it is likely that Matt will not either. However, if you ever come again, you may expect that you will find yourself face to face with God well before you intended. We will all attend your funeral and wish you God speed."

Ami Ruth had never spoken as many words in her life to a man other than her father and her husband. She was breathing heavily when she joined Aunt Elizabeth on the wagon. The two women rode halfway back to the farm before either of them spoke. Aunt Elizabeth asked, "What did you say to him, Ami Ruth?"

"I'm not exactly sure," she responded. "I was still thinking about what you said to him, and I think I just gave him a double dose that let him know where he stood with both of us. I can't believe we did that, but it feels good! We can be pretty sure that no one else will know what we said to him. We aren't going to tell anyone, and I'm sure he won't either."

* * *

Despite all the disruption caused by the night riders, one thought that was at the back of everyone's mind from the time Isaac came back from his first trip to Thornton Enterprises in Martinsburg was the possibility of money being hidden on the farm. Did Mr. Schendler hide money somewhere he could easily reach it when it was needed? Logic told the group that he did. He was selling wine and, perhaps, other products across the border in West Virginia where Union dollars were used. There was no place to use greenbacks in Virginia until after the war. So the question was, "Where did he hide the money?"

It did not make sense that he would have hidden it in the house or the barn. Both were up front and vulnerable to the deserters and renegades moving up and down the road in front of the farm. That left the grounds, the vineyard area, and the garden as possibilities. The winery was a consideration. However, it might be a lesser possibility since there were always men working there, and the risk of the money being discovered was greater in that location. Mr. Schendler might have buried the money back on the ridge behind the big house. If that were the case, they might never find it.

Each of the members of the family had been looking for the hiding place for weeks now. Ami Ruth had gone over the house, every room and every hallway. She was sure in her own mind that the money wasn't in the house. Aunt Elizabeth and Ami Ruth had looked over the barn as well with no luck. The smoke house was small with no obvious hiding places, and they had dug up the floor getting up the salt they needed for cooking. It just wasn't there.

Both of the ladies went to the garden every day and picked the vegetables needed for the table that night. If the money was buried there, it was not obvious where it might be. The entire garden was plowed up in the spring, and they supervised the plowing. The best of the possibilities in that location was along the fence at the back of the garden plot near the ridge. They had both taken a sharp stick and stuck it down in the unplowed dirt looking for a soft spot where it might have been dug up to bury the money. No luck.

Matt and Isaac looked over the wagons and the corrals. Sometimes the best place to hide something is in plain sight where everyone gets used to walking by a location every day. Soon it seems to disappear. Again, no luck.

It was now late in the harvest, and it was obvious they no longer needed ten workers in the field. Earlier in the week, they had moved several of the workers into the winery to help begin the crushing of the grapes, the next step in making wine. Matt and Isaac shared the supervision of the workers, one staying in the field and the other in the winery. Finally, they decided on the last day of work for the visiting crew. The following morning the field workers would be heading back north.

Matt had already counted out their pay. The men and Sparrow had been with them for six weeks, so each would take home eighteen dollars and an additional three dollars as a bonus. He placed the money for each in a small leather pouch, and Ami Ruth added a short note for each that thanked them for coming to help. She promised work for them next year should they be free to come back for the harvest.

Matt had not had another conversation with Tybee and Seabrook about the prospect of staying on the Schendler Farm permanently. He sought them out for a front porch conversation the night before the group was to leave. Matt and Ami Ruth were not sure what their two friends were thinking, but both knew that their visitors had friends in Pennsylvania to whom they felt an obligation.

Matt approached the subject slowly, telling them again that they hoped Seabrook and Tybee would stay here with them on the farm. Seabrook was the first to respond, telling Matt and Ami Ruth that they had loved their time in Virginia and wanted very much to stay and make this their home. Tybee reminded Matt that they had come to the Schendler Farm on a borrowed horse, and he felt obligated to take the horse back to the people who had loaned it to them.

Thus, almost before the conversation was started the question was settled. Tybee and Seabrook were staying, but Tybee would leave with the rest of the freed slaves to return the horse. Matt suggested that Tybee take the grey mare with him so he would have transportation back. There were handshakes all around, and Matt felt delighted that the family had grown by two. In fact, by the look of Seabrook's front profile, it seemed likely that the family might soon grow by three.

EVIL IN ALL OF ITS FORMS

The next morning, after breakfast at the winery, the freed slaves had the wagon hitched up and their meager belongings packed. Their journey home would take them up the back road and over the ridge toward West Virginia, then to Charles Town and Harper's Ferry, where they would cross the Potomac River through Frederick, Maryland, and on north toward the Pennsylvania line and Gettysburg. The trip would take about three days.

After they were gone, Matt and Isaac did an inspection of the vineyard, assessing what was left to be done following the harvest. They made note of the fact that the vines imported from France with the new variety of grapes had yielded little. It was possible they would not work in this climate, or perhaps, it would just take them another year or two to be productive. Matt resolved to be patient. It would not cost anything to leave them in the field for another year. If they still were not producing at the end of next year's harvest, it would be time to replace them with seedlings from the Norton grapes that seemed to thrive in Northern Virginia.

Matt and Isaac were up at the big house for lunch when they heard the warning bell in the winery begin to ring. Both raced out, mounted their horses, and raced down to the winery. The grey mare was at the hitching rack, and Jesse was at the door with a worried look on his face. He said, "Tybee is back and he is hurt bad."

It took a few seconds for Matt's eyes to adjust to the gloom in the winery after coming in from the bright sunlight. There he saw Tybee lying on a pallet on the floor, and his blood seemed to be everywhere. After briefly examining his friend, Matt turned to Jesse and said, "Take my horse and get Aunt Elizabeth, Ami Ruth, and Seabrook from the big house. Tell Aunt Elizabeth that Tybee has been shot and give her your horse. You hitch up the wagon from the barn for the other two ladies. We will need something to transport Tybee back to the house but we are going to have to get the bleeding stopped before we move him. It looks as if he has already lost a lot of blood."

Turning to the other men in the winery, he said, "Get me some water and any clean rags you can find. Use the cloths we use to strain out the seeds from the grapes. They are as clean as we can make them."

Pa was kneeling beside Tybee. "It looks as if he was shot in the left leg and in the chest just below the shoulder," he told Matt. "He is bleeding both in front and in back, so I think it might be a through-and-through up there. I don't see an exit wound from his thigh so the ball is still in there."

"Let's get some pressure on the open wounds and see if we can stop the bleeding," he continued. "You take the thigh, and I will lift him and see if I can handle both of the top spots. If I were guessing, I would say that the thigh wound was made by a Smith and Wesson minié ball and the chest wound has the earmarks of a rifle shot. I think it entered his back and exited through the chest area. If we are lucky, it missed his lung. It is well above the heart."

Just at that instant, Tybee began to rouse. His eyes came open, and though it took him a few seconds to get focused on his surroundings, he was awake.

Matt said, "What happened, Tybee? And what about the others?"

"I don't know," the injured man responded. "We done rounded a curve in the road just south of Charles Town and several shots be fired. Me and Jekyll was riding behind the wagon. I saw one, maybe two of our folks shot. I don't know how bad. We didn't have no guns, there weren't no place to turn the wagon around. I got hit in the leg early on and another shot got me in the back. Jekyll, he done rode with me a piece, but he weren't hit that I know of. He done sent me on back, and he done stay behind to see if he could help the others. If this here mare didn't know her way home, there be no way I would be here."

Tybee had just gotten the last words out when Aunt Elizabeth entered the side door to the winery in a swirl of skirts. Although she had brought supplies to deal with the wounds, she took one look at Tybee and said, "We need him in a bed up at the big house. Jesse is bringing the wagon. Let's move him outside ready to transport. If that chest shot missed his lung, he has a good chance."

Matt and Isaac had done the best they could to stem the bleeding, but it was still pouring out. The rags they used were already saturated with blood.

Isaac said, "Matt, you stay here and I will take Big Billy up to the barn to get the Winchesters. We need to head up the road and see about the rest of the group."

In a few seconds, he was gone. About halfway up the lane toward the big house, he passed the wagon headed to the winery. He stopped long enough to tell Seabrook that Tybee was badly wounded but was awake and had a good chance to make it. Seabrook had been holding her emotions together up to that point but now the tears began to come. Isaac galloped toward the barn where the Winchesters were stored.

Isaac met the wagon on the ridge road when he returned from the barn. Jesse was driving and Tybee was lying on a pallet in the back. "Jesse, when you get the boy where Miss Elizabeth wants him, you pick up some bandages and alcohol from the medicine chest," Isaac said. "Ami Ruth will help you with that. Bring the wagon back down to the winery. I need you to follow us up the back road toward Charles Town. We are not sure what we will find up the road, but we may need the wagon to bring back any other wounded."

"Yes, sir," Jesse said.

In just a few minutes, Matt and Isaac were headed up the ridge toward the West Virginia border and Charles Town.

It took about an hour for Matt and Isaac to reach the site of the ambush. The wagon was sitting just to the left of the road with one of its wheels broken. With a quick analysis of the situation, they could visualize the driver trying to get turned around in the narrow road and losing a wheel in the ditch on the side. A body was draped across the tailgate and two other bodies were lying on the other side of the wagon. There was a second wagon just ahead in the road.

Isaac raised his hand and both he and Matt froze. Then Isaac pointed at his ear and to the other side of the road. They could hear voices, low but consistent, back in the brush. Both quietly dismounted and took the Winchesters with them as they moved toward the sound. When they pushed through the brush, they had their rifles raised for quick response. The scene before them was beyond any they could have imagined.

There, hanging by his neck from a tree, was the body of Jekyll. At the base of the tree were three people. One was Simon. The others were strangers, an older white couple they had never seen before. When the older couple saw the armed men, they drew together with the man standing between the intruders and his wife. Their hands were raised.

Isaac's voice broke the silence. "Who are you?"

"We are the Schmidts," the man responded. "We live just down the hill. Who are you?"

"We are Matt and Isaac Mason. These are our people," Matt said.

"Who did this?" Isaac asked.

Mr. Schmidt said quickly, "We don't know. We heard the gunfire and came to see what had happened. When we crested the hill, we came on this scene. This young man is the only one still breathing, and he is just barely alive. All the rest are gone."

Matt put down his rifle and knelt next to Simon. He was just regaining consciousness. "What happened, Simon?" he asked.

The words came slowly. "We come 'round the curve, and they shot at us from both sides. Sapela, he tried to get the wagon turned 'round so we could make a run for it, but the wheel done broke and he done got shot." Simon stopped talking for a few seconds and his face took on a terrible grimace.

"Easy, lad," Isaac said. "Take your time."

"They done grab Sparrow, and she be screaming," said Simon. "Jekyll, he come riding in and jumped on the man who had ahold of her. They got him on the ground . . ." Simon's voice faltered as he looked at this friend hanging from the limb above him. "That is what they done to him," he said, his voice thick. "They was going to hang me too, but one of the men said they gone teach me a lesson and leave me to tell what happened to our kind from Pennsylvania who come to Virginia. They done held my hands against the tree trunk and smashed them with their rifle butts. Then they done it to my feet. Mr. Isaac, I can't move my hands or my feet. Then they done held me up to the tree trunk and hit me and hit me. I can't remember no more."

"Matt," Isaac said, "you help the Schmidts with Simon. I'm going to have a look around."

Isaac was back in a few minutes and motioned for Matt to come over near the edge of the clearing. "Son, I think they took Sparrow with them. I can see a trail of about ten horses leading off toward Charles Town. I bet these bandits are the same folks who were on our farm a few weeks back. I think they want us to think they are from north of the border, but at some point not too far up the road they will be doubling back. I am going to follow their trail and see where they have taken Sparrow."

"Pa, you can't go after them by yourself!" Matt said. "Ten men! That is too many for you to take on. Jesse is headed this way with a wagon and should be here before too long. I can—"

Isaac put up his hand to stop Matt from saying anything else. "Son, I'm going now. I'm not leaving Sparrow with that gang of cutthroats any longer than necessary. You take care of our people. Load them on the wagon and take them back to the farm. Take care of Simon. I will be okay."

With that Isaac was gone, and in a few seconds, Matt heard the hoof beats of Big Billy in a steady gallop headed up the road following the trail left by the bushwhackers.

The Schmidts continued to work on Simon's wounds. He had blood coming out of his nose, mouth, and one of his eyes. The bushwhackers had beaten him nearly to death. Matt thought he might live, but looking at his hands, he wondered if he would ever be able to move his fingers again. Both hands were swollen until it was hard to tell they were hands. In one place, he could see the bone sticking out from the flesh.

Matt took on the grisly task of moving the bodies to the edge of the road. He waited until the last to take Jekyll down from the tree, enlisting Mr. Schmidt's help to get him down. He then carried Jekyll to the edge of the road with the others.

Together, he and Mr. Schmidt carried Simon out by the edge of the road as well. They had hardly laid him down when Matt heard sounds coming up the road. He went quickly back into the brush and retrieved his Winchester in case the bushwhackers had come back. He was relieved to see Jesse coming around the curve driving their wagon.

"Lord Almighty, what happened here?" Jesse asked.

"I'm glad to see you, Jesse. It is a long story and one that will not be pleasant to tell," Matt responded. "Let's get these folks loaded on the wagon and head back to the farm. I'll tell you on the way. We have some graves to dig before nightfall, and Simon needs serious medical attention."

"Matt, where is your Pa?" Jesse asked.

"He picked up the trail of the bushwhackers and is following them. They have Sparrow, and he hopes to get her back or at least find out who did this to our people," Matt said.

Matt walked over to the Schmidts who were climbing into their wagon.

"I want to thank you folks for coming to help." Matt said. "This is a real mess, and we appreciate your Christian attitude toward these poor folks."

Mrs. Schmidt was crying. Mr. Schmidt said, "I never saw anything like this, not even during the war. This was just murder, killing unarmed folks just coming up the road. You have your work cut out for you when you get home." He spanked the horse with the reigns and his wagon moved off toward their house up the road.

By the time they arrived back at the farm, the ladies knew most of what had happened from Tybee. What they saw in the wagon was

THE WOUNDS OF WAR

even worse than they imagined. Jesse stopped for just a few minutes by the front porch in the wagon while Matt went into the barn and retrieved two shovels. Then they took the bodies across the front yard to the little family cemetery where Ami Ruth's folks were buried.

In a hard three hours, they had finished their grisly task. There were now four new graves in the cemetery; a total of six including Ami Ruth's parents.

Ami Ruth came out to talk to Matt just as they finished with the last of the graves. "Tybee is sleeping now. You were right about the shot to his chest. The bullet went in his back and exited through the upper portion of his chest. The bleeding has stopped. The ball in his leg was stubborn, and Tybee passed out before Aunt Elizabeth got it. The leg wound is still bleeding some, but we have it packed pretty tight, and he should be okay if something doesn't get infected. Aunt Elizabeth is working on Simon now. Nothing there is life threatening, but his hands and feet look terrible. I'm not sure he will ever walk again, and for sure, his hands are going to be a problem all his life."

"Tybee is a strong kid," Matt responded. "He will fight his way through this and so will Simon. Who would believe that the hatred of people is so strong that they would do things like this to people and believe they are in the right? The White Knights, a Christian organization! More likely Devils, every one of them." He spit the words out of his mouth.

"Matt, what about Isaac?" Ami Ruth asked.

"He is looking for the gang who attacked our people. They have Sparrow and he is following them to get her back or at least to find out who the bushwhackers are," Matt said.

"Several times Aunt Elizabeth has asked if your Pa is back yet. She is awfully worried."

"I am worried too," Matt said. "I wanted to go with him. Ten men are way too many for one man to take on. Pa did what he always used to do back on the farm in North Carolina when he wanted me to stay out of the way. He gave me a task and sent me to do it. In this case, he gave me the group to take care of and get back to the farm. He was gone up the road even before we had poor Jekyll out of the tree. Still, Pa is a veteran soldier, and he is a crack shot. He isn't following to confront them. He isn't looking for a fight. He is trying to get Sparrow free and to learn who the bushwhackers are. He has them outgunned even if he is only one man and they are ten. I am pretty sure none of them would have a sixteen-shot Winchester '66."

AN EYE FOR AN EYE

It was after midnight when Isaac and Big Billy trotted quietly down the hill behind the winery. There was a large bundle draped over the big horse's rump, behind the saddle. Isaac lifted the bundle off and laid it on the ground, unsaddled the horse, and went into the winery. He collapsed on one of the work tables there and was immediately asleep. He knew that if he went up to the big house he would awaken the entire household, and he was just too tired to respond to their questions. The sun was streaming in through the side door when he opened his eyes.

Isaac led Big Billy over the ridge with his bundle and walked him up to the porch in front of the house. He took the bundle and laid it carefully on the porch, and then took the big bay horse to the corral and put the feed bag on him. He watched Big Billy for a few minutes and then walked slowly to the back porch to wash up. As soon as he walked up on the porch, the back screen door swung open. It was Aunt Elizabeth. Before either could think, she was in his arms. Ami Ruth found them like that a few minutes later, still holding each other, silently letting the emotions settle. Neither was talking. He was home safe and that was enough for now.

By the time Matt came into the kitchen for breakfast, Isaac was sitting at the table. He picked up his coffee cup and motioned Matt outside to the back steps, where he told him what had happened.

"Matt, Sparrow is on the front porch," he said. "I'm afraid you have another grave to dig. I caught up with them at a little shack out in the woods. By the time I got there, only three of them were left. The rest had headed back south. They had beaten and abused her. I took down two of them before they really knew I was there. The third fired a couple of shots but nothing came close to me. He was hiding behind the door to the shack. I put a shot through the door and caught him in the throat. I checked the three bodies on the way into the shack and all were dead. Sparrow was lying on the floor without any clothes on. It was obvious what she had gone through.

"I wrapped her in a blanket I found in the shack and took care of her as best I could," Isaac continued. "I tied her on Big Billy and then I followed the trail of the rest of the bushwhackers until I knew they were headed south toward Winchester or perhaps toward the Loop. When I was sure, I let Big Billy have his head and he brought us home."

Matt took a deep breath, staring for a moment at the ground. "Pa, what should we do next?" he asked. "It seems right that we should make a report of what happened to the military office in Winchester. I'm not sure what they will do about it but, at the very least, there are three men who will not be coming home tonight. We need to tell someone where to find their bodies. Then do you think there is any hope of finding out who the others responsible for this are?"

"Matt, we already know who the leader of the White Knights is in this area. You picked out the voice of Mr. Mueller the night they were here. I think our next action is to get face to face with him. He may not have been one of the bushwhackers, but we can be sure he knows who the others were. I suggest that we take the morning to take care of poor Sparrow, let the horses rest, and then make a trip into Winchester. We need to get Simon to a doctor, and then we need to make a report to the military adjutant. Depending on the response we get, we can decide what to do next. Just in case, let's take the Winchesters along on this trip."

"Pa, it is a sad commentary on the state of things, but there is no doctor in town who will even look at Tybee or Simon," Matt said, shaking his head. "Aunt Elizabeth is as good as it gets out here in the Loop. Taking them into town is just a waste of time."

By lunchtime, Sparrow had joined the others in the little cemetery. As each shovel full of dirt was moved, Matt became more and more upset. By the time the group was sitting around the table for

THE WOUNDS OF WAR

lunch, Ami Ruth was very much aware that her husband was agitated almost to the limits of his emotions.

There wasn't any conversation around the table other than getting the ample bowls passed from person to person. Five of their friends were dead. Five who would be alive if they had not come to help with the harvest. Two were badly injured and looking at weeks and months of recovery time.

As the time for departure into Winchester approached, Isaac said to Matt, "Son, I want us to take Tybee and Simon into town with us. We are going to find a doctor for them if we have to break down a few doors."

Matt wasn't sure what his Pa had in mind, but he and Ami Ruth put feather mattresses into the back of the wagon, and Isaac carried both of the injured young men down the stairs and laid them onto their makeshift pallets. The ride into town would take about two hours, and it would not be easy for anyone injured as severely as those two were. Just before they were to leave, Aunt Elizabeth walked out with her little medical satchel and climbed up on the driver's seat with Matt. Isaac had the grey mare tied to the back of the wagon and was astride Big Billy. Except for Ami Ruth, the whole family was going to town.

Two hours later, they were tying the horses to the hitching post in front of the doctor's office. Matt began the slow process of getting the two patients up from their pallets and down off of the wagon. Isaac strode into the doctor's office, carrying his Winchester. Simon still could not put any weight on his feet, so Matt simply picked him up and carried him inside. By the time they reached the door Isaac was standing inside and directed him to take both young men back to the examining room. The people sitting in the waiting room watched silently and blank faced as Matt and Isaac helped Simon and Tybee to the back.

When they left the doctor's office about an hour later about half of the people who had been awaiting the attention of the doctor had left. Both of the patients had clean dressings on their wounds and a doctor's diagnosis to work from.

Tybee's wounds were clean and the bleeding had stopped. The doctor instructed Aunt Elizabeth to do all the things she already knew how to do, but she smiled graciously and nodded when it was appropriate. Simon's hands and feet were another story. The doctor said many of the bones in his hands and feet were broken and though some would heal themselves others would not. The swelling would have to go down a bit so he could examine the bones more closely. During war time, the doctor said, he would have simply amputated the worst breaks and let the others heal. That might be the best solution in this case, but he suggested that Simon come back in two weeks. He spoke in a low voice to Isaac, suggesting that he could bring Simon into the office through the backdoor and that the rifle would not be needed.

The young men were loaded into the wagon, and they were about a half block down the street when Matt asked Isaac, "Pa, these doctors don't take dark-skinned patients. How did you make that happen?"

"I learned in the army that doctors are mostly interested in helping people get well," Isaac said. "These city doctors are worried that if they serve slaves and former slaves, they will lose their white patients. And as is evidenced by the half-empty waiting room when we left, that would be true here. I just gave the doctor an alternative he could accept and a way to cover his backside with his usual patients. I told him to tell folks that I held a gun on him and made him take care of them. It was a true statement. He wasn't worried about my shooting him, but he liked the idea that he was 'forced' to take care of these new patients."

In a few minutes, they arrived at the military adjutant's office. The clerk gave them some papers to fill out, and Matt set about trying to describe what had happened in written form. Before he had finished, he had filled out the form, the back of the page, and had asked for two additional sheets of the clerk's paper. He handed in the paperwork and sat back down.

The clerk started to read what he had written, and then he suddenly stood up and disappeared back into an inner office. In a few

THE WOUNDS OF WAR

minutes he came back and ushered Isaac and Matt into the office of the adjutant.

Matt remembered the face of the military official from his visit to the Schendler Farm a couple of months before. That occasion had not been pleasant and this visit would prove to be no better.

The adjutant looked at the two of them and said, "This paper says there were eight people killed on your farm over the past twenty-four hours."

"No, sir," Matt responded. "Five were killed on the road north toward Charles Town. They had finished the harvest at our farm and were on the way home to Gettysburg. They were bushwhacked along the road and their wages stolen. The other three, probably local people, were in the process of abusing and killing one of our young women."

"So you claim that none of these people were killed on your farm. Is that your testimony to me?" he asked.

"Yes, sir," responded Matt. "One of the traveling group made it back to our farm and told us what happened. We went to find the group hoping some were still alive. Unfortunately, only one more made it out alive and he was badly injured."

"So was this incident in Virginia or was it in West Virginia, north of the border?" the adjutant asked.

"We are not sure exactly where the border is along that road, but we think the ambush happened in West Virginia," Matt responded.

"Well, in that case, you may have to take this situation to the police in Charles Town. I have no authority in West Virginia," the adjutant responded. "I will keep this paperwork and see that it is sent to the authorities in Charles Town. They will be the ones to investigate exactly what happened and what should be done about it."

Until now, Matt had been handling the give and take with the military official, but Isaac was growing more and more frustrated. He said, "Sir, the people involved were all from Virginia. They call themselves the White Knights of the Camelia. They are a bunch of hoodlums out to intimidate whites and blacks alike. They paid us a visit about a month ago and threatened us and our workers. These are, in fact, local people under your administration. If we take this to the West Virginia authorities, they are going to tell us that these atrocities were not committed by West Virginia people, and so it is the responsibility of your office here in Virginia to handle his matter."

"That may, in fact, turn out to be the case, but if it happened on West Virginia soil, they have to be the ones to deal with it, not me," he responded.

Isaac was already on his feet. Matt looked at the adjutant and said, "Sir, we will do our best to get to the bottom of this mess and will report to you what happens as a result. Until then, if you hear anything that will help us clear it up, we would appreciate a word from you."

"If I hear anything, I will be in contact," the adjutant responded calmly.

They were hardly in the wagon when Isaac said, "We won't hold our breath until we hear from that paper-pushing bureaucrat."

Isaac, Matt, Aunt Elizabeth, and the two injured men were nearing home when Isaac brought Big Billy around to the front of the wagon. He said, "Matt, let's take the horses and make a little side trip."

Aunt Elizabeth started to object, but the look on Isaac's face told her that she should not interfere in this matter. Her job was to take care of the patients, and their job was to deal with the attack on their people. As she watched them ride away toward the middle of the Loop, she knew they were going to the White Hall Store. She wasn't sure how she would get the two injured young men into the house without their help but knew that with Ami Ruth they would manage it.

When they had the store in sight, Isaac stopped Big Billy and spoke to Matt. "Son, let's split up here. I am going to ride up to the front door of the store. I want him to see me coming. You go around to the back of the store and wait for him to come out. When he sees me, I don't think he will stay inside and wait for me to come in."

It was just as Isaac said. Matt was in position behind the store when he heard Big Billy approaching the hitching post near the front door. In just a few seconds, Mr. Mueller came out the backdoor and began walking quietly toward the wood frame house next door where he and his wife lived.

Matt confronted him before he reached the house. "Good morning, Mr. Mueller," he said. "I wish you would stop where you are. My Pa wants to have a talk with you."

Mr. Mueller stared at the Winchester rifle pointed at his chest. He knew he could not escape to the house. In a few seconds, Isaac came out the backdoor of the store.

"Good morning, Mr. Mueller. It's a nice day for a walk. Let's, the three of us, just walk over there under that oak tree and have a short conversation."

Matt kept the rifle pointed at Mr. Mueller while Isaac checked to see if he had a handgun hidden under his apron. When he was sure Mr. Mueller didn't have a weapon, Isaac reached in his back pocket and pulled out a small leather pouch. "This was on the counter when I passed through the store a few minutes ago," he said.

"Pa, that is one of the pouches I used when I paid our people!" Matt said.

"I've never seen any leather pouch like that," Mr. Mueller objected.

Then Isaac's voice turned deadly serious. "Mr. Mueller, tell us who was on the raiding party that shot up our field hands on the road to Charles Town yesterday."

"How would I know? I was here in the store all day yesterday. You can ask any number of people who came into the store," Mr. Mueller said, but even as he talked, his voice told a different story. He was caught and the responsibility for the assault that killed six people belonged to the organization he was in charge of. Guilt was written all over his face like ink on stationery.

"Mr. Mueller, you brought a gang of cutthroats to our farm about a month ago," Isaac said. "You tried to intimidate us and you threatened our family and our workers. The events of yesterday was *your* group keeping *your* word to do harm to our people. Whether you were there or not, you were the person in charge. We hold you responsible for all the deaths as well as the abuse of the one young lady who was in the group.

"Three of your people paid with their lives," Isaac continued. "I suspect there are three families today who don't even know where to find the bodies of their men. The other murderers are still out there somewhere acting as if nothing has happened. You, sir, are here with us with a gun pointed at your chest. We could take your life right now and no one would blame us. But we want the names of the others of your group, and we want you to identify them to the adjutant in Winchester so he can hang them legally."

"Look, you Masons are way out of line," Mr. Mueller sputtered. "I'm a shopkeeper, a business man, not an assassin. I didn't kill your people, and I don't know who did."

"I'm about tired of talking to you and hearing your lies," responded Isaac. "You may not have been on the road north of our farm yesterday but you know who was. You are out of choices and out of time."

Isaac cocked the Winchester, and to Mr. Mueller, it must have sounded like thunder.

The shopkeeper's voice was very low when he spoke again. "Look, if I don't tell you, you are going to kill me. If I do, *they* will kill me. I didn't do it, and I did not send a group out to do it. I would swear on a Bible that is the truth."

Isaac took a deep breath, looked at Matt, and said, "Mr. Mueller, you may not be guilty of this atrocity, but you certainly were the one in charge when your hoodlums came to our farm. We intend to let it be known that you told us the names of the other seven bushwhackers. I suspect they will kill you when they hear you told. So this is your lucky day. You can disappear so far away they won't find you. We don't want to ever see your face again in the Loop or in Winchester. As of today, your store is closed for business. You and your wife have until tomorrow morning to pack up your belongings and move as far away from here as you can get. By tomorrow afternoon, we will begin spreading the rumor that you talked, and we have turned over the names to the adjutant in Winchester."

"Look here, Mason, I can't just pull up stakes and leave everything I own, the store, the house, everything!" Mr. Mueller cried.

"How much do you figure your store and house are worth, Mr. Mueller?" Isaac asked. "Are they worth your life? Because if you are still here by noon tomorrow, your wife is going to bury you."

"I can't, I just can't," Mr. Mueller responded.

"All right," Isaac said. "I'll give you three hundred dollars for the store, your house, and anything else that you can't get in your wagon. That will give you a grubstake to start over with. You may drive your wagon by our farm on your way out tomorrow, and I will hand you the money on the road by the lane. Bring the title to the store and the house next door with you, and we will handle the transaction right there on the road. If I am not right there, just wait. Don't pull down into the lane. We don't want you on our land ever again."

Mr. Mueller nodded dumbly, as if he could not speak.

"And one other thing," Isaac said. "If you think you can bring your gang of cutthroats along to shoot your way out of this, you are badly mistaken. We will be ready for you, and there isn't much cover up by the road in front of our farm."

With that, Isaac motioned to Matt, and they walked away, leaving Mr. Mueller standing under the oak tree. In a few minutes, they were mounted and riding up the road toward the Schendler Farm.

Around noon the next day, right on schedule, Mr. Mueller pulled his wagon to a stop at the edge of the lane by the road. Isaac rode Big Billy up to the meeting place with a leather pouch in his hand.

Mr. Mueller had nothing to say to Isaac and his wife sat staring straight ahead. Isaac handed him the leather pouch. Mr. Mueller reached in the bag that was by his foot and pulled out the deeds to the store and house. Both were already signed. Mr. Mueller looked in the pouch while Isaac was examining the papers. Isaac nodded to him, and Mr. Mueller rattled the reins on the horse's backside. In a few seconds, they were out of sight down the road. The Masons now owned the White Hall Store and the house next door.

The family also had a problem with the tax money again. The $300 they paid Mr. Mueller brought them just below the amount they needed to pay taxes on the farm if the assessment grew to $1,400 as Matt expected it would.

FINALLY, SOME GOOD NEWS

It did not take long to learn the names of the three bushwhackers. Funerals that take place without notice usually indicate that the person did not die of natural causes. The rumor mill, always active in such times, indicated that the military adjutant was looking for seven men who had been part of a shooting up in West Virginia. Isaac did not contact the adjutant in Winchester again, but two short conversations on the street in town generated rumors that traveled like wildfire, as Isaac knew they would. Some key people in the community were keeping a very low profile. None of this was lost on Matt and Isaac Mason.

Tybee continued to make a steady recovery, and soon he was leaving his bed for several hours each day. Aunt Elizabeth called him a quick healer and said she expected he would be back to normal in a few weeks. Simon was not so lucky. The next visit to the doctor's office gave him the dilemma of amputating several of his fingers and toes or taking the risk of having stiff hands and feet for the rest of his life. Simon decided cutting them off wouldn't hurt more than the pain he was already feeling. In the end, he had two good fingers on one hand and three on the other. He kept his big toe and two smaller toes on each foot. Once the surgery was over, it was just a matter of recuperation and learning to function with his remaining fingers and toes.

Toward the end of the first week in November, Aunt Elizabeth and Ami Ruth went down to the winery to clean up the rooms where the field hands had stayed. The work took most of an afternoon, and while they were there, they noticed that a hinge was loose on the big door that closed off the basement from the main floor. The door was nine feet high and about fifteen feet across, so it took several of the men to get it open and to brace it so the hinge could be fixed. While that was going on, Ami Ruth and Aunt Elizabeth continued their work in the two rooms where the field workers had lived.

The two ladies had walked in and out of the broken door a half dozen times before Ami Ruth paused to watch Jesse and another of the winery workers holding the door up to work on the hinge. She was headed back down the slope into the basement when something caught her eye, something she had never noticed before. She stopped in front of the large rectangular piece of wood that held the hook where the large door was attached when it was open, which was most of the time.

Ami Ruth remembered her parents talking about the big door. Her father had built it to shield the Underground Railroad visitors who had come from time to time before the war and while the armies of both South and North were coming and going in the region around Winchester. It had to be a big door because it was their intent to bring the visitors from the barn up by the big house to the winery in a wagon and to unload the wagon only after it was inside the lower area. And it needed heavy wood at both ends to anchor it. He had used two four-by-fours at the upper end which were sunk well into the ground. Before now, she had never noticed what was used at the lower end.

She stared at the large rectangular piece of wood, realizing she and others had passed it by hundreds of times. But until now she had never really looked at it. It was about five feet high and four feet across. Right in the middle of it was a joint, a crease. When she saw the crease, she had a flash in her mind back to when she was twelve or thirteen years old, watching her father building a table. It had what she called Schendler magic built under it. When you pulled the two halves apart, an apparatus lifted up and a leaf appeared that fit perfectly into the two sides to expand the table by a good eighteen inches. Mr. Schendler was working on two tables at the same time.

She knew what happened to the first table. It was in their kitchen. Until now, she never knew what happened to the second table.

The more she looked, the more she realized that she was standing in front of the second table top. Of course, this table had no legs and it was not finished on top like the table in the kitchen at the big house. This table top was stuck into the side of the wall and was being used as the lower foundation for the door that swung open and closed to seal off the basement area under the winery. Right in the middle of it was the metal eyelet that accepted the hook that was attached to the door. When the door was open, which was most of the time, the door hid the five by four piece of wood that anchored the lower end. When it was closed, light was blocked off and the entryway was dark. Unless you were looking for it, you would never know it was there.

Her heart beating fast, Ami Ruth retraced her steps to the top of the slope and asked Jesse when he thought they would be finished with the hinge. He looked up at her and said, "Miss Ami Ruth, we are almost finished now. Do you need this door closed?"

"No, Jesse, I want you to leave the door open, but I want you to take the wagon and find Matt. I think he and Isaac are in the vineyard on the north slope. The storm the other night took down several of the frames that support the grape plants there, and I think they took on that job on this morning. Ask him to come to see me at the winery before they go back up to the big house."

"Yes, ma'am," Jesse responded.

Ami Ruth rejoined Aunt Elizabeth in the two rooms in the basement. She was busting to tell her what she thought she had found, but she resolved to share it with Matt before anyone else knew what she thought was behind that four-by-five piece of wood.

About a half hour later, she heard hoof beats approaching the winery, and she hurried up the slope to the large opening that led to the basement. In a few seconds, Matt and Isaac came rushing in the side door. By then, Aunt Elizabeth had joined her at the entrance to the basement.

Matt had been working outside in the sun, and he had his shirt off and slung over his shoulder. Ami Ruth had a flashback to that time two years ago when she and her friend Mary Ann had taken some water out to Matt and her father when they were working on the corral fence. He had his shirt off then too. That was the first time she ever saw a young man, any man, without his shirt. That memory brought a smile to her face.

"Okay, what have we been missing this morning?" Matt inquired. "We were about done on the north ridge and thought we would soon be back up at the house washing up for a good lunch. Instead, we are back in the winery again. What's the crisis?"

Ami Ruth was obviously excited and smiling from ear to ear. "I'm not exactly sure what I have found, but if you and your Pa will help me, I think I have a solved a mystery," she said.

With that ambiguous comment, she turned and led the other three down the slope to the wall behind the swinging door. She reached up and pointed at the crease in the slab of wood that was just above her head. "It may be hard to separate, but I want you and Isaac each to take hold of the sides of the wood both above and below the joint. Then pull the two pieces apart. It should slide easily once it is started."

The two men positioned themselves on either side of the rectangular piece of wood, Isaac at the upper piece and Matt kneeling next to the lower end. Then both began to pull. It was just as Ami Ruth said: once they got it going, separating the two pieces of wood was not difficult.

The joint grew larger as the pieces of wood separated, and the ladies could see something behind the joint. As they reached a separation of about a foot, a tray seemed to come out of the wall behind the wood pieces as if by magic. On the tray was a box that was about two feet square and eight inches high.

By this point, the excitement was almost unbearable. Ami Ruth's voice was heard above the others shouting, "Open it, Matt, open it!"

Matt backed away and looked at the box. It had a latch on one side with a place for a lock, but instead of a lock, there was a small metal piece like a large nail stuck in the latch to hold it shut. Matt remembered someone calling that piece of metal a cotter pin.

Matt looked at the others. "Let's hold our noise down a bit," he said quietly. "We are all anxious to know what is inside the box, but I suggest that we take it up to the big house where we can have some privacy when we open it. We may have prying eyes and ears here in the winery. Pa, let's lift the box to the floor and close up the hiding place. Right now, we are the only ones who know where it is. Let's keep it that way. This wall safe may come in handy down the line."

Isaac stepped in and lifted the box to sit it on the ground. "Man, that box is heavier than it looks. What in the world did Mr. Schendler keep in there?"

In a few seconds, they had the table top safe closed up, and Matt strode back up the slope to ground level. He took the big door that had been standing about halfway open, grasped the handle, and pulled the door down to the four by four wooden anchor attached to the wall, placing the hook into its slot. He then stepped away and looked it over.

"You know," he said, "this is about as good a job of hiding something in plain sight as anyone could do. When the big door is open, the safe is covered by the door. When it is closed, it is dark in this passage way and you are concentrating on where your feet are planted as you come down the slope, so you aren't looking at the wall. If Ami Ruth had not remembered watching her Pa make the tables when she was a girl and seeing the hidden compartment inside, we would never have found it."

"Matt, we still don't know what is inside," his wife said impatiently. "Can't we hurry up to the house so we can open it?"

"C'mon, Pa, let's get this box on the wagon and take a quick trip up to the house," Matt said.

Isaac bent down to pick up the box, but Matt cautioned him, "Hold just a minute, Pa. That thing is too heavy for one person to carry up the slope and out to the wagon. Let me get one side of it."

Soon the box was in the wagon, and Aunt Elizabeth was rattling the reins against the backsides of the horses, Ami Ruth at her side, heading up the east ridge toward the big house. Matt and Isaac followed on horseback, each speculating silently about what was in the box that weighed so much.

It took both of the men to get the box up the back stairs and into the kitchen. They set it down on the kitchen table and waited until the women had joined them at the table. Then Matt took the cotter-pin out of the latch and lifted the lid. Their response was a gasp of surprise and wonder. Aunt Elizabeth was the first one to find her voice. "Oh my gracious," she said.

Then the words came in a rush with everyone talking at once.

"Good gosh, look at that."

"I've never seen anything like that."

"Matt, how much is there?"

"We're rich!"

"There are greenbacks and greybacks *and* hard money."

Finally, Isaac breathed his low whistle, "No wonder it was so heavy."

The box was divided into a large section and several smaller compartments. The large section was filled with greenbacks. Each bundle of greenbacks was wrapped so that they were all the same size. It looked like there were several different denominations of bills, twenty dollars, fifty dollars, and one hundred dollars. The rest of the larger section had greybacks, the now worthless Confederate money. In the outside sections, that were about two inches wide and ran along the side and end walls of the box, there were gold coins.

Matt picked up one of the gold coins and identified it as a twenty-dollar double eagle. He didn't count them, but there looked to be well over three hundred gold pieces in the box. That accounted for the weight. Aunt Elizabeth reached into the box and began intently examining several of the gold pieces.

Since Isaac's low whistle, no one had said a thing. Matt looked across the table at Ami Ruth who was sitting down with her head in her hands but with her eyes looking between her fingers at the box full of more money than any of them had ever seen, more than they had ever hoped to see.

Isaac said the words everyone was thinking. "Where in the world did all this come from? There must be thirty or forty thousand dollars here!"

Matt was holding several bundles of hundred dollar bills. "I think there is more than that, Pa," he said. "Maybe fifty to sixty thousand. Ami Ruth, where did this money come from?"

"Matt, I have no idea," she responded.

"Let's think for a moment," Aunt Elizabeth said, keeping a cool head as usual. "The double eagles were first minted in 1849 right after the California gold rush. Some of these coins have 1850 and 1852 dates on them. Mr. Schendler must have been saving this money for more than a decade when he was killed in 1863. We can never date the greenbacks without going to the government and probably raising questions from them we don't want to answer. But with those coins looking brand new and with dates on them that spread all through the 1850s, we can be sure he was putting this treasure box together for a decade and more. The greybacks were not issued until the winter of 1861, but they are worthless now anyway. If Lincoln had lived, the Union was going to buy our greybacks but that promise disappeared with his death."

"Ami Ruth, do you remember how old you were when you were watching your Pa build the two tables?" asked Matt.

She thought for a moment and said, "I think I must have been twelve or thirteen. No, I was thirteen because I remember that the war had just started. Pa must have been concerned when the war started that he needed a better place to keep the money. One of the early battles was fought all around us and into Winchester. He must have worried that one of the armies would come in and take our farm. He could see the need of having enough money—greenbacks, greybacks, and some gold—to take care of the family in case we lost the house or barn."

"That sounds right, Ami Ruth," Matt said. "He loved his farm, but he knew there was nothing here that couldn't be replaced. He was mostly concerned with your mother, you, and David. Of course, David was relatively safe up in Philadelphia. You and your mother would have been the ones most on his mind."

Ami Ruth continued, "Several around us were convinced that because we were Quakers both sides would leave us alone. Pa believed that neither side would care what our religion was, and they would take whatever they wanted to support their war effort. That is why he let the animals out of the corrals and drove them up onto the ridge. He knew we could get them back, but Yankees or Rebels, whoever came, would have a hard time taking them if they were in the woods."

"I think the idea of the table top safe came to him when he started working on the kitchen table," Ami Ruth added. "He was a master with wood. He made all our cabinets and most of our furniture over the years. I think he saw a table with a hidden leaf in a store somewhere. He knew he could make it here at home. Once he saw the plan, he knew he could put a tray where the leaf had been in the other table and the money could be hidden in the wall behind that big door." Her eyes filled with quick tears and her voice trembled a little. "That was my Pa."

"Well, Ami Ruth, he has certainly left us a legacy," said Isaac softly. "I knew after just a few days here that he created this farm so that it would be self-sustaining. Some items could be bought at the store if his womenfolk wanted them, but the farm could stand on its own feet. So anything he sold at the marketplace, either in Winchester or up in Martinsburg, became money he could hide away in case it was needed down the road."

"Ami Ruth, your Pa was a fine farmer and businessman, but he was a loyal Quaker too," Matt added. "He would be pleased to know that we uncovered his gift to us just at the time when many of his neighbors are facing the loss of their farms because they do not have the money to pay the new taxes."

"Matt, what are you thinking?" Ami Ruth asked wonderingly.

"I am trying to think like your Pa would under these circumstances," Matt said. "He always said that if a neighbor needed anything he had, all he had to do was ask. We have plenty of money for our own needs with this treasure trove you uncovered. If your Pa was here, he would be figuring out how to use it to ease the burden of those around us who are in need. We now own White Hall Store. You and Aunt Elizabeth are helping to run a barter store at the Meeting House that could be moved to the store, which is more centrally located. We could set up a bank in the store for use by our neighbors so they could borrow the money they need to pay their taxes."

"That's a wonderful idea!" Ami Ruth said, hugging her husband.

"I like it too, Matt, but let's don't call it a bank," Aunt Elizabeth said. "Banks charge interest, and we don't want to charge interest. I know we could get rich charging interest when our friends and neighbors have no other alternatives. But there are more than twenty verses in the Bible that tell us not to charge interest. Moses wrote such to us in Exodus, Deuteronomy, and Leviticus. Even King David wrote about the evil of charging interest in the Psalms."

"That is fine with me," Matt said. "If it isn't to be a bank, what shall we call it?"

"Let's call it a cooperative," Ami Ruth said. "The barter store is a cooperative. Each person brings what they have available to trade, and hopefully, takes home what is needed. That is what we will do with the money—give each family what they need. We can make it more of a universal effort by asking others who have enough for their taxes to invest what they have available in the cooperative to help their friends and neighbors."

Around the table, it was almost unanimous. Only Isaac had not spoken to the idea of setting up a cooperative and giving away the money. He said, "You three are the most amazing people I have ever had the privilege to know. We found a treasure and you were deliriously happy. But deciding to give it away makes you even happier. I am proud of you because I think you are doing exactly the right thing. I never met Mr. Schendler, but I know he would be pleased with his family and this unselfish attitude."

"More important," Aunt Elizabeth said, "I think God would be pleased."

PLANNING FOR A BRIGHTER TOMORROW

Matt, Ami Ruth, Aunt Elizabeth, and Isaac stayed at the table for a long time after supper that night, talking about the best way to set up the new cooperative. Some of the conversation concerned the barter store but most was about how to share the money they had found.

All agreed that the first thing to do was enlist the help of Mr. Ridgeway, the current moderator and convener for the group that had been meeting each week at the Society of Friends Meeting House. The original Quakers in the Loop had named the building Hopewell Meeting House when it was built in the 1700s, and never had that name been as fitting as it had become during this crisis. Everyone had been working toward solving the problem that plagued all the farm families, and all had been filled with hope that God would direct their leadership to a solution.

Matt resolved to ride over to the Ridgeway farm the next morning. With the field workers gone, the pressures of meal preparation had lessened, and Aunt Elizabeth suggested that Ami Ruth ride along for the visit. The Ridgeway farm was about three miles away on the far side of the Loop, and it took about an hour to reach it. Mr. Ridgeway was out in the field when they arrived, but Mrs. Ridgeway was very pleased to have a visit from the young couple. She sent someone to find Mr. Ridgeway, and in a few minutes, the three were sitting on the front porch with cups of cold cider.

Soon Mr. Ridgeway came around the edge of the porch, dressed for work in a pair of bib overalls, his boots covered with mud. He was not a big man, but he was built thick and his face was almost brown from working in the sun. Mr. Ridgeway wasn't sure why he had been called back to the house but was delighted to see the farm's young guests.

He opened the conversation with a question. "Matt, I have heard the rumors around the Loop about the visit of the White Knights to your farm and the attack on the farmworkers who were headed home to Pennsylvania. I also heard that three of the White Knights were killed. I was hoping you might fill me in on some of the details."

Matt, however, did not intend to talk about his family's involvement in the confrontations and steered the conversation directly into the purpose of his visit—that of paying the new taxes. "Perhaps we can talk about that later," he said. "I have come to share some information with you and to seek your counsel. I want you to know that several things have changed for us over the past two weeks, and these things have little to do with the face-off with the White Knights, though their presence in our community is a constant concern to us, as I know it is with you."

Mr. Ridgeway nodded, his eyes riveted on Matt's face. "They're a serious problem and we don't seem to be in a very good position to protect ourselves from their violence."

Matt continued, "First, I want you to know that we have bought the White Hall Store. Mr. Mueller decided that with the turmoil surrounding the White Knights, he and his wife will be better off living somewhere else. We all know that the store was not doing well because most of the people in the Loop were buying nothing as they tried to save money for their taxes. So Mr. Mueller agreed to sell us the store and the house next door. As you may know, the store has been closed now for about a week. We want to work toward reopening it and, perhaps, moving the Friends barter store from the Meeting House to the White Hall Store."

Obviously pleased, Mr. Ridgeway leaned forward in his seat and his expansive face broadened into a big smile. He glanced at his wife, whose face also wore a broad smile, and said, "I had a feeling that God was at work when the women came up with the idea for the barter store! I knew something big was about to happen. Moving the store to White Hall would allow us to open it every day and make it into a continuing cooperative for all the farms."

Ami Ruth smiled at Matt, knowing that opening the store every day was in his plans all along. Matt's eyes told Ami Ruth to stifle her smile. Both of the young Masons reacted to Mr. Ridgeway's comments as if he had just come up with a very good idea. Matt had hoped that the idea of opening the White Hall Store as a cooperative could be presented to the Meeting House group as Mr. Ridgeway's idea and that was exactly the way it was turning out.

"It was our hope that you could appoint a committee from the ladies who would work toward helping us get the store open and stocking its shelves with trade goods from our farms," Ami Ruth said.

Mr. Ridgeway responded with enthusiasm. "We will do just that! I was in Mueller's store just before it closed and the shelves were bare. I understand why Mr. Mueller would sell it since it seemed to have died with this tax crisis. Reopening it as a barter store cooperative will certainly revive it. And getting several of our women into the store to clean up the place, and perhaps put some new paint here and there, would dress up the place considerably. I think reopening the store is a great idea."

Mrs. Ridgeway chimed in, "It never fails, young people come up with young ideas, and I knew when the two of you were planning to get married that this would be a union that would be good for all of us!" she said.

"Thank you, Mrs. Ridgeway," Matt said, smiling at his bride. "Mr. Ridgeway, I have another item for you to consider that may become very important over the next couple of months."

Mr. Ridgeway again leaned forward in his chair with anticipation. From the expression on his face, it was obvious he was thinking, *What could be better than what Matt and Ami Ruth have just presented?*

"I think I remember the total tax obligation that was still uncovered by our neighbors around the Loop at around thirty thousand dollars," Matt stated. "Am I correct with that number?"

Mr. Ridgeway thought for a few seconds and then responded. "I think our original poll several weeks back made the tax obligation closer to sixty thousand dollars, but all the work and effort by our people had reduced that number to around thirty thousand dollars by the time we took the latest poll last week. Several were at their wit's end with trying different things to make and save money. We may not be able to reduce that total very much farther by the deadline at the end of November. Several are at the end of their rope."

Matt asked, "What if we had a sort of bank, maybe call it a cooperative, where we could loan the money to our neighbors, enough so that they could pay their taxes? They could pay the cooperative back over the next year or two."

"Matt, you know that most of our farmers had their money in the Winchester bank, and it closed when the war ended and made their greybacks worthless," Mr. Ridgeway responded, disappointed. "I don't know where we would get enough money to help our neighbors."

"If we were to open the discussion next week at the Meeting House, inviting those who had enough money for their taxes and some to spare to deposit what they didn't need right now into a cooperative for those in need to draw from, how much do you think we would get?" Matt asked.

"I don't know," Mr. Ridgeway said. "But for sure we couldn't come up with thirty thousand dollars."

"I think we might," Matt said.

Mr. Ridgeway shook his head slowly. "Matt, I wouldn't want to set up such a thing, get everyone's hopes up, and then not be able to come through on the promise of such an enterprise." he said.

"Mr. Ridgeway," Ami Ruth said, "I think we may be shorting God just a bit in this effort. Such a proposal is like Gideon putting out the fleece. We need to give our people a chance to underwrite such a challenge. I think we would be surprised what came from the effort. Several of our farms are very prosperous during good times. And we may be surprised just how many of our people have set aside savings for just such an occasion as this. We need to give them a chance to answer the challenge."

Mr. Ridgeway still sounded doubtful. "There is considerable risk in presenting something like this, getting everyone's hopes up and then not being able to help everyone who needs it," he said. "I think several are resolved that they can't meet the tax deadline. They are anticipating that their farms are going to be forfeited, and they will have to move. To give them hope and then dash those hopes would be beyond cruel."

Matt leaned forward in his chair and lowered his voice, as if someone might be sitting under the porch listening. "I would not want this guarantee to go beyond this conversation because I think it would inhibit others from participating in the cooperative bank or whatever we end up calling it. I am sure we will have enough money to cover everyone's needs for meeting the tax burden. I even think we may have enough available to help each of the farms with seeds and supplies they will need for planting next spring."

"Matt, how could you possibly make such a guarantee? No one farm has that much money!" Mrs. Ridgeway burst out, her hands clutching her glass so hard it seemed it would shatter. "This seems almost impossible!"

Ami Ruth's voice reflected Matt's low tone, "I am hopeful that nothing is impossible when God is involved," she said.

Mr. Ridgeway looked at his wife. "From our own situation, I am sure we could contribute something to the cooperative," he said. "We have enough for our taxes and some left over. I'm sure there are others capable of doing the same thing. We just need a way to handle the process. It is a great idea and one that will help solve this problem and can be used in the future for us to help each other. All right, Matt, if we do this, how would we set it up?"

"I'm no banker," said Matt. "But it does not look like a difficult process. We create an accounting process for both income and outgo. Everyone who has a gap between what they have available and what they need for the taxes should be able to take out as much of a loan as they need for that purpose. We will deal with the tax problem now and look down the road in February for the spring planting needs. When we reach a time when the cooperative is no longer needed, everyone who put money in could take it out in the same proportion of their deposit."

"How much interest would you charge, Matt?" asked Mr. Ridgeway.

Ami Ruth smiled at Matt and responded, "We don't envision charging any interest. The Bible tells us many times not to charge interest to our friends and neighbors. I think this is another time where we put God's word to work."

"How will we pay for the work of running the process if we don't charge at least some interest?" Mr. Ridgeway asked.

Matt said, "First, the bank—let's call it a cooperative—can be housed in the White Hall Store. Aunt Elizabeth or someone like her who knows how can be the bookkeeper. Money can be taken to the store as it is needed for transactions."

"Matt, where will you keep the money to be sure it is secure?" Mr. Ridgeway asked.

"We have a place that was created by Mr. Schendler before he was killed. No one would find it in a hundred years," he responded.

"I think we need to keep this new 'cooperative' as quiet as possible. If we were using the bank in Winchester, word would be on the street almost before we started. And word of the cooperative will leak out eventually, but we want this to be as low-key as possible. I hope we can get through the tax obligations at the end of November before the community begins to find out what we are doing. Once we are past the end of November, we can close up shop until February when some of our farmers will need help in setting up for the planting season."

"What about paying back the cooperative?" asked Mr. Ridgeway.

"We would need to limit the times when the cooperative is open for paybacks. But I don't anticipate there would be much income for the cooperative until after the harvest in the early fall next year," Matt responded.

"I don't know, Matt," said Mr. Ridgeway, sounding doubtful again. "It sounds like a Godsend, but some of us would be getting most of our savings tied up for a year and more. I'm not sure how many would contribute."

Ami Ruth said, "Well, we won't know until we put it in front of our people. Some may be uneasy with what we are doing, but I think most will view it as what you called it just now, a Godsend."

The young couple got up a few minutes later, thanked the Ridgeways for their hospitality, and climbed onto their horses. Matt and Ami Ruth were about a mile down the road before either of them spoke. Ami Ruth pulled the grey mare up next to Big Billy and said, "Matt, did that conversation go the way you expected?"

Matt smiled at her. "It did. In fact, I'm not sure it could have gone any better."

"Matt, we did not talk to Aunt Elizabeth about taking charge of the cooperative, or the store either for that matter. I'm not sure how she will react."

"Well, if not Aunt Elizabeth, then someone else like her who is known to be dependable and trustworthy. She knows and understands the cooperative approach for the barter store. This approach to sharing the money is just taking the concept a step further. She has been with us for two years now. She may be ready for a new challenge," Matt said. "She came to stay at our house as a favor to David and to help you. You have been standing on your own feet for months now. I'm sure she sees you as a finished product."

Ami Ruth laughed. "I'm not sure I think of myself as a finished product, but I will take that as a compliment" The two rode on in companionable silence until they reached the lane that ran down to the house. Matt stopped Big Billy and Ami Ruth came up beside him.

Matt was feeling reflective and the words seemed to pour out of him. "I can't look down this lane without thinking of that time more than two years ago when I happened onto this very spot. The rain was just pouring and the wind was blowing so hard it seemed to be raining sideways. I had been leading Big Billy because it was so dark we couldn't see the road, and I was afraid of him stepping in a wagon rut. I was looking for someplace where we could get inside and out of the rain. There was a bright lightning flash, and I caught sight of your barn down at the end of the lane. In a very real sense, it was the only port in a storm. When we came closer, I saw the eight-pointed star on the side of the barn and knew I had come to a Quaker farm. It gave me great confidence that everything was going to be all right."

"I have much the same feeling when I look at the farm," responded Ami Ruth. "I can't help but look across the yard in front of the house to the cemetery where my folks are. I was very fortunate to have them as long as I did. I knew my Pa was a great man, but I didn't know just how great until the last couple of weeks. He was always thinking ahead to the future. He always saw his purpose in life in reflection to the Bible and its lessons. He put everyone else's needs ahead of his own. How could he have known how important the money would be down the road? He set it aside for us and it makes it possible for us to help our neighbors. But he couldn't have known the mess we would be in, could he?"

It was a question left hanging in the air as Matt and Ami Ruth rode together down the lane to the hitching post in front of the big house. There was security in their feeling of warmth toward each other. There was security in the feeling that they were doing the right thing for the farm as well as for their friends and neighbors. Along with the security, there was the feeling of strength.

Matt helped Ami Ruth down from the grey mare and held her for just a few seconds before they climbed up the steps to the porch together.

At the top of the stairs, they stopped. Matt said, "Standing here and looking out on all those memories, it makes me think we have lived a lifetime together here on your Pa's farm, and we are only eighteen. I wonder what we will have seen and experienced when we are standing here thirty years from now?"

Ami Ruth smiled. "I don't know what we will be thinking then, but I do know we won't be standing here alone. Matt, we are going to have a baby."

FAMILY COUNCIL

Most of the Schendler family discussions happened around the table in the kitchen after breakfast or supper. Each morning and evening, everyone was there and the more they talked, the less inclined they were to leave each other's company. That was especially true of the discussion that began that evening following supper about the White Hall Store and Aunt Elizabeth's proposed role in running the store and the cooperative.

Matt related to the group the substance of the conversation he and Ami Ruth had with Mr. and Mrs. Ridgeway earlier that day. He told them they had reached agreement that the barter store would be moved to White Hall and would be open every day. The cooperative, if it was approved by the Meeting House group, would function within the store with everyone having equal opportunity to share in the process. The key, of course, was having someone who could be trusted by everyone to handle both the store and the cooperative in a business-like manner.

Matt looked at Aunt Elizabeth and said, "The consensus between us and the Ridgeways was that you are the logical person to take over the operation of the store and cooperative, Aunt Elizabeth."

Aunt Elizabeth had been stirring her coffee and the stirring stopped. There was a few seconds of silence and then she responded. "How did you come to that conclusion?" she asked. "I have no experience running a store and certainly none running a bank."

"The most important thing right now is trust," Matt responded. "And you are among the better known Quakers in the Loop. You have worked on many of the farms. They call on you when a new baby is coming."

Ami Ruth added, "You helped set up the barter store in the Meeting House, and you have spoken out to the group in the meetings. Even if you haven't been on their farms, everyone knows who you are. And we can attest to how well you handle the bookkeeping for the Schendler Farm. You are the obvious choice."

"But we have so much to do here on the farm," said Aunt Elizabeth, "and, I still have two mighty sick boys to take care of. What about the meals for the workers?"

Ami Ruth responded, "You are right that we have much to do here. However, I have Seabrook here to help me, and though we know we won't do it as well as you would, we can get the meals on the table."

"We didn't mean to just dump this on you all at once, Aunt Elizabeth," Matt said. "When David asked you to come to the farm to fill in for Mrs. Schendler, he meant for you to live here forever with the family. We mean for you to be here with us too, as long as you want to be. We see this venture at the White Hall Store as a short-term solution to the tax and store problems."

"Let me give this some thought," Aunt Elizabeth said. "Would I be living in the house next door to the store?"

"It would probably work best if that were the case," Matt responded. "Then you could walk out your backdoor and open the store in just a few minutes. That doesn't mean we would move you out of your room here in the big house. That room is yours whenever you want it and for as long as you want it."

"Let's talk again tomorrow," Aunt Elizabeth said.

Later that night when things had quietened down in the house, Matt and Ami Ruth could hear voices just below their window on the front porch. Both knew it was Aunt Elizabeth and Isaac.

When Matt opened his eyes the next morning, he could already hear noises in the kitchen. He rolled over and reached for Ami Ruth, but she was already gone. The only evidence she had been there was the impression of her head on the feather pillow. He was almost dressed when she came back into their bedroom.

"Have you and Aunt Elizabeth talked about the store and her moving there?" Matt asked.

"We haven't," she responded. "But it is obvious she is in a very good mood, even humming some while she is cooking."

When the four of them were again around the table, Matt asked the question everyone wanted to know the answer to. "Aunt Elizabeth, have you given the proposition of the store and the cooperative some thought?"

"Yes, I have, Matt," she responded, smiling broadly. "I want to do it. I may need some help to get things up and running, but I want to do it."

"Good!" Matt said. "I hoped it would seem like the thing to do, kind of like another chapter of service to others which has been the pattern of your life."

Matt left the table and walked into the living room, returning in a few minutes with some papers in his hand.

He said, "Aunt Elizabeth, I know you will do well at running the store, and before too many weeks have passed, everyone in the Loop will know your name and what you are doing for them and for us. Ami Ruth and I want you to not only live in the house and run the store, but we want you to be the owner of both of those properties too."

With that comment, Matt pushed the papers he had been holding across the table. "Here are the deeds to the house and the store signed over to you. You are now a property owner."

Aunt Elizabeth's face revealed her overwhelming surprise. Isaac leaned back in this chair and began to laugh as Ami Ruth reached over and took her aunt's hand. Aunt Elizabeth began to cry softly. Between the muffled sounds they heard her voice, "I'm not sure what to say,"

"There isn't anything to say," said Ami Ruth. "This isn't a gift, it is something you have earned by giving yourself to us over the past couple of years and to many other families in the Loop before that. Everything you have today has been earned by working for others. It is your just due."

Aunt Elizabeth exclaimed, "I was looking for my reward in heaven and didn't anticipate that it might come right here and especially not at this troubled time!"

"God takes care of his own, Aunt Elizabeth, and for sure, you are one of his chosen ones," Ami Ruth said.

Later in the day, Aunt Elizabeth and Isaac took the horses and rode over to take a closer look at the store and the house. No one had been inside either since the Muellers left, and they needed to take an inventory so they would know what it would take to get the two properties up to speed.

The next morning while Matt was still in bed, Ami Ruth hurried into their bedroom and announced, "Matt, Aunt Elizabeth is gone!"

Matt sat up straight in the bed, "Gone! Gone where?"

"She left a note and it doesn't tell where, just that she and your father will be gone for a week or so. She says she will explain when they get back."

"Good night," said Matt. "What is she up to? What are *they* up to?"

"Oh, Matt," Ami Ruth said, her voice filled with excitement. "You don't suppose they have gone off to get married, do you?"

"Get married? My Pa and Aunt Elizabeth, married? That will take some getting used to," Matt responded.

"Well," she said, "we won't know until they get back, but wouldn't that be wonderful?"

Matt's mind was moving a thousand miles an hour. *My Pa and Aunt Elizabeth*. It was too much to absorb all at once. This would take some thinking time. A week. They would know in a week!

THE ONE CONSTANT
IN LIFE IS CHANGE

Spring came in strong in 1866 with a windy March followed by a rainy April. Much had changed for the Mason family and the Quaker families in the Loop north of Winchester.

Aunt Elizabeth and Isaac were indeed married in their one-week sojourn from the Schendler Farm. Considering how close they had become in recent weeks, it was not a great surprise to Matt, Ami Ruth, and the others on the farm.

The move to the White Hall Store for Aunt Elizabeth and Isaac was among the biggest changes. The movement of the barter store from the Hopewell Friends Meeting House to White Hall and the opening of the cooperative "bank" for use by the Quaker Friends in the Loop created an entirely new atmosphere in their close-knit community.

The result of the loan capability of the cooperative generated an even greater spirit of kinship among the farmers in the Loop. That was especially obvious when the congregation met on Sunday at the Hopewell Friends Meeting House. With that attitude was a new feeling of strength in their unity and faith that, whatever the challenge, together they could handle it. Not one farm was lost to the tax man, much to the disappointment of the Northerners who had moved to Winchester to take advantage of the crisis created by the heavy tax burden. When they found they could not prey on the misfortune of the local farmers, they moved on to other opportunities elsewhere.

That also seemed to be true of the White Knights of the Camelia, the local chapter of the Ku Klux Klan. After the ambush of the farmworkers on the road to Pennsylvania and the loss of their leader and three of their number, they seemed to fade from sight.

Perhaps the biggest change that occurred for Aunt Elizabeth was being disassociated from the Society of Friends fellowship at the Hopewell Meeting House. There were many things that could cause a person to be disassociated from a fellowship. They included exhibiting violence against another, joining the military, attending a different church, and marrying outside of the faith. In marrying Isaac Mason, Aunt Elizabeth had indeed married outside of the faith. In the weeks following, as their marriage became known to the Society of Friends, a discussion was held in the Meeting House and a vote was taken to disassociate the group from Aunt Elizabeth.

Being disassociated from the Society of Friends was not a surprise to Aunt Elizabeth. She had witnessed such discussions during her years as a member of the group. However, it was no less a shock when it occurred. What that vote meant was that she could no longer participate with the group in Sunday services. It did not mean that she could not join her family sitting on the back row of the sanctuary as an observer while services were going on. It did not mean that they could not share the work with her in the barter store. So from that time on, Aunt Elizabeth and Isaac continued to arrive at Sunday services with Matt and Ami Ruth. All of them dutifully sat on the back row, though not as participants.

For Ami Ruth and Matt, the baby that was due began to dominate their lives. Seabrook and Tybee's baby was born in February and gave the household a practice run through the process of birthing a baby and of caring for a newborn. Aunt Elizabeth and Mrs. Poteate came to help with the birth, and Ami Ruth watched everything that happened very closely. She knew she was next.

Seabrook's baby was a little boy who everyone said right away looked just like Tybee. Much to Matt's pleasure, they named him Matthew. He was Matthew Hart, son of Tybee and Seabrook Hart of the Schendler Farm.

Over the next couple of days, Matt kept going back to look at the baby again and again. It was as if he couldn't stay away. Matt looked very closely at the little guy, but despite everyone's declaration that "he looked just like Tybee," Matt just couldn't see it. His skin was light, not at all dark like Tybee's. He did have a full head of hair, but except for the lobes of his ears, this was a light-skinned baby.

Aunt Elizabeth was aware of Matt's fascination with the baby and walked in one morning with him looking down into the crib at the little fellow. "Matt, this is the third time you have been in to look at this baby this morning. Does it make you think of your own that will be along in a few months?"

"It's his skin color," said Matt. "This looks like a white-skinned baby."

Aunt Elizabeth laughed. "Matt, I'm guessing that you have never seen a Negra baby just after it was born. At birth, their babies are very light skinned. As they grow older, the skin darkens. If you want to know the eventual color of a Negra baby, you look at the lobes of their ears. That color is very close to the color their skin will be when they are grown."

As Aunt Elizabeth left the room, she saw Matt looking down at the baby again and shaking his head. She thought, *Ami Ruth's mother used to say something from time to time that was appropriate now, "Wonders never cease." And for sure they don't.*

Tybee was a proud father, but Matt knew when his baby arrived he would be even prouder. He didn't care if it was a boy or a girl. At least he kept telling himself that. Down deep inside—surprise, surprise—he was pulling for a boy.

* * *

The spring came and went. The cooperative bank provided the financial support for the necessities for planting and the crops were sowed. The White Hall Store provided the necessities for the farm families, and Aunt Elizabeth proved to be a marvelous store manager and banker for the Loop families, just as everyone knew she would.

Late in the spring, Isaac and Aunt Elizabeth moved back to the farm, and their presence eased the pressure on Matt and Ami Ruth with the baby's birth expected to be less than a month away. Aunt Elizabeth rode over to the store for a few hours each day but resumed her responsibilities with breakfast and the evening meals to take some of the burden from Ami Ruth. Matt had made two new excursions up to Martinsburg with wagons full of wine, and the farm's coffers were beginning to be refilled. Matt didn't have to think twice about where to keep the money. He opened up the big door to the basement and placed the money in the safe just as Mr. Schendler had envisioned. He was sure it was the best hiding place on the farm. There were now two separate boxes in the wall safe, one for the family money and the other for the money being used by the cooperative.

The work on the farm and in the winery continued to occupy Matt's time as he and Ami Ruth awaited the arrival of the baby. Isaac was again there each day to fit into the supervisory responsibilities of the farm. Matt concentrated on the winery and the vineyards, and Isaac keep watch over the gardens, the barn, and the animals. Virtually all the farm animals had been retrieved from the ridge behind the barn, and they had two new litters of pigs.

Big Billy continued to welcome regular visitors of the equine sort as the farmers in the region brought their mares for breeding. Matt created an arrangement with Mr. Raymond of the Circle One Horse Ranch, north of the West Virginia border, to bring his one bay mare to the Schendler Farm when she was ready. Matt traded four of the piglets, six chickens, and three sessions with Big Billy for ownership of any colt that came as the result of Big Billy's efforts with the mare. Matt had in mind that those two beautiful animals would produce another fine stallion that would enhance the reputation of the Schendler Farm as the top breeding stable in the region.

Big Billy—or King William as he was beginning to be known—had his two-night visit with Mr. Raymond's mare in the early summer, and within a month, it was obvious that the mare was going to foal in the spring of 1867. Matt was excited to learn of his good fortune and to know that there were going to be two births on the farm that would help make their lives complete: their baby and Big Billy's colt.

* * *

THE WOUNDS OF WAR

It was late in the day in mid-June when Seabrook rode the grey mare to the winery to fetch Matt. Hearing the hoof beats, he ran to the door, and Seabrook did not even dismount. "Miss Ami Ruth say you best come on up to the big house," she said. "She feeling poorly and say the baby is on its way."

Matt leaned back into the door of the winery and called for Jesse. "Jesse, take your horse and go to the White Hall Store and find Aunt Elizabeth," he ordered. "Tell her it is time, the baby is coming. Let her have your horse. Then hitch up the wagon at the store and go fetch Mrs. Poteate. Aunt Elizabeth can tell you how to find their farm."

Before Matt could get the cinch tightened on Big Billy's saddle, Jesse was headed up the back road at a gallop.

When Matt ran in the backdoor of the big house, he found Ami Ruth and Seabrook in the dining room where they had put the spare bed for Tybee when he was recovering from his gunshot wounds. They thought it would be a much better place for the baby to be born than on the second floor. It was easier for the ladies to get to and gave them easy access to the water and stove in the kitchen.

He knelt down next to Ami Ruth's bed, and she placed her hand on the back of his neck. She smiled at him and said, "He is coming, Matt, any minute now."

Matt felt instant panic. "Any minute now?" he asked.

"Yes," she responded. From the other side of the bed, Matt saw Seabrook's head shaking side to side.

Seabrook said. "This baby coming, Miss Ami Ruth, but I think it be some time yet before he be here."

Matt gulped and then relaxed. He wanted the baby to arrive but not before Aunt Elizabeth was here to take charge of the process. He had some experience helping farm animals birth their young but dealing with a real human birth was well beyond any experience he ever wanted to have. In his mind he was calculating how long it would be before Aunt Elizabeth would be here. Maybe an hour? Maybe a little more? It was a couple of miles over to the White Hall Store, and Jesse had just left to get her headed this way. He wanted the baby to come but was hoping it would wait a couple of hours at least. By the sounds Ami Ruth was making, she was ready for it to come anytime.

Seabrook stayed close to Ami Ruth while Matt went into the kitchen to stoke up the fire in the stove. He wasn't sure just how this birthing thing worked but he had heard you needed lots of hot water. He walked outside onto the back porch and filled up several pans with water at the pump and brought them back into the kitchen ready to put on the stove when Aunt Elizabeth instructed.

Matt then walked back into the dining room and sat down on the edge of the bed next to Ami Ruth. She reached out her hand and he took it. She reached over and took his other hand and put it on the bulge on her stomach.

"Can you feel the baby, Matt?" she whispered.

Indeed he could. He smiled and nodded at her and said, "It will be just a little while now. Don't worry. Aunt Elizabeth is on her way." He did, indeed, hope that was a true statement.

At that instant, he felt Ami Ruth begin to squeeze his hand. He gritted his teeth and almost made a noisy response, but he resolved that she could squeeze as hard as she wanted to, and he would not utter a sound.

The process went on for more than an hour. Her abdomen would get tight, she would squeeze his hand, and both of them would grit their teeth to keep from yelling.

With Aunt Elizabeth's arrival, everything changed. He heard her firm tread in the kitchen and the splash of water as she washed her hands. She walked into the dining room still wiping her hands on a dish towel.

She surveyed the scene and said briskly, "Okay, Matt, we don't need you here anymore. You get yourself a cup of coffee and go to the front porch with Isaac. Seabrook and I will be fine here with Ami Ruth, and when Mrs. Poteate arrives, you send her in. Otherwise, you stay out of the way. This is women's business, and we will take care of it without your help."

Matt was all too happy to let Aunt Elizabeth take charge. He bent down and kissed Ami Ruth just as her stomach began to tighten again, then fled out the door. He stood for a few minutes in the kitchen thinking about the reality of having a son or daughter in a few hours or perhaps in a few minutes. Aunt Elizabeth had told him to get a cup of coffee and go to the front porch and that is exactly what he did. There were times when it was prudent for men to take orders from women, and this was certainly one of them.

His father was smiling at him through his full beard when he arrived on the porch and took his place beside him in the rockers. Matt was preoccupied with the birthing activity going on inside but had a quick memory of a picture of Stonewall Jackson with a full beard. He thought for the first time how much his father resembled the Southern icon general who died following the great Confederate victory at Chancellorsville.

Isaac smiled and said, "Son, I remember the night you were born. Just like you, I was sent outside by the lady who came to help your Ma. I tinkered around in the barn for a bit and then went and sat on the front porch just like we are tonight. It seemed like hours, but I shall never forget hearing your first cry from inside. You announced your coming with a good strong cry, and I knew you were a boy before they invited me back inside."

"Pa," Matt asked, "how long will it take, you know, for the baby to come?"

"I don't have that much experience with birthing babies, Son, but with you, it didn't take long. I do understand that it is different with every birth and some take longer than others," Pa responded.

When Isaac and Matt were together, there was usually a continual flow of words back and forth between them, but not today. There were a few of the usual sounds: the breeze in the trees, the chirping of cicadas in the distance, Big Billy making his presence known at the fence, but none of the usual chatter.

After what seemed like hours, a shrill sound pierced the air. It was unmistakably a baby's cry. Matt was on his feet and headed across the porch toward the front screen door like he had been shot out of a gun.

Isaac laughed and said, "Hold on, Son. It isn't time to go in yet. They have the baby, but there is still some work to be done with both the baby and Ami Ruth. Just sit down and be patient. They will call you before too long."

It seemed way too long, but finally, Seabrook appeared at the screen door. She said, "You come on in now, Mr. Matt." And Matt went in to see his new son.

Ami Ruth was sitting up on pillows on the bed, and the baby was wrapped up in a small blanket in her arms. She hardly looked up at him when he came in the door, but when she did, she gave him one of her biggest smiles and said, "Look what we did, Matt."

Matt leaned over and kissed her on the forehead and collapsed on the edge of the bed. He had to sit down, or he was sure he would have fallen. It was as if all the strength had left his legs. He heard Ami Ruth whisper, "Do you want to hold him, Matt?"

Matt looked nervously at Aunt Elizabeth and she nodded. "You can hold him, Matt. He is delicate but he won't break."

Matt took his new son and held him up to the light, which caused the little fellow to blink his eyes a couple of times. Matt thought about taking him out on the porch to show his Pa, but a quick glance at the door to the living room told him his Pa had followed him into the house and was standing just a few feet away.

Matt walked over to him and held the baby up. "Look here, Pa. Isn't he something?"

Isaac smiled and responded. "Son of mine, this is a sight I wish your mother could see."

Elizabeth spoke to both of them from across the room. "Oh, she sees this baby. She is here right now with us watching her family grow."

* * *

It was hard to imagine life being any more complete for Matt, Ami Ruth, and the family at the Schendler farm. The family schedule took on a life of its own over the next several months as the baby occupied Ami Ruth's time while Matt and Isaac worked through the fall harvest in the vineyard. Simon, gravely injured by the bush whackers a year ago, had made a significant recovery and returned to his home in Pennsylvania. As he promised, he returned to help with the fall harvest in the vineyard and brought several friends along to help.

Just as they had done a year ago, they posted sentries to keep watch for a possible visit from the White Nights of the Camelia. There had been no reports of new activities by that white sheeted bunch for months, but with additional black faces on the scene, it did not make sense to take chances.

Matt made two more trips north with casks of wine for the winery in Martinsburg. The additional income was stored in the safe under the winery and the totals stored there continued to grow. The farmers in the Loop had begun to pay back the monies borrowed earlier to pay taxes and plant their crops in the spring. Virtually everything they had decided as a family more than a year ago seemed to be working out as planned.

The schedule eased somewhat during that winter of 1866–67, and Matt found himself more and more preoccupied with the growth and development of his son. The little guy was crawling all over the house and took constant watch and care. That was especially true when Tybee and Seabrook's son, Matthew, was in the house. Little Stephen tried every way possible to keep up with Matthew, who was almost five months older and was already beginning an unsteady walk from room to room. When Matt came in for lunch, he would always plan an extra hour to sit with Stephen just to watch what new thing he had learned to do.

* * *

So the family settled into a schedule that included the constant work on the farm with their weekly visit to the Friends Meeting House on Sunday morning.

TO POLITIC OR NOT, THAT IS THE QUESTION

Little Stephen had just passed his first birthday when the family loaded into the wagon for their weekly sojourn to the Meeting House. Aunt Elizabeth and Ami Ruth rode in the wagon while Isaac and Matt rode alongside on Big Billy and the grey mare. As they approached the Meeting House, it appeared to the family that the number of horses and buggies were somewhat larger than usual. Matt thought to himself, *I wonder what is going on that has attracted so many people.*

The group slipped in, and seated comfortably on the back row, they could survey the entire congregation. Mr. Joshua Ridgeway was in his usual place at the front of the room playing the role of convener. The right side of the room was filled with men, some still wearing their traditional straight-brimmed hats and others holding them on their laps. The women were all seated on the left side of the center aisle and dressed in almost identical fashion with long black skirts partially covered by aprons and white blouses partially covered by lightweight black jackets or vests.

Matt thought to himself that *Quakers are strong in their unity not only in spirit but also in the way they dressed.* He smiled to himself, wondering what the reaction would be if a woman in a bright red dress walked in the back entry. He surmised that they would be scandalized, but within minutes they would recover, greet the newcomer, and do whatever was necessary to make her feel welcome.

The service went as usual with several members expressing their thanks for blessings their family had received over the past week and others asking for prayer in dealing with both health and farm issues. By the mental clock Matt carried in his head, they had been in the Meeting House for about an hour when Mr. Ridgeway began to make preparation to close out the meeting.

At that point, portly, bearded Mr. Benjamin Thomson stood to be recognized. He asked, "Could I please ask your indulgence for a short discussion on something that I think needs our attention? It does not relate to our worship, so perhaps we could close out the worship service and then stay for a few minutes."

Mr. Ridgeway looked around the room and noted several nodding heads. He said, "If there is no objection to Mr. Thomson's suggestion, we will stay and listen to his thoughts after our meeting is closed." Nodding to one of the oldest men in the Meeting House, he said, "Mr. Poteate, would you please pronounce the benediction to our worship service?"

When the prayer was over, Mr. Thomson strode down the center aisle to the front of the room. His ruddy face was somber as he addressed the gathering. "Friends, we have weathered many problems that seemed overpowering at the time," he said. "Each time we have met a new problem, we have gained strength from each other and have managed to pass each challenge. I think we have a continuing problem that may take a new approach if we are ever to solve it." He paused, allowing his words to sink in. "We have a history of staying out of local politics, out of conflicts that are not of our making, out of wars fought over slavery and other issues that are not ours. We have been here in the Winchester area as a people since the early 1700s, and every time there is a new challenge given to us, it comes from outside of our group and relates in one way or another to either the state or the federal governments."

Several voices were raised from the men's section of the Meeting House. Most of their words were indistinguishable but "Amen" was repeated several times, and it was obvious that Mr. Thomson's words were appreciated.

He continued, "Throughout our time here, we have stayed out of fights that were not ours. We have judged that the politics and government of the 'English' was not to be our concern. We answered to a higher power. But each time we get a government initiative, we become victims of whatever new challenge they decide to send us. That was true with the war that they fought all around us and most certainly it was true with the taxes they put on us to pay for their war."

More voices were raised and more voices saying "Amen" could be heard from the men's side, with some of the women joining in from the left side of the room.

"I think it is past time that we get involved in the politics of the region," Mr. Thomson concluded. With that comment, he retreated up the center aisle to his seat.

Silence fell over the room for a moment, and then a small murmur started and grew stronger. Soon almost everyone was talking at once.

Mr. Ridgeway stood, motioning for quiet, and the noise immediately disappeared. "Would anyone else care to speak to this issue?" he asked.

Several hands were raised, and young Mr. Thomas Moon was recognized by the convener.

Thomas Moon was a short, thick man with a beard growing sparsely on his chin. "I am sure that what Mr. Thomson says is accurate," he said. "But I'm not sure entering politics with the English will solve our problem. Wherever Quakers are, we have tried to maintain our separation from the rest of the world. We don't want to be dragged into their fights and run the risk of losing our way of life."

The noise level of the group rose again and several voices shouted out the familiar "Amen". Hands shot up around the room, but when elderly Mrs. Poteate stood up, Mr. Ridgeway immediately acknowledged her. She turned around to face the group from her second row seat. Everyone knew Mrs. Poteate. She had been in many of their homes helping to deliver babies, including Matt and Ami Ruth's baby just last June. Matt smiled inwardly as he recalled that occasion, then strained to hear her soft voice as she addressed the group.

"I am not sure to what extent we need to get involved in every aspect of the politics and government of the English," she said. "I do think we need someone to represent us when discussions are going on that will affect us. We should not forget that when we came here in the 1700s, it was a short move south from Pennsylvania. That state began as a land grant to William Penn, who was a well-known Quaker. Our Loop also began as a land grant to Quakers. William Penn welcomed Quakers from all over the world to his territory and, eventually, to his state. Benjamin Franklin's parents were Quakers. In fact, most of the leading merchant families in Pennsylvania were Quakers. As a people, we have not always set ourselves aside, and often we have prospered when we worked alongside the English instead of going it alone. I would support running one of our number for office in this area, and I think we should all be in support of becoming active in local affairs. To do so may be the best solution to future problems. At least it can't hurt."

Mrs. Poteate sat down and the noise level again began to rise. Mr. Ridgeway soberly regarded the raised hands among the congregation. "We have gone on long enough today," he declared. "When we come back together next Sunday, please plan to stay a little later, and we will resume this discussion. If we are to choose one of our number to run for office in this area, we will decide at that time. In the meantime, we need to think about who might represent us and what office could have the most benefit for our community. Do I hear a motion for adjournment?"

Several voices from the group responded affirmatively, and Mr. Ridgeway said, "Hearing no disagreement, this meeting is adjourned."

Isaac rode along ahead on Big Billy as they headed home while Matt rode alongside of the wagon. Matt and Elizabeth were more than halfway home when she finally spoke. "Well, what do you think, Matt?" she asked.

Matt was caught with his mind wandering. As was normal for him since Stephen had been born, he was thinking about his new son and Ami Ruth and anticipating their life on the farm in future years. His initial response to Aunt Elizabeth was a startled "About what?"

Aunt Elizabeth looked up at him and spoke quietly, "About having someone from the Quaker group to represent us in the government," she said.

"Oh!" Matt said, jolted back into the discussion at the Meeting House. "I don't know, Aunt Elizabeth. Doing something like that is not for me. We have way too much work to do on the farm, and now we have the responsibility of the cooperative bank, the White Hall Store, and growing the winery business. I am not sure who would take it on, but I don't think it would be very productive for us."

"Look at it another way," Aunt Elizabeth said. "Whoever takes it on will become an important leader in the Quaker community. We are probably the largest voting bloc in the region, and if we can exert some influence in one area, there may be others where we need to make our presence felt."

Matt laughed. "Aunt Elizabeth, you are the right one to represent us. Unfortunately, you can't run for office and can't even vote. Maybe our first initiative should be to let women vote."

Matt laughed again, but Aunt Elizabeth wasn't laughing. She looked Matt in the eye and demanded, "Why shouldn't women vote? If the truth were known, women make most of the family decisions, and spreading our influence to the public arena should do nothing but enhance our way of life. At the very least, you would cut the number of wars in half or totally eliminate them. Women don't solve their problems by fighting."

To his surprise, Matt noticed a vein pop out in her neck. He thought better of further conversation and was relieved when they rounded the bend and he could see the lane to the big house. He turned in and gave the grey mare her head down the lane. By then, Aunt Elizabeth was thinking about what to prepare for lunch, and Matt was again thinking about chores on the farm and little Stephen. The prospect of electing a representative to run for office from the Quaker community slipped well into the background.

RESOLVING THE ELECTION ISSUE

It was early August when the Quaker group again convened at the Hopewell Friends Meeting House. Early August in Northern Virginia brings cooler evenings but warmer middays. The Meeting House was well placed in a grove of oak trees, and so the building, which was mostly of rock construction, was well protected from the sun and it was generally cool inside.

The family was again sitting in their accustomed seats near the back wall of the Meeting House. Isaac was sitting on the aisle closest to the door with Aunt Elizabeth next to him. Matt, Ami Ruth, and the baby were down the row.

During the services, little Stephen became restless, and Ami Ruth took him out the backdoor. Shortly, Isaac followed her outside. Thus, Matt and Aunt Elizabeth became the lone occupants of the back row. When the meeting came to a close, Mr. Ridgeway took the floor at the front of the room and suggested a ten-minute break before they convened for the business meeting. Everyone seemed to be anticipating something major happening, something that had never happened before in their congregation. They were considering entering the world of politics and government, something they had avoided for most of the hundred years since the Loop community was formed.

Finally, Mr. Ridgeway called the meeting back to order and opened the floor for discussion.

Once again, Mr. Thomson was the first to ask for the floor. "Last week, I suggested that we do whatever is necessary to gain representation to these various bodies where decisions are being made that affect us," he said. "I hope that many of you gave that matter serious thought over the past week. I think it is a good first step in defending ourselves from being taken advantage of by the English."

Several voices were raised in support of Mr. Thomson. Mr. Ridgeway asked if there were others who would like to speak.

Mr. Moon, who had also spoken to the issue the week before, rose to his feet. His voice was low. "When we were here last week, I wasn't exactly sure where I stood on this matter," he admitted. "I must say that it has been on my mind all week. Our history in dealing with the English is not good, and I am not sure of what level of success we might have, but I believe we should give it a try."

Several in the room voiced their approval of Mr. Moon's comment.

Mr. Moon continued, "The issue goes beyond having a representative. We have to have a representative who can draw some support from the English as well as from the Quaker voters. Otherwise it will appear that it is an 'us' against 'them' situation and that won't improve our lot with the important issues. We have to look around the room here and choose someone who has relationships in Winchester and who has friends beyond our Quaker community."

"Mr. Chairman, Mr. Chairman," shouted a voice from the back of the room. "Is the floor open for a nomination?"

Mr. Ridgeway raised both of his large, weathered hands. He said, "Friends, we have two issues to settle here. First, we have to decide if we want to get involved in local political and governmental issues. Second, we need to decide who will represent us in the next election if we do want to get involved.

"So with that in mind, the chairman will entertain a motion from the floor regarding the issue of whether or not we will get involved in the political and governmental process in the area."

Several hands went up around the room, and Mr. Ridgeway called on Mr. John Poteate.

Mr. Poteate was seated about halfway toward the front of the men's section. He slowly stood and faced the group. It was easy to understand why Mr. Ridgeway had called on Mr. Poteate. He was among the oldest men in the congregation and both he and his wife had provided leadership in many past difficulties. He was respected both for his years and his wisdom.

He said, "Friends, we have tried over the years to maintain our separation from the English and have often found ourselves in difficulty. Resolving to get involved in the politics of the region may yield us little, but we can't do worse than we have in recent years, having to pay for their war and losing much of the marketplace for our farm products."

There was a murmur across the room as he paused for a few seconds, gathering his thoughts.

He continued, "I make a motion that we do get involved in local governmental issues and that we begin by electing a representative to go to Richmond in December to represent us in the writing of a new constitution for the State of Virginia."

Almost immediately, several hands shot up, and Mr. Ridgeway again called on Mr. Thomson.

The portly farmer's response was brief and to the point. "I agree with Mr. Poteate and second the motion," he declared.

The noise level rose to a loud buzz, and Mr. Ridgeway lifted both hands for quiet. "Is there any discussion?" he asked. He waited just a few seconds and said, "Hearing none, I would like a show of hands as to how many favor this motion."

Hands were quickly raised, and he began to count. Before he had covered half of the room, he spoke again. "The measure has passed. We will get involved in local political and governmental process in this region."

"Now," Mr. Ridgeway said. "The first election to face us is this fall in early November when the region is to elect a representative to go to Richmond where a new state constitution is to be written. I now entertain nominees for the man to enter the election process to become a representative to the State Constitutional Convention."

Almost immediately, Mr. Moon was on his feet. "Mr. Chairman, Mr. Chairman," he said.

Recognized by Mr. Ridgeway, he said, "I believe that as the idea of entering the political arena was Mr. Benjamin Thomson's, he would make a fine representative for our group. Therefore, I nominate Mr. Thomson." Immediately, muted discussion began among both the men's and women's sections.

Mr. Ridgeway raised his hands again for quiet and recognized a man from the back of the room. It was Mr. Richard Beeson.

Mr. Beeson's family had been in the Loop since the first land grant back in the early 1700s. Mr. Ridgeway realized as Mr. Beeson rose to speak that he was a quiet man and not one who had spoken often to the group. As he surveyed the room, Mr. Ridgeway's eyes met Aunt Elizabeth's. He realized that Elizabeth was a Beeson and that Richard was her father's brother. In fact, most of the people in the room were related either by blood or by marriage to other families in the congregation. There were several natural family alliances in the congregation, just the kind of situation where conflict could occur.

Mr. Beeson, a lean man with a leathery face and a distinctive hook nose, said "I am sure that Mr. Thomson would make a very good representative for us. I am also sure that several other men in the group would represent us to the outside world as well. We have many here who have great ability. Some of our people are better educated than others and perhaps could make a stronger contribution to whatever responsibility falls their way."

Heads were nodding, but Mr. Ridgeway could see that several of the men were whispering among themselves as Mr. Beeson spoke. Mr. Ridgeway suspected several had met prior to this meeting and perhaps had already decided who they would vote for. If so, he could anticipate the possibility of disagreement and perhaps some hard feelings coming out of this discussion.

Mr. Beeson concluded, "And so I believe that we have a convener who has served us well, and I think Mr. Ridgeway would make a fine representative to the State Constitutional Convention. I therefore place his name in nomination for that role."

Before anyone else could ask for the floor, Mr. Ridgeway stood up at the front of the room with both hands raised. "Friends, I am calling for another ten-minute recess from these proceedings," he said. "Let's take a rest before we resume our deliberations."

Many men and women walked outside for some fresh air, while others huddled together in the back of the room. Mr. Ridgeway walked around both inside and outside, stopping here and there to speak or listen to conversations. When the ten minutes were almost up, he returned to the front of the room and waited for the group to gather again.

When the people had again settled into their seats, he said, "When Mr. Thomson made his suggestion at our last meeting, I had a fear that competition might develop and cause dissention and perhaps some hard feelings among us. I know you realize that we are not electing someone to represent just our Quaker qroup in Richmond at the convention. Instead, we are electing someone to run for election in this district of the State of Virginia to represent the entire district."

Many heads were nodding and murmurs of support were heard across the room. Mr. Ridgeway had read the group well.

"We have come through a very difficult time over the last year," he said. "Some of us almost lost our farms. Others were facing serious financial difficulties. We hung together and the end result is that we are closer as a group than we have ever been. Anything that pulls us apart cannot be in the center of God's will for our community. If the decision to identify someone to represent us is going to create dissention and bad feelings among some of our number, then I think we need to rethink how we are going about it."

"What would you suggest, Mr. Ridgeway?" a man asked.

"I suggest that we go to the word of God for our solution to the problem," he replied. "We don't need to create factions within our group when God gave us a plan to make such a choice. We can find it in the Old Testament when Saul was selected by God as King. It is in Samuel 10: 20–24."

Several of the congregation were already reaching for their Bibles and turning to the book of Samuel.

Mr. Ridgeway asked, "Who can read it for the group?"

Mr. Beeson was the first to rise to his feet and read aloud,

"Then Samuel brought all the tribes of Israel near, and the tribe of Benjamin was taken by lot."

Mr. Ridgeway stopped him and said, "We already have all our families gathered here. So I have placed a bowl on the table in the front of the room. I want someone from every family to write their family name on a piece of paper and put it in the bowl."

There was much moving around and sharing of paper and pencils, followed by designated family members walking to the front of the room to deposit their slips of paper. Finally, the task was done and every family had a name in the bowl.

Mr. Ridgeway then asked Mr. Moon to pray for God's will in this process. Mr. Moon came to the front of the room and stood behind the table with the bowl on it. The room fell silent while Mr. Moon prayed. When he finished, Mr. Ridgeway asked Mrs. Poteate to come forward and draw a name out of the bowl.

The elderly lady approached the bowl almost timidly and reached her hand in as though God Himself was handing her the right piece of paper. When she withdrew the paper she gave it to Mr. Ridgeway.

He opened the paper, read it, and said, "God has chosen the Mason family."

There was an instant response from the group. There was only one Mason that they knew of in the group and that was Matt, one of the newest members of the congregation and also one of the youngest.

Raising his hands again, Mr. Ridgeway asked Mr. Beeson to read the next verse in Samuel.

He stood up again and read,

"Finally, he brought the family of the Marrites near man by man and Saul, the son of Kish, was taken by lot."

Mr. Ridgeway looked to the back row where Matt was sitting and said, "Matt we need you to complete the scripture. Could you come forward and place the names of all male members of your family in the bowl?"

Matt began to frantically search for a piece of paper, but Aunt Elizabeth calmly placed two slips of paper in his hand. He walked to the table and placed the two slips into the bowl. Again, Mr. Ridgeway asked Mrs. Poteate to draw a piece of paper out of the bowl.

She reached into the almost empty bowl and withdrew one small slip. Mr. Ridgeway said, "The name on the ballot is . . . Isaac Mason."

At that point there was an almost universal upheaval from the congregation. It was a name no one expected, a person that was not even a member of their congregation—an English! The words were indistinguishable in the loud buzz of voices, but it was easy to discern that the speakers were both surprised and upset.

Matt had retreated to the back row and whispered to Aunt Elizabeth, "Do you know where Pa went?"

She responded, "I don't know, but I think you will find him with the horses."

Matt said, "I think I had better find him and get him in here." He left by the backdoor to look for Isaac and, indeed, found him among the horses.

"Pa," he said, "You need to come back inside and see what is going on. They have elected you to run for representative from this district!"

Isaac looked like he had been struck by a thunderbolt. "Lord, son," he said, "the last thing I want to do is get involved in politics. What must they be thinking?" But he accompanied his son back into the Meeting House.

Mr. Ridgeway was again addressing the group. "Mr. Beeson, would you read the rest of that scripture for us?"

Mr. Beeson stood once more and began to read.

"This is Samuel 10: 23–24: *Then they ran and fetched him from the baggage, and when he stood among the people he was taller than any of the people from his shoulders upward. And Samuel said to all the people,*

'*Do you see him whom the Lord has chosen? There is none like him among all the people.*'"

As Mr. Beeson finished reading, Matt and Isaac appeared in the backdoor. Mr. Ridgeway motioned for Isaac to come down front and be presented to the people. Isaac walked to the front of the room but looked anything but comfortable.

"This is the man that God has chosen for us," Mr. Ridgeway said. "He is someone who is known by reputation even if you have not met him personally in the year he has been among us."

Mr. Thomson's booming voice came from the back of the room. "Mr. Ridgeway, with all due respect, you can't be serious. Isaac Mason is a fine man and one we are all proud to know. But he isn't one of us! We need someone we can all get united behind. Our little election today means nothing. We have a general election to win and everyone must enter that effort unified in the conviction that we have God's man leading the way. This is a man who carries a Winchester with him, who fought in the war, who knows more of fighting than of politics and government process. He isn't a Quaker."

Several other voices were raised in support of Mr. Thomson. Isaac listened for a while and then found a seat on the men's side close to the front. Mr. Ridgeway let the group vent for a few moments and then gestured for silence.

He said, "We have heard from several who believe this is not the way to go. Is there anyone who would speak in favor of Isaac Mason as our candidate for representative to the State Constitutional Convention?"

No one moved for the longest time, and then Mr. Poteate stood up and began to slowly walk down the side aisle to the front of the room. Mr. Poteate was approaching eighty years of age. Age had stooped his back and reduced his height to slightly more than five feet. It was obvious when he walked that every step brought him pain.

He stopped for just a few seconds as he faced the group, blue eyes peering out from his weathered face, as if he was not sure what he was going to say. That illusion disappeared with his first few words.

"I think Isaac Mason is exactly the right one to play this role for us," he said in a surprisingly strong voice. "He has many things to recommend him, but the most important is that he can get elected.

First, he isn't a Quaker. That is good, not bad. Quakers have never done well in elections. The general population does not know or understand us. Any of us who attempted to be elected in this area in a general election is carrying a handicap before we even file for election."

Mr. Poteate's voice had started out strong with his support for Isaac but the longer he talked the lower his voice became. People began to lean forward to hear what he was saying.

He continued, "Second, he already has a reputation in this region. He stood up to the Ku Klux Klan. He fought in the war and was wounded at Gettysburg. The Masons hired the only black field hands in this entire area. That isn't so important here in Frederick County where we don't have many former slaves, but over in Clark County, where many of the votes are going to come from, there are more former slaves than there are white people. They will be voting in this election. Those folks know which family hired their people and gave them a fair wage. And he is a Mason. We all know the Mason family and their reputation of service to Virginia."

By this point many in the group were beginning to nod their heads in agreement with what Mr. Poteate was saying.

"Last but most important," said Mr. Poteate, his voice rising again, "we used God's plan to choose this leader. Mr. Beeson read it right out of God's Holy Word. I am not so quick to discount God's hand in the process. When God ordains something, who are we to say, "No" to it?"

With the last of his words spoken, Mr. Poteate began to make his way slowly back up the side aisle.

Mr. Ridgeway quickly reassumed control before there was more discussion. He said, "We have heard from several speaking for and against what we have done here in the last twenty minutes. I would like to hear from Isaac Mason."

There was silence. It seemed that the last thing Isaac wanted to do was to address this group. But he slowly stood to his great height, reminding some in the group of the scriptures about Saul that said, "He was taller than any of the people from his shoulders upward." And so he was.

Isaac looked over the group and said, "I am not sure I am the person for this job. Many here can do it better than I, and getting involved in politics has always been the last thing I ever thought I might do. I do not agree to take this on. But I do agree to think about it and to report back to you in a week or two with my best thoughts on the matter. I do thank you for your confidence in me, and I will consider whether or not I feel it is misplaced."

With that, Mr. Ridgeway moved quickly to adjourn the meeting. A number of the people came toward the front to shake hands with Isaac, but most simply walked out the backdoor headed for home. It was a mixed acceptance, to say the least.

Aunt Elizabeth and Matt were both anxious to talk with Isaac about the election and what had transpired, but he trotted Big Billy ahead of the wagon, making any conversation with him impossible. It was obvious that he wanted to think about what had happened without hearing from the two most important people in his life.

A SURPRISE VISITOR FROM THE DEEP, DARK PAST

Isaac's challenge from the Quaker community was never far from the minds of any of those on the Schendler Farm over the next few weeks. Isaac did not attend the next meeting at the Meeting House but sent word by Matt that he would appear to give his answer to the group at the next Sunday gathering. In the meantime, Matt and Isaac were occupied with the normal work on the farm. Matt tried several times to open a discussion with Isaac on the subject of the Meeting House vote, but Isaac was keeping his own council on the subject.

Days and nights on a farm follow a pattern of work by the seasons. In late August, the focus is on preparation for the harvest that will come in a flurry in late September through the end of October. What was normal for the fall season continued until one day, an event occurred that changed the future for all the family, but especially for Isaac Mason and his new bride.

Matt and Isaac had been at the winery for most of the morning when Seabrook rode the grey mare over the hill and down to the side door. She came in out of the bright sunlight and stood there for just a few seconds while her eyes adjusted to the relative dark inside. The smell of fermenting grapes was almost overwhelming and surprised her anew every time she entered the winery.

Matt and Isaac were working on one of the crushing machines but both stopped when she walked toward them.

She said, "Miss Ami Ruth done sent me down here to fetch Mr. Isaac." Isaac and Matt looked at her for a few seconds awaiting more information.

"There are a couple of mens who have come to see Mr. Isaac and be waiting for him on the porch," she continued.

Isaac slipped his gloves off, looked at Matt, and said, "We about have this finished anyway, Matt. You go ahead and finish up and then come on up to the big house. It is almost time for lunch anyway. I have no idea who has come to see me, but I suspect it may have to do with you as well."

Matt nodded and turned back to the machine. Isaac followed Seabrook out the side door. There were two horses hitched to the post just outside the door, Big Billy and the grey mare.

Isaac said, "Seabrook, let's take Big Billy and leave the grey mare for Matt. You slide up behind me, and we will ride double back to the big house. Big Billy will hardly know there are two of us."

It was a short ten-minute trot up to the big house, and Isaac let Seabrook off at the back steps. He rode Big Billy around to the front of the house and saw the two men, one of whom was holding two horses out by the big oak tree close to the gate. The other was sitting in one of the rockers on the porch with a glass of cider in his hand.

When Isaac walked up on the porch, the man put his glass down and stood up. Isaac, not yet up the last step, noted that this was a very big man, almost as tall as he was, though somewhat older. He was aging well, with dark hair greying at his temples but no evidence of the expanding waist line that appeared on some men later in life. Isaac estimated him to be in his late fifties or early sixties.

The man greeted Isaac with a firm handshake and a careful smile. He said, "Isaac, I have not seen you since you were a little boy, maybe four or five years old. I am John Murray Mason, your father."

Isaac's words of greeting died in his throat. He had heard of his father from his mother and her people in Lexington, Virginia, where he grew up. But he had no memory of ever seeing him.

Isaac collapsed into the rocker, and John Murray Mason sat down next to him. Isaac could not take his eyes off of the big man. He had dark skin like Isaac's, like a man with a heavy suntan, and his eyes were brown. Isaac had always wondered who in the earlier generation had given him the dark skin. Here he was. Here was the man he always wanted to ask a thousand questions.

Finally, Isaac found his voice and formed some words to break the awkward silence. "Sir, tell me again who you are, and while you're at it, who is the man out by the tree who came with you?"

John Murray Mason answered slowly. He nodded toward the man holding the two horses. "My friend is here to keep watch over me and, hopefully, to keep me safe. I still have some enemies in this region and many people remember me from before the war. Sometimes I travel with three or four bodyguards, and sometimes I take just one along on short trips. This time, I thought it would be less obvious if it was just two of us riding out on the country roads into the Loop. Besides, this is Quaker country, and it is not a place where you would expect violence. And, Son, I am your father."

"How did you know where to find me?" Isaac asked.

John Murray Mason responded, "Oh, I have always known where you were, from Lexington to North Carolina, and during your time with General Lee and the Army of Northern Virginia. It has been even easier to keep up with you since you joined your son here in Northern Virginia. The stories in Winchester about your confrontation with the White Knights and the bushwhackers are a part of the day-to-day rumor mill. If I believed everything being said about you, I would think you were seven feet tall and a one-man battalion with a Winchester rifle in each hand."

Isaac laughed softly before he responded, "The rumors are very much exaggerated of course, but I have thought that considering the visit of the White Knights and the ambush of our fieldworkers, it was not a bad idea for those who would do us harm to know that if they come looking for trouble here, they will find it."

John Murray Mason continued, "When I hear anything about someone named Mason, I am going to listen. We have a long and proud history here in the Winchester area. You, of course, were not a part of that until just recently. Now you are writing some new history for our family. Son, I have always been proud of you."

"Mother always told me we were from Winchester," Isaac said, "and she told me about you and the Mason family. She said I should be proud to be a Mason because the family had a long and illustrative heritage. So tell me, where you are living now?"

"I have been in Canada ever since the war ended," John Murray Mason responded. "I am visiting in Winchester mostly to find out the state of our old house and to see if it can be repaired enough to live in. When things have settled down, we want to move back here to our home in Winchester."

Just at that moment, the conversation was disturbed by the sound of hoof beats approaching from around the side of the house. Matt, riding the grey mare, trotted up to the edge of the porch and slid off of the horse, eyeing the two men as he tied the mare to the hitching post.

When he reached the top of the stairs, the two men stood up and his Pa said, "Matt, I want to introduce you to your grandfather, John Murray Mason."

Of all the things he might have imagined his Pa to say, the last on his mind would be an introduction to his grandfather. Like Isaac, Matt was momentarily speechless. He had never met any of his father's people, not even his grandmother. His Pa had told him that he had two uncles and some cousins in Lexington who were Masons.

When Matt's mother died back on the little farm in North Carolina, and he began his trek north to find his father, he intended to go through Lexington, and perhaps, to look up some of his father's relatives there. Unfortunately, his trek through war-torn Virginia took him up through Lynchburg where the military hospitals were on the east side of the mountain range, and he missed going through Lexington.

John Murray Mason reached out his large hand and Matt timidly grasped it. He could not help but notice that the hand was very much like his father's. He heard himself mumble, "Nice to meet you, sir."

The big man settled back down into the rocker, and Matt retrieved a stool that was sitting against the wall. He had just set it down close to his Pa when he heard a sound at the door and Ami

THE WOUNDS OF WAR

Ruth walked out onto the porch. Isaac and John Murray Mason stood immediately and Matt introduced his wife and explained she was the daughter of the Schendlers, who had owned the farm for many years.

John Murray Mason said, "Ami Ruth, I knew your father. He was a very good man and one respected both in the Quaker community and in Winchester. Everyone knew him as a very competent farmer but also a man whose word you could trust and who always met his obligations. I was sorry to hear that he and your mother were lost toward the end of the war. We lost so many of our best in that five-year nightmare."

Ami Ruth was moved toward tears by his words. She responded, "I'm pleased you knew him, sir. We all knew who you were even though your duties took you away from the region so often and for so many years. It did not dawn on me that Matt and Isaac were a part of your family. I guess I should have added two and two together. I have heard Isaac say that his father was originally from Winchester." She paused, wiping her eyes on her apron. "I hope I am not interrupting, but I assumed that you men would want some lunch, so I have taken the liberty to set up a table in the dining room for you. Seabrook is bringing in the food now. If you would like to wash up on the back porch, we can serve lunch in just a few minutes."

Matt and Ami Ruth exchanged a smile, and he heard himself say, "Thank you, Ami Ruth."

Ami Ruth paused for a few seconds and said, "Matt, how about the man out by the tree? Should I set a place for him at the table too?"

John Murray Mason smiled at Ami Ruth and said, "That is a very hospitable offer, but he will stay in front of the house where he can survey the road and the lane that comes into the house. I'm sure he would appreciate knowing you had made such a generous offer."

"Well," Ami Ruth said with a smile, "we will take him out a plate anyway."

The conversation around the table was surprisingly casual and relaxed. John Murray Mason set them all at ease by asking Matt questions about what he grew on the farm and how he marketed his produce.

"We have about everything a farm needs to be self-sufficient," Matt said. "We like to think that if things went bad again like it was during the war, we could stand on our own feet and take care of our family. Our primary market is in Winchester, but we have sold to the White Hall Store before it became a barter store. The wine products all go up to Martinsburg in West Virginia."

Trying to keep the conversation light, Isaac decided to save his most important questions for his father until lunch was over. As he ate, his mind was working overtime, compiling a list that had begun when he was a fatherless boy growing up in Lexington.

Finally, lunch was over and Matt, Isaac, and John Murray Mason retreated to the front porch. The older men took the rockers and Matt sat on the low stool. Matt noticed that the man was still under the oak tree, but he was sitting on a blanket and holding a dish that had obviously been brought to him from the kitchen by Ami Ruth or Seabrook. That visitor might not be a part of the discussions that were going on, but he was certainly going to receive the hospitality of the Masons that every visitor would always receive.

Over the next couple of hours, Matt became a very interested listener as his father and grandfather talked about the past, about Isaac's mother, the Mason family, and the events of the war that had so affected Virginia and the South over the past five years.

Isaac's most important question was the one that had been in his mind the longest. "Sir, how was it that you and my mother were not together while I was growing up?"

John Murray Mason was silent for a few seconds as he contemplated his answer. Then he responded in a very soft voice, "Isaac, your mother and I were very much in love at a very young age. My father was not for my marrying anyone at that time, and he had someone in mind from a well-to-do family in Winchester for when I was of age. Your mother and I had other ideas, and we ran off and got married, but it didn't take long for them to find us. My father was waiting on the porch when we arrived back at the house. Within a few days, he had the marriage annulled and had sent me off to Virginia Military Institute down close to Lexington. About six weeks later, I received a letter from your mother telling me that you were on the way. I left VMI in the middle of the night for Winchester."

Matt's eyes met his grandfather's and he asked, "Just how old were you when you got married?"

"I was eighteen that year and your grandmother was sixteen," he responded. "The fact that Isaac was on the way did not seem to impress my father at all. He arranged for your mother to move to Lexington to live with some of our people there. He sent me in the other direction, off to the US Military Academy at West Point, New York. I tried to be a good cadet, but my heart was just not in it. Almost every thought was of your mother in Lexington. My world came to an end when I heard that your mother died in childbirth. After that I just didn't have the heart for anything."

With that comment, Isaac sat up straight in the rocker and it stopped moving. He said, "My mother died in childbirth? No! My mother lived until I was in my late teens. She died of cholera during the epidemic of 1845."

"Son," replied John Murray Mason, "the woman who raised you was my cousin, Marian. She never married and you became her whole world. It was the proudest day of her life when you went off to Virginia Military Institute. Unfortunately, she did not live to see you finish your first year there."

Isaac was shaking his head. "That seems impossible. The woman who raised me wasn't my mother? My mother died when I was born? Why did no one ever tell me?"

"You were living with enough confusion in your life without a father around, and I think everyone thought it best if you felt you belonged to Marian," he replied. "Marian wrote me many letters about you, and she sent me a number of pictures of you when you were growing up. I remember one that was taken in the livery stable where they had to go to get you weighed and measured. You were standing in front of the measuring tape that was stuck on the wall, and it showed you to be somewhere north of six feet and four inches. She told me you weighed in at 220 pounds."

"I remember that trip to the livery stable," Isaac responded. "One of the men said they ought to enter me in the county fair in the boar competition. They were sure to get a blue ribbon."

John Murray Mason continued, "I knew then you were the biggest Mason on record. Your great-grandfather, George Mason IV, was about six foot two, and I am right at six foot three now, though I used to be an inch taller. As I look at Matt, I think you still have him by an inch or so, but he may still be growing."

Just at that moment, Ami Ruth came through the screen door with a tray of glasses and a pitcher of cold cider. She smiled at the elder Mason as he took a glass and said, "Just a half glass please."

After the three had tasted the cider, Isaac asked his second most important question. "Sir, why did I not know you when I was growing up? I knew my father was living and was somewhere else, but I never knew why I wasn't with you."

"That is just one important thing of many that I need to apologize to you for," said John Murray Mason. "By then I had remarried, and you had become a well-kept family secret. Even my wife did not know about you until we had been married for several years."

Matt ventured a question, "Sir, I have read that you were appointed by Jefferson Davis as ambassador to England and France during the war."

"Yes, I was in Europe going back and forth between London and Paris for the last three years of the war. Before that, I was a prisoner in a Yankee jail for almost a year. I was elected to Congress in 1836 and to the Senate later. I stayed there until Virginia left the Union in 1861. At that point, I went to work for the State of Virginia and the Confederacy."

Matt quickly followed his first question with another. "Would you tell us about the stay in prison?"

"No," his grandfather responded, "That is certainly a story worth telling, but I'll let that one sit until we are together again. For now, I have something else of importance to talk with Isaac about."

"Should I leave?" Matt asked.

"Oh, no, this concerns you too," his grandfather replied.

John Murray Mason looked at his son and smiled. "Isaac, the State of Virginia is getting ready to hold a convention in Richmond to write a new constitution. Rumor has it that the Quaker community would like for you to be the representative from this area. I understand that they voted to make you their candidate to run for political office."

Isaac looked down and then back into the face of his father. "Yes, sir. But I don't see how I can do that. I just don't have any experience with being a politician. Even what little education I have was at VMI, and it was basically military training. I learned a lot about marching and shooting a musket, but they certainly didn't teach me anything about running for office."

"Son, let me share a bit of family history," John Murray Mason said. "Your great-grandfather was one of the authors of the first constitution of the State of Virginia. Very specifically, he was the author of the state's Bill of Rights. Later, he was a contributor, along with James Madison and Thomas Jefferson, to the US Constitution and was the sole author of the first ten amendments to the constitution, the section that we call the Bill of Rights. Isaac, if I were a citizen of Virginia instead of Canada, I would be running to represent us in Richmond if for no other reason than to hold up our family heritage."

"Sir," Isaac said. "I have known for a lifetime about the Masons of Winchester and their involvement in the creation of the Union government, as well as the government of Virginia. All of you had training and background in what to do and how to do it. I am a farm boy from Lexington who moved off to farm in North Carolina. Even if I wanted to uphold the family heritage, I would not know how to do it."

"Son, all of life is a leap of faith. There is no set of qualifications that would keep you from running for political office. On top of that, you are a Mason. We have many in this region who would vote for you just because you are a Mason."

"I had not thought about that," said Isaac. "But for sure, there is a loyalty oath to deal with. It requires that a person say that they did nothing to aid the war effort against the Union. After four years with General Lee and the Army of Northern Virginia, I can't very well say

I did nothing during the war to aid the cause of the South. Because of that, they would never let me run for office even if I wanted to, and I am pretty sure I don't."

"Don't be too hasty in making that decision, Isaac," John Murray Mason said. "The South is in disarray and needs good leadership wherever it can be found. People in this area already speak of you in admiring tones. You have stood up to the military leadership and to the Ku Klux Klan. You were in the midst of the fighting for their cause during the war, and you were wounded at Gettysburg. Those are pretty good credentials."

"But what about the loyalty oath?" Isaac asked.

"First, there are several different loyalty oaths. The one that might affect you is a concern, but one needs to read the loyalty oath like a lawyer," John Murray Mason responded. He reached into his coat pocket and pulled out a piece of paper. "The oath has lots of words that anyone could attest to and just a few that pertain to your situation. Those words say, 'I have never voluntarily born arms against the United States since I have been a citizen of, and I have voluntarily given no aid or encouragement to persons engaged in open hostility thereto.'"

He tapped the paper with his finger. "In your case, the phrase 'since I have been a citizen of' is very key. You were a citizen of North Carolina and the United States until that state withdrew from the Union. Then you were no longer a citizen of the United States. So from a legal perspective, you are cleared to vote, to hold office, and to serve in any capacity you choose here in the State of Virginia. Now if you wanted to go to Congress, that might be a different situation. Congress can decide to seat you or not, no matter what the State of Virginia says. In fact, as it relates to getting elected here in Virginia, the loyalty oath may be of help to you. Most of the white population cannot take that oath because they were, in fact, involved in the war effort in some way. They are not reading the oath like a lawyer. That means they don't think they can vote or run for office. For your situation, that means they can't vote against you for someone else.

"The Quaker community was not involved in the war effort and most could sign that oath anyway. So the people who want you to represent them can all vote for you. The other potential voters are mostly former slaves. To your credit, they know that this farm has hired several of their number to work here and that you are paying fair wages. Because of that, many of them will vote for you. You have a ready-made constituency and the most important issue in running for office is, can you win? That answer for you is a resounding *yes*."

MAKING A MOMENTOUS DECISION

Matt and Isaac sat on the porch after John Murray Mason left and talked. Both had many questions for the next visit, but the curiosity about the family was kindled and it was not soon to be extinguished.

"Pa," Matt said. "You never talked about your father to me when I was growing up. I never knew we had family in Winchester."

Isaac thought for a few seconds before responding. "Son, it didn't make much sense to talk about something that was never to be. The Mason family put me and the woman I thought was my mother in Lexington to get us out of the way, and it wasn't likely that would ever change. My father married again, and somewhere out there, I have eight half-brothers and sisters. After meeting my father and hearing that the mother I knew was not my mother, I am not sure what to think at this point."

"Is this the first time you have met your father?" Matt asked.

"Yes, it is," he responded. "He said that he saw me when I was about four years old. That would have been before he began to hold public office. I don't remember it. He didn't come south to Lexington where we were but that one time that I know of."

"But you knew about him and the family when you were growing up?" Matt asked.

"Yes, my uncle, James Mason, in Lexington told me much about the Mason family when I was a boy. I could even follow my father's career in the newspaper. When I was growing up, he was a congressman representing the Northern district of Virginia. Then he became a Senator. In fact, during the 1850s, he was president protem of the Senate, which meant he was third in the line of succession for the presidency of the United States. Had the war not come, he might well have run for president in 1864. There was never a doubt in my mind that my father was a great man."

"Pa, what about his comment on being in a Yankee jail?" Matt asked.

"It is a little hard to remember," Isaac responded. "That would have been what the South called the Trent Affair. When he was sent to England shortly after the war started, he was on a British ship called the *Trent*. The Yankees captured the ship en route and took him to Boston. I think the British finally got him out of there by threatening to join the South in their war against the Union. But it took a good long while for him to be released. It made headlines all across the South. Your grandfather became a very well-known name during those early years of the war, kind of a symbol of Southern resistance in the face of overwhelming oppression."

"Pa, what are you going to do about running for office?" Matt asked.

"I'm not sure, Son," he responded. "Until this discussion with him, it was never a serious consideration. I'm not sure he is right about the oath one has to take in order to be a functioning citizen of the United States again. I am not sure I want to test it, but I will give it serious consideration. Elizabeth may be the key decision maker in whether or not I get involved in my father's world, in politics. It would take me away from home way more than I want to go. And I really don't have any training or background that would prepare me for playing such a role. The best I can say is that we shall see."

Matt smiled at the last three words: *we shall see*. He said. "Pa, when Ma used to use those words, it almost always meant no."

Isaac laughed. "It did, didn't it? Well, in this case, I just don't know. I know I am not prepared for such a role, and I am not sure how to get prepared. But I will give it some thought and talk to Elizabeth." Isaac laughed again. "We shall see."

* * *

That evening, it was Elizabeth who guided Isaac out to the rocking chairs on the front porch. Conversations could take place anywhere, but it had become a family pattern to take serious discussion to the rocking chairs at the front of the house. There you were able to sit in the gathering dark and have absolute privacy. At least that is what one would think. Those on the porch seldom gave a thought to who might be just above the porch sitting in the bedroom on a loveseat close to the open window. On this crisp early fall evening, that is exactly where Matt and Ami Ruth were as Isaac and Elizabeth took their places in the two rocking chairs.

There was a chill in the air, and Elizabeth snuggled into a warm blanket while she waited for her husband to tell her about the conversations with his father earlier in the day. Big Billy, the grey mare, and two of the cows were grazing on the front lawn. It had become a practice to let the grazing animals into the front yard every week or two during the summer months to keep the grass in check. That would not work with sheep since they pull the grass out by the roots, but horses and cows take a bite and break off the grass blades so the grass keeps growing.

Elizabeth was anxious to hear about the conversation between Isaac and his father. The only discussions she had heard earlier were around the table at lunch, and they were casual and superficial. She was anxious to hear Isaac talk about his father, and she had some questions she wanted to ask.

"Isaac, tell me about your father," she began.

"I met my father for the first time today," Isaac responded. "He says he saw me when I was about four years old. I don't remember that. When I was a boy and asked about my father, I was always told he was away doing important business. When I was old enough to read, I could follow his career in the weekly newspaper in Lexington. He was a congressman, then a senator, and for the years in the 1850s, he was speaker pro tempore of the Senate, which made him third in line for the presidency of the United States. He spent the years of the war in England and France representing the interests of the Confederacy."

Matt and Ami Ruth listened closely to hear Elizabeth's comment and her next question but her voice was just too soft. Ami Ruth leaned over and whispered to Matt, "Your grandfather is a really great man, Matt."

Instead, they heard Isaac's deep voice carry on the wind. He said. "The shock of the afternoon was learning that my mother died in childbirth and the woman I thought was my mother was actually my father's cousin."

Elizabeth spoke, and this time they heard her. "I've heard you say that your mother died in the cholera epidemic of 1845."

"Yes," Isaac answered. "I was off at VMI that year. She was struck by the disease and was gone in three days, before I even knew she was sick. If I had known, I could have ridden to our home in Lexington in less than an hour and been with her, but I didn't even know. They told me she was gone, and I was to come home for the funeral. When it was over, I never went back to VMI. I never knew where the money was coming from to pay for college, and I knew I didn't have enough for tuition, let alone room and board."

Once again, the two eavesdroppers upstairs could hear Elizabeth's voice, but it was too muffled for them to know what she was saying.

When Isaac responded to her, he said, "I went to work on my Uncle John Mason's farm just outside of Lexington for the next year. By then, I was eighteen and I went looking for a farm of my own. I found it in North Carolina, just a ways outside of Mt. Airy. It wasn't at all the quality of farm my uncle had or what Mr. Schendler created here at the edge of the Loop. But I thought with some hard work, I could make it into something, given some time and effort. Unfortunately, by the time Matthew was old enough to be of significant help, the war came along and—to quote Matt's mother as she recited her favorite Robert Burns poem—'The best laid plans of mice and men often go astray.' Well, for sure, they do. We were beginning to make really good progress on that little farm when the war came along and changed our lives forever."

They rocked in silence for a moment.

"Elizabeth," Isaac said, "John Murray Mason says I should run for representative to the constitutional convention in Richmond in

December. He evidently heard about the discussion and election at the Meeting House last week. I know he was pleased to meet me, but I think the real reason he came was to urge me to get involved in the politics of this region of Virginia, kind of follow in his footsteps."

"What do you think?" she asked.

There were a few seconds of silence and then Elizabeth asked a second question. "What about the oath?"

"My father says that the oath should not be a problem and, in fact, may be helpful to me if I decide to run for office," Isaac said. "He says I was not a citizen of the United States when I joined the war effort, and thus, the oath doesn't apply to me."

"Do you think he is right?" asked Elizabeth.

"I honestly don't know," Isaac responded, "and it is likely I would not know for sure until I actually filed for the election."

"Isaac," Elizabeth said, and there was a bit of steel in her voice, "the Quaker community has asked you to represent them. Your father says you should do it. What is your reluctance?"

"My name is Mason," Isaac said, "but I am far from being a Winchester Mason like my father or my great-grandfather. Both of them had college degrees and were lawyers. Both of them were raised in a family where someone else made the living and they served the people. I have no education and no background that would qualify me to hold office. The farm I created in North Carolina was a struggling operation. I left to be a soldier and my wife got sick. My son pretty well raised himself while I was gone. The only thing I have ever been good at was being a soldier. What makes you or any of these people think I can do well at this role they seem to visualize me in? No, I don't think so. I don't think I can do it."

Elizabeth took a few seconds to reflect on what Isaac had said before responding. "I know you are concerned that you may not be capable of the responsibility of representing these people. I know that you look inside yourself and wonder what is there. I wish you could see yourself as I see you. You say that Matt raised himself. Isaac, he had a father until he was thirteen, through the formative years. You never had a father at all. Both of you are products of a mother's love and her education. Both of you have the courage to stand in front of loaded guns and speak for the right. Both of you are respected for the men you have become. Both of you are destined for great things, despite any shortcomings you may think are inside of you just below the surface.

"Isaac, great men are not born, they are made." Elizabeth continued. "They are made by the times they live in, by the influences that shape their lives. You are a giant to these people. You can stand comfortably with one foot in the Loop with the Quaker community and one foot in the English world. You have shown your courage and you have, at the same time, shown that you know who common folk are and what is needed to make their lives better. Who else that you know could do better for these people than you?"

Upstairs, Ami Ruth leaned over to Matt and whispered, "Amen."

Several minutes passed, and it had become silent downstairs. Ami Ruth was drifting off to sleep, her cheek pressed to Matt's shoulder. He whispered, "Let's go to bed."

ACCEPTING THE CHALLENGE

~~~~~~

In the days that followed, Isaac's mind was focused on the challenge of accepting the will of the Quaker group to represent them in the election for representative to the State Constitutional Convention in Richmond. He had thought about little else since leaving the Meeting House on Sunday. Having his father come to visit, along with his late night discussions with Elizabeth, had kept the issue of his possible future in politics front and center in his mind.

Every time he came up with justifiable reasons why he shouldn't take on this responsibility, he would think of even more reasons why he should. Certainly, he felt unprepared for such a responsibility. What did he know about writing a constitution? He had never even read a state constitution. He could envision being at the convention in Richmond with all the lawyers and businessmen and having little to contribute to the discussion. If he was to do it, he certainly needed to see a copy of the current Virginia State Constitution. He also needed to see what the US Congress had passed that set requirements for a new constitution for any state that petitioned to come back into the Union with full statehood.

Then he would think of all the things he would rather be doing than holding up his family heritage as a politician trying to meet the needs of the entire State of Virginia. He would think, *No, I won't do it.*

Then he would think of the words of support from Elizabeth, who obviously wanted him to take it on and give it his best shot. John Murray Mason had said that the state was looking for good leadership wherever they could find it. And his father felt not only that he was qualified but that he could win the election.

Several times Matt tried to talk to his father about the dilemma. Each time Isaac found some excuse not to discuss it with him. He knew Matt would support whatever he decided to do but felt this was a decision he had to make for himself and by himself.

Finally, on Friday, two days before they were to return to the Meeting House, he resolved to accept the challenge and run. He would make every effort to become the representative of this region to the State Constitutional Convention. If he was elected he would give it his best shot. If not, he would assume that God had spoken and it was not a challenge he should be involved in. That morning at breakfast, he told the family what he had decided to do. There were a few nods but no comments. Elizabeth, Matt, and Ami Ruth all had smiles on their faces and that was all the assent he needed.

This time, when the Masons arrived at the Meeting House, there were four adults together: Isaac, Matt, Elizabeth, and Ami Ruth. Little Stephen was left at home with Seabrook and her son, Matthew.

Isaac was feeling somewhat philosophical when he entered the Meeting House on that fateful day. His mind moved fleetingly to little Stephen, his grandson, at home. They named him, Stephen, after the character in the Bible who had stood up to the Pharisees. The religious leadership had stoned him for having a different perspective of God than they did. Isaac thought there was some parallel between that story and his dilemma regarding the decision to run for representative. He could envision everything going wrong and everyone being disappointed in him. He had not felt so much tension since Gettysburg.

The meeting ran very much as usual with the Mason family sitting together on the back row. Matt and the others waited patiently for the meeting to adjourn and for Mr. Ridgeway to call everyone together to hear Isaac's decision on his willingness to run for office.

Finally, the time came, and Isaac strode to the front of the room to tell the people what they were waiting to hear. There was a buzz of low conversation as he stood before them, taller than anyone in the room.

Mr. Ridgeway asked for silence and nodded to Isaac to take the floor.

Isaac was very aware that he was addressing the Meeting House group for the first time in a new role. He was beginning to see himself as a leader and knew that if he were to take on that responsibility, he could not speak from a position of weakness. He was determined that his remarks would be positive, strong, and leave no doubt that he was committed to giving the best he had to the task and that he could do what was required.

His eyes swept the room, seeming to glance into every face before he spoke. Then he said with a firm voice, "I have given this task you have set before me lots of thought over the past two weeks. I know that there are those in this group who have better qualifications than I to take on such a responsibility. Still, I don't own a farm nor do I have children to take care of. I am free to devote my time completely to the task at hand. I recognize my own shortcomings but believe, with my wife Elizabeth's help and the support of others of our number who have such expertise, that I can learn what I need to know to fulfill the responsibilities of the job. With that in mind, I will take on this responsibility on one condition."

Isaac paused and a soft murmur rose from the group. A man's voice finally asked, "What condition?"

Isaac replied, "The condition is that everyone in this room, everyone in the Quaker community, will support my election. I would like to see your commitment and ask everyone who would support me to please stand. If you think I am not equal to the job or you feel others are more capable, please stay seated."

When Isaac concluded his surprising request, Mr. Ridgeway quickly walked back to the front of the room and stood beside him. He extended his hands to the group, palms up, and lifted them upward. On that signal, every person in the room stood. That included even the aged Poteates, who had difficulty standing. Matt watched carefully, looking especially for Mr. Thomson, who had objected to Isaac as their choice just last week. Mr. Thomson was the last to leave his seat, but he rose with the rest of the group. And in the back of the room, Ami Ruth and Aunt Elizabeth were hugging each other and the smiles were unmistakable.

With everyone standing, the group began to applaud. As the applause grew, there were cheers and even a rebel yell or two. The response was so loud that the crowd in the usually quiet Meeting House could have been heard a mile down the road.

The Masons were on the way home when Isaac pulled Big Billy up next to the wagon. He looked down at Elizabeth and she smiled up at him. He swallowed hard as he often did when she looked at him that way.

"Okay, folks," he said. "What do we do now? We are in it and we need a plan for the next several weeks as we get ready for the election."

Elizabeth said, "The first thing we need to do is to get the filing papers from the military office in Winchester. Once we have them filled out and filed, we will have to mount a campaign. We will want to get an article in the newspapers in Winchester telling the people that you are running. It may keep some others from filing for office. I think we will need some petition signers promoting your candidacy. There is much to do. We are just getting started."

Over the next week, the necessary papers were filed along with the signing of the required oath that had been so much on Isaac's mind. Nothing was said then or later about the oath by any of the military administrators or the locally elected officials. Isaac surmised that may have had something to do with the influence of John Murray Mason, but he never knew for sure. Isaac heard that two other men had filed for the office of representative to the Constitutional Convention. One was a former slave from Clark County and the other was a businessman from Winchester.

Elizabeth took on the role of campaign manager, and shortly, there was an article in all three of the Winchester newspapers, the *Journal*, *Times*, and *News*. All were new to the community, having started at the end of the war in 1865 and each had a different constituency in and around the community. Placing an article in each publication would cover most of the reading public in the region.

A few days passed before there was a family council around the supper table regarding the campaign. They had one month until the election, and there was no shortage of ideas on how to get Isaac's name in front of potential voters.

Isaac listened intently to every idea and turned them down one by one. He was not for bearing the expense of having signs printed to put in yards in the city and along the roads. He was not for hosting a big dance and inviting everyone to come to celebrate the election. He was not for going here and there making speeches. He did not believe he was much of a speechmaker and rejected the idea that he could sway anyone's vote in his direction.

Finally, Aunt Elizabeth presented one idea that everyone but Isaac agreed with, and faced with the unanimity around the table, he gave in. They would hire the local music makers who had played at Matt and Ami Ruth's wedding to set up their instruments in both Winchester and Berryville on a Saturday afternoon when the farmers came into town to buy supplies and visit with their neighbors. They would play until they gathered a crowd and then Isaac would come out of the group of listeners and speak. That would give them an opportunity to know who he was.

Ami Ruth offered to write a speech for him, but Isaac said that anything he said would be short and sweet and he would handle it. So it was settled. Their entire election campaign would be the three articles in the newspapers followed up by three more closer to the election. His only speeches would be in Winchester and Berryville, with the help of the music makers.

The next weekend the family followed the music makers into Winchester and found the streets busy as usual on a Saturday afternoon. Farmers from both the Loop and points south had come to town. Country and town folk were on the streets shopping or visiting with friends. When the wagon pulled up with the music makers, no one knew what to expect, but the people on the crowded streets soon warmed to the spirited music and a large crowd gathered to enjoy the festivities.

THE WOUNDS OF WAR

Shortly before Isaac was scheduled to climb up on the wagon and speak to the crowd, Mr. Thomson approached the family. He said, "I have a thought that might be of help."

The Masons were glad to see him, and Isaac, especially, was pleased to see a familiar person who was offering help. At that moment, just before he was scheduled to make his first-ever public speech, he was wondering if all this was a good idea.

Aunt Elizabeth responded to Mr. Thomson with a wide smile. "We are glad to see a friendly face. What do you have in mind?"

Mr. Thomson said, "My family has had both a farm in the Loop and a business here in Winchester for many years. I am well known both in town and with most of the farmers, even those who are not in the Loop. I would count it a privilege to be allowed to introduce Isaac to these people."

Elizabeth's eyes met Isaac's and with a nod of their heads both agreed for Mr. Thomson to play the role of master of ceremonies.

In a moment, the music makers stopped playing, and Mr. Thomson climbed up on the back of the wagon. It was obvious that many in the crowd recognized him. He raised his hands to get their attention and began to speak in his very strong voice. "Friends, most of you know me," he said. "I am Frederick Thomson. My family has been in this community since before the city was incorporated. We have done business with most of you at one time or another. I am here today to introduce you to a man I believe will make a fine representative for us to the Virginia Constitutional Convention. Many of you have heard of him though you may not have met him face to face. His name is Isaac Mason."

There was a murmur in the crowd, and many nodded their heads while others whispered to each other, perhaps telling what they had heard about Isaac in past weeks.

Mr. Thomson continued, "Isaac Mason has links to this community through his family, the Mason family, who are well known to us because of their service in past years. He is also linked to us through his son Matthew, who is married to Ami Ruth, the daughter of David Schendler, a man many of you knew before his untimely death at the hands of Union deserters back in '63. Matt and Ami

Ruth are the owners of the Schendler Farm just north of town. Isaac Mason and his wife, Elizabeth, who is a Beeson, are the owners and operators of the White Hall Store in the center of the Loop north of town."

He paused and surveyed the crowd, continuing, "I am sharing the Mason, Schendler, and Beeson names because I want you all to know that Isaac Mason is one of us. If you have heard his name prior to now, I want you to know that the stories are true." He chuckled just a bit. "Well, almost all the stories are true. He isn't actually seven feet tall, but he is a mighty big man, and he is big enough to carry the load for all of us down to Richmond to create a constitution we can live with that will help get us back into the Union and will serve the people of Virginia long and well. Friends and neighbors, I am pleased to introduce to you Mr. Isaac Mason."

Matt's eyes met Elizabeth's and both smiled. Neither could imagine a better introduction. Mr. Thomson, reluctant as he might have been a few weeks back in the Meeting House, was certainly in their camp now, and he had done his part to support Isaac. It took a burden off Isaac that Mr. Thomson had introduced him as if he was a part of the community. He didn't have to justify his presence. He knew he couldn't talk about his experience in the war. He had decided to focus on the future and Mr. Thomson had given him just what was needed to do that. The rest was up to him.

Isaac climbed up into the wagon and took a few steps toward the back to get as close to the crowd as he could. Looking out over the crowd, he focused on several individuals in the back and began to speak to each one as if they were the only ones there.

"Good day! I am very pleased to meet every one of you," he said with a forceful voice. "We don't know each other, but I anticipate this may be the first of many times I will come to you in the future if you elect me to represent you in Richmond as we create a new constitution for the State of Virginia. If you trust me with that responsibility, I will listen to each of you if you have advice for me in helping to construct the final document."

Many in the crowd were nodding their heads, and when he finished with that last sentence, several began to applaud.

Isaac continued, "We have put an article in each of the local newspapers, telling you of my candidacy to represent you in Richmond. Given this responsibility, there will be an article each week bringing you along with me each step of the way, telling what the difficulties are and how we are handling them." He paused and smiled. "By now you have found out that I am not a speech maker, so I am going to step down and let the music makers play some more of that rousing music for you. I am going to stand over on the walkway for a bit and any of you who would like to talk to me further, I would invite you to feel free to come over and visit."

With that Isaac stepped down over the front wheel. Hands were still clapping when he arrived on the walkway and the music makers began to play.

By the time the family was on the way home, everyone was in a very good mood. It had been an exciting day, and they couldn't have asked for a better reception of Isaac from the people. Isaac pulled Big Billy up by the front of the wagon and smiled down at Elizabeth, who was riding on the front seat next to Matt.

Elizabeth said simply, "Isaac, I was so proud of you."

"Pa, where did you learn to speak to a crowd like that?" asked Matt.

"Well, Son," he responded, "I guess once you learn something, you never forget it. Before you were born, I was a student at Virginia Military Institute for a year. I received instruction in how to talk to a troop of soldiers. The man giving the instruction told me to know what I was going to say before I started talking and to look for someone on the back row to talk to so I would feel like I was talking to just one person. Then he told me to imagine that I was the only person in the group who was wearing any clothes, that everyone standing before me was totally naked. Something about that vision made me relax. Before today, I had never tried it. But it worked like a charm."

When Isaac finished his response the whole family was laughing. "I hope there weren't any really pretty women in that crowd, Pa!" Matt said. Aunt Elizabeth poked him in the ribs with her elbow but was too tickled to speak.

Three weeks remained until the election and the same pattern was followed in Berryville the next Saturday. As promised, each of the three weekly Winchester newspapers wrote an article about Isaac's candidacy on the front page. One of the newspapers accompanied the article with a drawing of Isaac standing on the wagon speaking to the people. When Elizabeth saw it, she could only shake her head. Whoever said it earlier was right: with his full beard and his military posture, Isaac did look very much like Stonewall Jackson.

THE ELECTION
AND BEYOND

Much to Isaac's surprise, he won by a landslide. Of the 730 votes cast, 512 of them were for Isaac Mason. The former slave from Berryville came in a distant second, but there was no doubt who the people wanted to represent them.

The family had ridden into Winchester the evening following the election. It took about three hours for the votes from the outlying areas to come in, but all were counted in the military adjutant's office by about 10:30 p.m. Isaac stayed outside while the others went inside to get the word. When they came out, there was no mistaking the smiles on their faces. He had won! Amazing!

The next morning after breakfast, Isaac walked out to the rockers on the front porch. It was a crisp day, but he didn't feel cold at all. He thought about what had just transpired. His father, John Murray Mason, was right. He said Isaac could win and he did.

Winning, however, created a whole list of new problems for him, and it was those problems he was thinking about when Matthew joined him on the porch.

"Now what, Pa?" Matt asked.

"Son, that is just the question I have been thinking about. I have just learned something about elections. They are a lot like commencements at VMI and other colleges. They are both the end of something and the beginning of something else. An election gives you the will of the people, but now the real work starts. Whoever wins, and in this case it is me, is now in the soup and the fire will begin heating up almost immediately."

"Do you know when you will be going to Richmond?" Matt asked.

"Everything starts down there the third of December," Isaac responded. "I have less than three weeks before I have to leave. But the work starts now. I have lots of homework to do before I go if I am to make a contribution to the constitutional process. I have to do everything I can to make sure I represent these people well and that the new constitution that comes from our efforts in Richmond fulfills both the letter and the spirit of Union requirements."

Isaac thought for a few moments before continuing. "One other thing, I have to do is to lose the word *Union* from my vocabulary. Every time I say it, there is a vision in my mind of the enemy in their blue coats waiting for us behind their cannons on Cemetery Ridge at Gettysburg. If I think that way, lots of other people must think that way too. They are no longer the enemy. The war has been over now since April of '65. As hard as it is to remember that fact, it has to be in the front of my mind every minute. We are no longer the Confederacy and the Union. We are the United States of America. The quicker we get a vision of one people and one nation in our minds, the quicker we will be able to resume our lives and begin the healing process that will allow us to move forward together."

Isaac climbed out of his rocker and stood for a moment, looking down at Matthew. Suddenly, a big smile split his face. "Son," he said, "this is a farm, and if I know anything about farms, it is that the work is never done. Let's go make a dent in whatever work is waiting on us."

* * *

The weeks passed quickly as Isaac made preparation to begin his new role as a representative of the people of Northern Virginia to the State Constitutional Convention. During that time, he read the former constitution and went into the military office in Winchester to acquire a copy of the action by the US Congress that necessitated that Virginia and all other states in the former Confederacy rewrite their constitutions.

It was required that each new constitution have three major provisions. They were to remove any provisions supporting slavery, provide full citizenship to all persons born or naturalized in the United States, and insure that all men of legal age had the right to vote.

By reading the former constitution of Virginia, Isaac could easily see what had to be removed from that document and where the new wording had to be inserted. He felt certain that most of the original constitution could remain as it was. As he read it he envisioned the men who were given the responsibility to write that first constitution. He had heard from his father the role his grandfather, George Mason IV, had played in the writing of that document, and he was aware also that James Madison, who later became president, was a coauthor. The two men had copied some of the document from the earlier writings of Thomas Jefferson, though Jefferson was not involved directly in the writing of that first Virginia constitution.

As the days passed, Isaac became more confident of his ability to contribute to the process of drafting a new constitution. He even drafted several sentences that could be utilized to make the necessary changes without altering other parts of the original document. He began to feel good about the role he would play.

Finally, it was time to begin his travels. He packed his saddle bags for what he expected would be a three-week stay between the beginning of the work and a three-week break scheduled for the Christmas season. Richmond was about 140 miles away, and he anticipated it would take him about a week to reach the city. He hoped to be there a day before the beginning of the convention. Thus, he planned to leave Winchester on the twenty-fifth of November to give him time to arrive in Richmond sometime during the day on the second of December.

ON TO RICHMOND

On the morning of Isaac's departure, Matt had Big Billy saddled and added two extra bags behind the saddle. He also put the carrying case for the Winchester 66 alongside of the saddle within easy reach. Isaac lingered for several minutes with Elizabeth on the porch before he came down the steps to where Matt was holding the big bay horse.

"Pa, do you have everything you need?" Matt asked.

"I think so, Son," he responded. "I have some money and shouldn't have difficulty getting anything I need along the way if I forgot anything. I plan to stay in Marshall, Opal, and Fredericksburg the first three nights so if I am missing something, I am sure I can pick it up on the way. After that the road is pretty good and straight south to Richmond. It should take me five or six days. I plan to stay at the Richmond Hotel right downtown, so you can reach me there by telegraph if you need to."

"Pa, I want you to know that Ami Ruth and I are very proud of you," said Matt. "No one we know of could do as good a job for the people as you."

"I hope you are right," Isaac responded, putting a firm hand on his son's shoulder. "I certainly intend to give it my best shot."

With that last word Isaac hoisted himself up onto Big Billy and turned the big bay to head out the gate and up the lane. He paused for just a second to look back over his shoulder and wave to Elizabeth, who was still standing on the porch leaning against the post at the edge of the steps. Matt turned to follow his Pa's glance, and when he looked closely, he saw that Elizabeth had tears in her eyes. He realized it was the first time they had been apart since their wedding. When Matt turned around again, his Pa and Big Billy were making dust heading up the lane toward the road.

* * *

The days on the road were mostly easy riding for Isaac. He simply gave Big Billy his head and the big red horse ate up the miles with his hooves. Big Billy liked to run at a light gallop, which is easy on the rider and isn't as tiring as moving at a faster pace. Each hour on the road, Isaac stopped and walked a bit to give Big Billy a rest, but he doubted the big bay really needed it. They made Marshall easily the first night, and he found a rooming house where he could stay. A restaurant across the street solved his problem for supper. He was in bed early and up before sunup. It was a pattern he followed each day and night on the way to Richmond.

It was Sunday evening when he arrived at the edge of the state capital. He slowed Big Billy down to a fast walk as he headed into the city, looking for the Richmond Hotel. He had heard that it was right downtown and four stories high, so he couldn't miss it. At one point he was looking down the street into the center of town and saw several buildings that were four or more stories high. Any of them could be The Richmond. He climbed down off his horse and addressed a man sitting on a bench close by.

"Sir," he said, "can you tell me how to find the Richmond Hotel?"

The man looked straight at him as though he was not there. Isaac started to speak again when he heard a voice coming from behind him. "I'm sorry, sir," the voice said. "Jason has not been himself since the Battle of Fredericksburg. He cannot answer your question."

Isaac turned to see a man dressed in Confederate grey pants and boots topped by a loose cotton shirt. He smiled to himself to see the familiar uniform and knew he had found an ally there on the streets of Richmond.

"Sir," he said, "I am Isaac Mason from Winchester and I have come for the Constitutional Convention that is to be held here in the Court of Appeals building over the next several weeks. I hope to stay at the Richmond Hotel, which I understand is right downtown close to the court building."

"Welcome to Richmond, Mr. Mason," the man responded. "I'm afraid you will be lucky if they have any room left, but you can give them a try. Just go two more blocks south and one block to the west. It is a big red brick building. You can't miss it."

"Thank you, sir," Isaac said, turning toward Big Billy.

The man continued to speak as Isaac mounted the big horse. "Mr. Mason, if they don't have a room for you at the hotel, try Miss Milly's Boarding House a block west of the hotel. I understand the rooms are cheaper, and she serves breakfast and supper for her guests."

Isaac thanked the friendly man for his advice. As he continued down the street, he reflected on Southern hospitality and the natural friendliness of Southerners. He made a right turn and saw the hotel in front of him. The man was right; he couldn't miss it.

About thirty minutes later, Isaac tied Big Billy to the hitching post in front of Miss Milly's Boarding House. The hotel was, indeed, full and Miss Milly's seemed to be the next best option. Shortly after he knocked, the door was opened by a smallish lady wearing a big smile and a spotless white apron, accompanied by kitchen smells that made this option seem so much more like home than the hotel would have been. He immediately felt good that the hotel had been full. "Welcome," she said. "I'm Milly Blake."

A few minutes later, he found himself standing at the door of a vacant room talking to his new landlady. "I'm sorry, Mr. Mason," she said. "Supper was over about an hour ago and I have cleaned the kitchen. I could fix you a sandwich with some milk or cider if that sounds good to you."

Isaac smiled his biggest smile and said, "Miss Milly, I will anticipate your good cooking in the morning at breakfast. Right now, I need to get my horse bedded down for the night. Can you point me toward the closest livery stable?"

Miss Milly led him down the steps to the front door and stood on the porch with him. She pointed back the way he had come. "If you go back to the Richmond Hotel and go around back, you will find the livery stable that serves the hotel."

"Thank you, ma'am," Isaac said and led Big Billy away toward the hotel.

The livery stable was just where Miss Milly said it would be, and the attendant was more than pleased to accept his Union greenback for the first week of Big Billy's stay there.

The attendant said, "Sir, you are getting a bargain at a dollar a week for that big horse. We ought to be charging at least another fifty cents."

Isaac smiled and replied. "Son, you just take good care of my horse, and I will see what I can do about a bonus for you at the end of our stay. Now can you tell me where I can find a bit of supper at this late hour?"

The young man replied, "The food service at the hotel stays open until ten o'clock, so I'm sure you can find something there."

When Isaac entered the backdoor of the hotel a few minutes later, he found the food service open just as the boy had predicted. Shortly, he was seated at a table covered with a snowy white cloth, a delicate china cup of hot coffee in his hand.

He looked around the room to see who else was eating late on a Sunday evening. The room held about fifteen tables and several were occupied. Most of the latecomers were men dressed in more formal attire, but there were three ladies in the room, each sitting with a man. Isaac smiled to himself and thought, *People watching is fun. I wonder where they are from.*

His eyes were drawn to the doorway that came into the eating area where two men had just entered. Both were dressed in a more casual way, like Isaac, and looked like they had just come off of the road after some long travel. He watched as the maître d' ushered them to a table on the other side of the room.

The waiter arrived at Isaac's table and placed a bowl of water in front of him. He looked at the bowl and was totally puzzled. He looked up at the waiter, smiled at him, and said, "That is mighty thin soup, Son."

The waiter leaned down close to him and whispered, "It's a finger bowl sir." As he stood there, Isaac noticed he was holding a white towel. This was a first for Isaac. The waiter had brought him a bowl of warm water so he could wash his hands!

Isaac put his hands into the water and swished them around, then the waiter reached forward with the towel as he withdrew them. After Isaac had wiped his hands on the towel, the waiter took both the towel and the finger bowl away.

Isaac looked around at the people at the other tables to see if anyone had been watching, but all seemed preoccupied with their food and table conversations. He was about to relax when the waiter was back at his side offering him the evening's specials from the kitchen. All the selections sounded good, but Isaac ordered roast beef—a rarity at the Schendler Farm—sides of vegetables, hot rolls and apple pie.

In no time, the waiter was back with his meal on a large tray, everything served in pretty china dishes and bowls. Isaac realized he was even hungrier than he had thought and everything smelled very good. He dug in.

Twenty minutes later he was on his second cup of coffee when he looked up to find a man standing there with his hand extended. He was a big man with a mustache and chin whiskers that covered much of the lower half his face. His voice was low pitched and he had a very confident demeanor about him.

Isaac stood to take his hand and the man said, "Are you Mr. Mason?"

Isaac responded that he was, indeed, Isaac Mason.

The man continued, "My name is Wade Hampton. I am from South Carolina."

Isaac wasn't sure of what to say to Mr. Wade Hampton but responded, "Would you like to join me for a cup of coffee?"

The big man said, "I certainly would. My friend won't mind my joining you for a few minutes." He settled into a chair, and the waiter hurried over to take his order.

"Mr. Hampton, your name is familiar. Have we met?" Isaac asked.

"Mr. Mason, were you in the war?" his new companion asked.

THE WOUNDS OF WAR

Suddenly it hit him. "I know who you are! You are General Wade Hampton, second in command of JEB Stuart's cavalry."

Wade Hampton's face expanded into a big grin and he said, "You are right. I was at every battle from Bull Run to Gettysburg and was on the way to relieve General Lee at Appomattox Court House when the war ended."

Hampton reached up and pulled the hair away from his forehead to show a vicious scar. He said, "I got that at Gettysburg. I have another almost like it on the back of my head that I got at Brandy Station. They almost got me twice, but I am still above ground. How about you?"

"I don't have any scars you can see," replied Isaac. "I was an artillery man with General Lee from '61 through Gettysburg. After Pickett's Charge, I was wounded in the leg and captured. I was in a Union prison camp in Maryland for the remainder of the war."

"So what are you doing now?" Mr. Hampton asked.

"I am living with my son on a farm outside of Winchester," Isaac replied.

"I know that country well," Mr. Hampton said. "We fought four battles around Winchester. Every time we came, we put those Yankees on the run." Then his voice lowered to a whisper. "We lost some good men there."

Isaac nodded and continued, "We were beginning to grow this farm just north of Winchester when they started talking about revising the Virginia State Constitution so Virginia can fit back into the Union. I ran for office to be the representative from that region and am in Richmond to see if I can contribute to the process."

Hampton said, "I am here for the same meeting you are. Governor Richardson of South Carolina sent me up here to see how you folks do it. We are planning to write our new constitution next year, and the governor thinks we would benefit by seeing how Virginia handles the details of that effort."

"Mr. Hampton," Isaac said, "if I am not too bold to ask, why did you pick me out among all these visitors to the city to speak with?"

"Oh!" he responded. "I almost forgot my purpose for coming over to disturb your supper. We took our horses to the livery stable, and I saw a beautiful bay horse there, a full hand taller than anything else in the stable. I asked the attendant whose horse that was, and he looked you up on the register for me. He said he didn't think you were staying at the hotel but thought you had gone into the hotel restaurant for supper. He told me to look for the tallest man in the restaurant and one who is the spittin' image of Stonewall Jackson. And here you are. And, by damn, with that full beard, you do look like old Stonewall!"

Mr. Hampton, despite his deep South accent, had been speaking rather rapidly until that point. Then his voice lowered a bit and he spoke very slowly. "I was wondering if that beautiful horse was for sale," he asked.

Isaac smiled. "No, sir, the horse isn't mine to offer. It belongs to my son. He wouldn't part with it. Not only is it the most amazing horse in our area, but it has become an income producer on the farm. We have a standing stud fee for him, and he gets a lot of company from our area and from north of the border in West Virginia and Pennsylvania. In fact, we just bred him to a bay mare from a horse farm in West Virginia and hope to get another just like him in the spring."

"I am, indeed, sorry he isn't for sale," Hampton said. "I raised a horse just like him in South Carolina before the war. He went to war with me. I lost him at Brandy Station when a saber knocked me off of him and put me in the sick wagon for a couple of weeks. I sent people to search for him, but we didn't have any luck. I thought he might be still wandering around the battlefield but I suspect the Yankees took him back to Washington, with them. If you saw Butler—I called him Butler—on the field without a rider, you certainly wouldn't leave him there. He was the best horse in the Southern army, the best of the best."

With that last comment, Mr. Hampton reached across the table for Isaac's hand. Both men stood up and Isaac said, "General Hampton, it is, indeed, my pleasure to meet you and have the opportunity to get to know you a bit. This is a proud moment for me that

I will be pleased to share with my son who, incidentally, survived Pickett's Charge when he was only fifteen."

"Please give your son my greetings," Hampton said. "And tell him that if he ever decides to sell that beautiful animal to make contact with me in Charleston by telegraph. I will head toward Winchester the next day."

Isaac's mind was full of memories when he lay down in his bed at Miss Milly's later than night. Visions of the war loomed in his mind. Imagine meeting one of the great generals of the war here in Richmond almost two and a half years after the fighting ended! Imagine, also, that he lost his big bay horse, Butler, at the same place Matt told of finding Big Billy a few weeks after that battle. Matt had wondered whose horse he had found and imagined that it must have been the mount of some great general. No one else would have had such a beautiful horse. Still, Isaac thought to himself, *Finders keepers.*

THE COURT OF APPEALS BUILDING

Isaac was up shortly after daybreak and made his way downstairs to the breakfast Miss Milly had promised him last night. He wasn't disappointed. When he arrived at the table, he was pleased to find that she had three other men who were staying with her. The smell of baking biscuits and frying ham filled the room, and the table held a number of bowls and platters carrying a delightful array of aromas into the air.

The other men looked up and nodded to him. One passed him a platter of scrambled eggs, and when he looked over the edge of the closest bowl, he was delighted to see it was full of steaming grits. He immediately had a memory of the table in his little house near Mt. Airy in North Carolina. His wife, Mary, used to always set the grits in the middle of the table so they would be available to all sides of the table. The butter was always close by to flavor the grits. His eyes moved over the table and located the butter. Both were in easy reach and, shortly, both were filling the empty side of his plate. Staying at Miss Milly's was, indeed, going to be a very good decision.

He and two of the other men lingered a bit after breakfast for a second cup of coffee. One of the visitors was attending the constitutional convention. The other was a salesman who traveled in a wagon and carried general use items that were usually purchased in general stores.

"Yes," he said. "My usual route is from Raleigh, North Carolina, to Washington. I come through here about once a month. Miss Milly's Boarding House became a regular stop on my route about five years ago, and she sees me going and coming each month. I wouldn't stay anyplace else."

Isaac noted the time and excused himself. He had been told that the Court of Appeals building was about a half-mile away, and he intended to walk rather than to have Big Billy standing outside all day. He wasn't sure what accommodations they had for horses at the building but knew Big Billy would be more comfortable in the livery stable.

Miss Milly gave him directions at the door, and he put his carrying case under his arm and began his walk down the unfamiliar streets toward the court building. He assumed he was about halfway when he heard a noise down the road ahead of him. It was hard to recognize the noise, but shortly after the first sound, he began to hear people yelling. He broke into a trot heading toward the commotion.

When he rounded a corner, he could see the Court of Appeals building on a hill several hundred yards away. The building appeared to be covered by smoke or dust that made it difficult to see what was going on. By the time he reached the bottom of the hill and started up the slope, he was already in a full run. All around him, other people were running, some away from the building and some toward it. Many of them were yelling, but he couldn't make out what they were saying.

When he was about fifty yards away, he realized part of the building had collapsed. The wall that he could see was still standing but the roof was gone. Two men were standing and gesturing toward the building. Isaac yelled at them, "What happened?"

"The roof just fell in!" the taller man said. "We think the walls are going to cave in any minute. There are people still inside!"

Isaac ran toward the building but yelled back at the men, "Get the fire department and some medical people headed this way!" He didn't look back to see if they were moving to carry out his directions.

By the time Isaac reached the wall that was still standing, he was covered in dust. He could hear people's voices inside the building, some moaning and others yelling for help. Isaac ran along the wall looking for an entrance. Finally, he found it, a door that seemed to lead inside. He turned the handle, but it wouldn't budge. He stepped back and looked for another possible entrance into the building but didn't see anything promising. He took a couple of rapid steps toward the door and hit it hard, with all of his 260 pounds. The door splintered and he grabbed the door facing and tore the rest of the door off of its hinges. He was inside.

The dust was as thick as smoke, and Isaac could only see a few inches in front of him. He pulled out his handkerchief and tied it around his face to cover his nose and mouth. He could breathe but he could hardly see. He heard a sound a few feet in front of him and moved toward it. There was a man lying on the floor, pinned down by two fallen rafters. He cleared them away and picked the man up and started toward the door he had just come through. He knew that under ordinary circumstances he would not move an injured person, but if the walls came down on top of him, he wouldn't be injured. He would be dead.

When Isaac was outside the door, he carried the man over to the grassy area and laid him down. He could see several people just down the hill and yelled to them to come this way. "Make this man as comfortable as you can," he said. "The medical people should be coming, and they can take over when they get here. There are many people injured inside. I will bring them here to you when I find them."

Isaac headed back toward the doorway and disappeared inside. The dust was just as thick and seeing anything was very difficult. He was feeling his way along a pile of bricks when he heard a moan. Again, he found a man on the floor with bricks and pieces of wood on top of him. He lifted him free of the debris and put him on his shoulder. He would have carried him in his arms, but he needed his hands free to guide them through to the door to the outside.

When he arrived at the grassy area, he laid the injured man down near the first one and the people who had gathered there began to minister to him. Isaac headed back toward the door. One of the helpers yelled at him, "Sir, the wall is going to fall. Don't go back in!"

Isaac heard him but knew from the sounds he was hearing that there were still many injured people on the other side of that wall. He disappeared inside.

This time the dust in the air seemed thinner and he could see better. As he went farther into the building, he reached a point where he saw open sky. The scene inside the walls was horrible. There were still hundreds of people inside, most were injured but many appeared to be dead. Isaac bent down to check a man who was just to his right. It was obvious that he was already gone. A second man was close to him and was still moving.

Isaac partially lifted the injured man and heard him yell in his ear, "Look out!" He looked up just in time to see the wall he had just come through swaying. He dropped the man back on the floor, picked up a piece of the broken table top he had just lifted off of him and pulled it over the two of them. Isaac's body was shielding the man and the table top was across his back, not totally covering him but enough so that his body would not catch the brunt of the falling debris.

Bricks were falling all around them, and Isaac felt the blows on both of his arms and the right side of his head. When the debris settled, Isaac pushed the trash off of the two of them and picked the man up again. Blood was running down the right side of his head and onto his shoulder. The door he had been coming through was gone and so was the wall. To get the man out, he had to climb over the debris of the fallen wall. Soon they were outside, and Isaac was putting the man down next to the others he had carried out earlier.

Isaac started to go back in, but one of the women who had come to help grabbed his arm. She said, "Sir, you can't go back in there! You have a head injury and are bleeding. We need to clean your wounds."

Isaac said, "Thank you, ma'am, but there are still several hundred people in there, and they need to get out." Isaac pulled away and was soon back in the building.

It seemed like hours, but probably was not nearly as long, before Isaac saw firemen and others with stretchers moving in and out of the building, carrying people out to those waiting to care for them. He wasn't sure how many people he carried out, but when he fell exhausted on the ground next to the injured, there was a long line of people lying side by side in the grass under the trees. Isaac finally became one of them.

THOUGHTS OF HOME

Isaac wasn't sure how he got back to Miss Milly's Boarding House, but when he came to himself, he was lying under a blanket on the hard floor of the room he had occupied the night before. When he lifted his head, he saw his dusty clothes lying in a pile by the door. He lifted the top blanket and looked under it at his body. He was in his underwear, but the dust he saw on his clothes had been washed off of his body. At first inventory, he didn't feel anything broken, but when he moved his left arm, the pain was intense, and when he tried to move his fingers, he felt a sharp pain in his forearm. His head ached.

He pushed himself up on his right elbow and felt a wrapping on his head. He had a compress on the side of his forehead that was held in place by a piece of cloth that was wrapped all the way around his head. He looked back over at his clothes and saw a bowl of water there that was about the same color as the dust on the pile by the door. *Those clothes are throwaways,* he thought. Not only were they dirty beyond washing but he couldn't imagine he would ever want to put anything on again that would remind him of the horror he had seen in that Appeals Court Building.

Just then, he heard footsteps on the stairs and Miss Milly appeared in the door. "So you are awake," she said.

"I think just barely," Isaac responded, his voice a croak. "How did I get here?"

"Mr. Miller, one of the men staying here, said he found you wandering on the street. He said you were in a bad way. He thought of taking you to the hospital, but read the note one of the doctors had pinned on your shirt, and it said you had a concussion and a green stick fracture of the left forearm. The doctor said you needed bed rest and would recover in due time. Mr. Miller thought you could get the rest you needed here as well as the hospital, which he knew was covered up with more patients than they could handle."

"Do I have you to thank for cleaning me up?" Isaac asked.

"Well, Mr. Miller took your clothes and put them in a pile over there," she answered, suppressing a small smile. "I tried to wash the dust off of the rest of you, though I didn't do a very good job. You will want to spend some time in the washroom when you feel up to it. Your beard and your hair are a mess. Let me know when you are ready, and I will bring you some hot water and a couple of scrub cloths. I'm afraid your clothes are a lost cause."

Isaac nodded toward the pile of clothes and said, "Don't bother yourself with those. When I am up, I will empty the pockets and dump them in the trash. Except for the shoes, there is nothing there I want to salvage." He paused and grimaced. "I expect I need to put this arm in a sling. Do you think you could help me with that?"

Miss Milly said she was sure she could. When she left the room, Isaac lay back on the blanket. In a short moment, he was sleeping the sleep of exhaustion. When he first woke up, it was midafternoon. By the time he was awake again, he could smell breakfast cooking downstairs. He moved to get up and felt muscles he hadn't felt since his days moving cannons for the Army of Northern Virginia, and his arm was aching. A sling made of a large red bandana was lying on his chair. He pulled on his other pair of pants, struggled into his shirt and headed for the privy out back and then toward the washroom. In a few minutes, he arrived at the table with the other guests.

Now there were only two other men and Miss Milly sitting at the table. She rose to seat him and poured a cup of coffee in a thick brown mug. She leaned down close to him, checking the bandage on his head and the sling around his neck that cradled his injured arm.

"Which one of you is Mr. Miller?" Isaac asked of the two men at the other end of the table.

The tall man sitting next to Miss Milly smiled and said, "I'm Miller, Mr. Mason." Isaac recognized the delegate to the constitutional convention from yesterday's breakfast. The other man was the traveling salesman.

Isaac stood up and reached for Mr. Miller's hand. "I want to thank you for taking care of me yesterday. Evidently, I was in a pretty bad way."

"You were, for sure," Mr. Miller said. "I found you about three blocks from here. I wasn't sure at first if it was you. If you hadn't been the biggest man on the street, I would have passed you by. You were so covered in dust that I could hardly see your face. You didn't know me, and you didn't seem to know where you were going. I tried to talk to you, but you were not talking back. I knew you had a head injury and thought Miss Milly here would be the one to doctor that wound and get you cleaned up."

"You were right about that," Isaac said. "She may have missed her calling running a boarding house. She would make an excellent nurse."

Miss Milly smiled and said, "During the war, that is exactly what I was doing. We fought two major battles here between '61 and '65. We treated more than ten thousand injured and buried three times that many. You had a vicious head wound, but it isn't the worst I have seen by far."

Isaac realized he was famished. Breakfast yesterday was the last time he had eaten anything. One by one, the bowls on the table made their way to him, and he emptied each one in turn.

Isaac listened to the conversation among his new friends while he savored the coffee, grits, and biscuits.

In between mouthfuls, he asked questions of his table mates. "Tell me what the word is on the street about the tragedy?" he asked.

The two men started to speak at the same time, but Mr. Miller dropped away, showing deference to the strongest voice. "It is a mess," said the traveling salesman. "The report today is that there are more than forty dead and the death toll is rising every hour. There are more than two hundred in the hospital and some of those will not make it."

"Does anyone know what happened, what caused the collapse?" Isaac asked.

The man responded, "It will probably be weeks before anyone knows what caused the building to collapse. That building was more than eighty years old, and it evidently just couldn't take the crowd that had come to participate in creating the new constitution."

Mr. Miller picked up the story. "Evidently, the crowd of watchers had filled the balcony and, without any warning, it just fell in. Everybody upstairs fell about thirty feet with the balcony, and those under it were all crushed. The balcony pulled the ceiling down on top of everyone, those in the balcony and those on the floor. It was a tangled mess. I was not inside so I didn't get injured. The front wall fell in immediately, and in just a few minutes, both of the side walls fell in too. Some were able to escape through the side walls before they fell in, but most were just caught inside. Do you know where you were when it happened?" he asked.

"I'm not sure," Isaac responded. "I don't think I was inside yet, but I was close. I remember running toward the building and carrying some people out. I think I was inside when the wall collapsed. I don't remember anything after that."

When breakfast was over, Isaac went back to the washroom and finished cleaning himself up. He then went onto the front porch and sat there in a rocker for a while. Miss Milly came out and sat with him.

"How are you feeling now?" she asked.

Isaac responded, "Ma'am, I'm still very sore all over and I can't grip my hand. My head seems all right most of the time, but the dizziness comes and goes. I am sure I am going to be fine. You did some fine nursing on me, and I am grateful."

"If you want to read about the tragedy, you can get the *Richmond Enquirer* newspaper down at the corner store," Miss Milly said. "I'm sure they can tell you more of what happened and why than any of us who saw or heard about it from a distance."

Isaac thought for the first time about his people back home. "Can you tell me where I can find a telegraph office?" he asked.

Miss Milly responded, "There is one about three blocks away past the corner store I mentioned to you earlier. If you feel up to it, you could probably walk to it in about five minutes."

Isaac slowly walked down to the corner, feeling every step in his legs and back. He stopped at the store, bought a newspaper, and sat on the bench in front of the store to read the headlines. One article on the first page announced that the constitutional convention had been called off until after the first of the year. That was the information he was looking for to plan what he needed to do over the next week. He now knew he could head for home whenever he felt able.

As he continued on toward the telegraph office, twice his head began to spin and he had to stop and lean against a building to get his bearings. He knew something about concussions, having seen several during the war. He had never had one himself and was gaining respect for the effects of such with each step. Finally, he found the telegraph office and was soon standing across the counter from a small balding man with a green visor on his forehead. He followed the man's instructions on how to send the first telegram he had ever sent.

The wording was simple and to the point. He wrote, "Tragedy here. STOP Two slight injuries. STOP Starting home tomorrow or the next day. STOP All will be fine. STOP"

Isaac retraced his steps to Miss Milly's, including the short stops every half block to let his head clear. When he arrived, he slowly climbed the stairs to the bedroom, lay down on the bed, and woke up with the sun coming in the window and the smell of bacon in the air.

Breakfast was very much like yesterday, though Mr. Miller had left the night before. He had come to Richmond for the convention, and with the postponement, there was no need to stay over another night. Isaac had enjoyed his exchanges with Mr. Miller and missed him at the table. Miss Milly did her best to keep up the conversation, but the tragedy seemed to be the only thing they all had in common, and Isaac was not in a mood to talk about it further. Instead, he was thinking about home and whether or not he should get Big Billy and strike out for northern Virginia that day.

By the time he had climbed back up the stairs, he had made up his mind to leave as soon as he could pack his belongings. It didn't take long to gather up his things. He carried everything downstairs and met Miss Milly in the dining room where she was cleaning up the table.

"I'm going to leave you now, Miss Milly," he said.

THE WOUNDS OF WAR

"Oh, Mr. Mason, are you sure you are up to such a long trip so soon after your injury?" she asked.

"I think the dizzy spells have stopped," he responded. "There is no reason for me to hang around here. I'm going to head for home and take it easy on the way. I should be there in five or six days."

Miss Milly shook her head. "You paid for the whole week. I'll get your refund for the days you haven't used."

"No, ma'am," Isaac said. "Count the extra as your pay for nursing services. I have felt secure with you taking care of me with your nursing skills. I'll be back the first week of January and would appreciate it if you would hold a room for me. I wouldn't want to stay any place but here."

Isaac put his bag over his shoulder and headed for the livery stable behind the Richmond Hotel. Big Billy was in the first stall just inside the door and whinnied when he saw Isaac. When Isaac reached for the saddle, his hand touched a piece of paper that was stuck just inside the saddle horn. He retrieved it, unfolded it, and read the short note that was signed by Wade Hampton, the man he had met in the hotel dining room.

> Mr. Mason,
>
> It was nice visiting with you at the hotel earlier in the week. I could not help but stop and admire this beautiful animal on my way out this morning. Please tell your son of my offer. I would, indeed, like to have this big bay as a stud horse on my farm near Charleston.

The signature was very ornate. With lots of curls and flourishes and in big letters it said, General Wade Hampton.

When the attendant saw him lead Big Billy out of the stall, he came running from the other end of the livery stable. The young man lifted the saddle off of the stall and hoisted it across Big Billy's broad back. It took just a few seconds to hook the cinch and get the bridle on. Big Billy never liked taking the bit in his mouth and gave the attendant some resistance, but Isaac's hand on his nose steadied him. In a short minute, the big horse was ready for the road.

"When the building collapsed, the hotel emptied and left me with a bunch of refunds to make," said the young man. "They have just about cleaned me out."

Isaac smiled and responded. "You keep the rest of the money for the week. I will be back in early January when the convention begins. Big Billy likes it here, and I will be staying at Miss Milly's Boarding House a couple of blocks over. We will see you then."

* * *

At the same time Isaac was headed for home, Matt was in the barn saddling the grey mare to head toward Richmond to search for his Pa. Word of the tragedy in Richmond had moved rapidly through the Loop. Even before the Winchester newspapers carried the story of the collapsed building, the very building his Pa was going to for the convention, all the neighbors knew of the potential for the Mason family's loss.

Matt led the grey mare out of the barn just as a strange horse and rider turned down the lane toward the big house. Matt met the young man just inside the gate and was handed an envelope. He said, "This was waiting for us when we came into the office this morning. We thought you ought to have it right away."

Matt tore open the envelope and quickly read the short message inside. The dread he had been feeling that was such a weight on his mind lifted immediately. Matt reached in his pants pocket and pulled out a shiny half dollar. He handed it to the boy and shouted a "Thank you!" over his shoulder as he headed for the house.

When he entered the front door, he was doing his best not to yell at the top of his voice. He knew Ami Ruth would be upset if he woke their little guy. He found Aunt Elizabeth in the kitchen, caught her around the waist and lifted her off of her feet.

Matt had difficulty getting the words out. "He's okay," he finally said. "We have a telegram with good news from Pa. He has a couple of minor injuries and is headed home!"

Before he got the last words out, Ami Ruth joined them in the kitchen and the three of them were hugging and laughing and crying in the middle of the floor. All their voices joined in one big sigh of relief. And just at that instant, right on cue, they heard the sound of Stephen making his presence known in the other room. They all laughed.

It was five very long travel days before Isaac rounded the bend and saw the lane in front of him and the big house under the trees in the distance. The trip had been much more difficult than he had anticipated. His arm hurt with every throb of his pulse, almost in the same rhythm as Big Billy's hooves hitting the ground. Several times he had felt himself getting dizzy. Each time he stopped and climbed down from Big Billy until his head cleared. He knew that falling off of the big horse was a distinct possibility. But now he was home. He could relax, sleep for a couple of days, and let Elizabeth take control.

AFTERMATH OF
THE TRAGEDY

Newspapers all over the states of Virginia, Maryland, Pennsylvania, and North Carolina made the tragedy at the Court of Appeals building in Richmond their front page story. Much of their narrative focused on the loss of life and the many injured. Every article seemed to report different numbers. The best guess was that there were more than nine hundred people inside the building when the balcony collapsed. Forty-five were evidently killed outright with another two hundred or more injured. Some of those who were injured died later that day.

As was often true with newspaper reports, various officials pointed the finger of blame at every conceivable person in authority, including the Union Military Administration, the governor of the state, various state legislators, and even the maintenance staff of the facility. The major Richmond newspaper, the *Daily Richmond Enquirer*, was still printing headlines and running major stories about the tragedy ten days later.

One of the stories focused on heroes of the tragedy, the policemen, firemen, doctors, and nurses and one civilian no one seemed to be able to identify. That story was reprinted in the *Winchester Times Newspaper*.

LOCAL OFFICIALS SEARCH FOR CIVILIAN
HERO OF APPEALS COURT TRAGEDY

Many eyewitnesses have reported seeing a man going over and over into the damaged Court of

Appeals building to bring out the injured. He carried many to safety, sometimes coming out of the damaged building carrying an injured person over each shoulder. He was described as a big man with a full beard and covered in dust from head to toe. At one point, witnesses told of watching him disappear through a side door into the building just before the entire east wall fell in. No one believed they would see him emerge again. But shortly he was seen climbing over the debris carrying out yet another body. This time they said it was obvious that he was injured. Dr. Josiah Smith, who was tending to the injured said, "He had a head injury and one of his arms was hanging at his side. He stayed for a moment, but before I could get a look at him he headed back over the fallen wall into the interior of the building."

The unknown hero's last rescue was a woman who had blood streaming from a head wound. She appeared to be totally unconscious. When he laid the woman down in the long line of injured he had carried from the building, he collapsed on the ground next to her. "Several efforts to revive him did not succeed and I left him there with a compress on his head wound, hoping nature would affect a cure," Dr. Smith said. "I was examining all of those rescued, some of whom had expired and others who were in various stages of distress. When I finished examining each of them, I pinned a note on their shirt for the doctors at the hospital so they would know where to begin their treatment. The big man with the beard who had saved so many did not regain consciousness. I wrote a note saying he most likely had a concussion and a green stick fracture of his left arm below the elbow. I projected bed rest and immobilizing the arm for a few weeks so it could heal."

However, when the wagon came to take the injured people to the hospital, the man was no longer there. He had appeared like an Angel and saved so many and had disappeared without a trace. He never appeared at the hospital for treatment on his own. In fact, no one knows who he is.

A joint statement was issued by the offices of the Governor of Virginia and the Mayor of Richmond. It asked the following:

"Who is the bearded hero of the Appeals Court building tragedy who saved so many lives at great risk to himself and then disappeared before anyone could thank him for his valiant service and his sacrifice? If anyone knows who this man is, please contact the Governor's or Mayor's office so we can share his name with the Richmond community and the State of Virginia who owe him so much.

Signed
Francis Harrison Pierpont, Governor
Joseph A. Mayo, Mayor

THE WOUNDS OF WAR

The story in the local *Times* newspaper continued:

> No one in Winchester would have known of the efforts of the Richmond leadership to find the hero of the Appeals Court Building tragedy if it hadn't been for the diligence of the reporters of the *Daily Richmond Enquirer* newspaper. We picked up the story from the front page along with the drawing that had accompanied the story.

We want everyone to know that we know who he is. Please see page two.

On the inside page, the *Times* newspaper reprinted the picture that had appeared on its front page a month ago. It was of Isaac standing on the back of a wagon making his first speech in front of the people of Winchester. Underneath the headline said:

ISAAC MASON OF WINCHESTER IS HERO OF APPEALS COURT TRAGEDY!

The *Winchester Times* has learned that Isaac Mason, who lives in the Loop north of Winchester and is our Representative to the Virginia Constitutional Convention, is the civilian hero for whom Governor Pierpont and Mayor Mayo are looking. When we saw the drawing they included with the Enquirer's front page article earlier this week, it was easy to compare with the front page drawing of Mr. Mason that was printed a month ago in this newspaper.

A *Times* reporter went to the Schendler Farm where Mr. Mason lives and asked him directly if he was the person described in the *Enquirer* story. He responded that he had been hit on the head and didn't have much memory of the events in Richmond. Actually, we had our answer before he responded. He had a bandage on his head and his left arm was in a sling. These are exactly the injuries sustained from the disaster by the hero who was described in the article from the Richmond newspaper.

Read the report from *The Richmond Enquirer*, then look at both drawings and form your own conclusions. We are satisfied we know who the hero is. He is one of ours.

AUTHOR'S NOTES
The History Behind *The Wounds Of War*

The Wounds of War is a fiction-based-on-fact story. It is written as a sequel to the novel *Journey to Gettysburg*. As is obvious by the title, *Journey* is focused on events related to the Civil War. *The Wounds of War* picks up the story at the conclusion of the war and is focused on the events that followed and their effects on the Quaker community that was in place then and is still today just north of the city of Winchester, Virginia. Though the characters and the setting are the same, the sequel stands on its own as a story of the Reconstruction period and the challenges unique to that period of history.

Matt Mason and his new wife, Ami Ruth, are fictional characters who came together as teenagers following the Battle of Gettysburg and were married shortly after the war was over. *The Wounds of War* begins with the wedding of the two young people. As the wedding is going on, Matt's father, Isaac Mason, returns from his years in a Union prison camp and joins the cast of characters. Ami Ruth's Aunt Elizabeth is the fourth main character in the story.

The Mason family is caught up in the throes of Reconstruction, the heavy taxation that threatens to take their farm, their involvement in the Underground Railroad that helped slaves escape their servitude in the Old South, and the efforts of the Ku Klux Klan to assert their control over the region during that tumultuous period. The family's Quaker foundations are threatened as their beliefs opposing both slavery and the war come into question.

Here is some historical background that will enrich your understanding of the book.

- The Community of Winchester and the Surrounding Territory

Several Native American tribes called the Shenandoah Valley home during the period leading into the 1700s. The Shawnee Nation occupied the northern section of the valley around present-day Winchester. The British were always concerned about coexistence with the Indians and wanted a strong settlement in that region to act as a buffer between the Indians and the settlers moving west from the coastal area. Thus, land grants were given to many to create farms and small towns in that region.

George Washington came to Winchester at age sixteen as a land surveyor to help with the land grant process. He was charged with the responsibility of surveying the land in the area and making it ready for settlement. Lacking money to pay the young Washington, the British paid him partially in land. Thus, Washington became one of the largest landholders in the region. While there, he became involved in local militia activities and helped build Fort Loudoun, which is still a landmark in the area. Washington lived there for several years until he married and moved back close to the Potomac in eastern Virginia. When he moved back east, he sold off most of his land for farms in the area. One of the stipulations for the sales was that any farmer who bought as much as a hundred acres of his land had to agree to plant at least twenty percent of the land in fruit. Because of that requirement, one can still find many apple orchards in the area today.

- The Quaker Community

The Quaker community arrived in the region just north of Winchester in the 1720s. Their reason for coming was a land grant given to a hundred Quaker families who migrated southward from Pennsylvania. Each family was to receive a thousand acres suitable for farming. The Loop, as it was referred to by the Quaker community, ran from just above Winchester on the map north to the Potomac River in a large oval. Situated in the South central area of that Loop was a store that came to be called the White Hall Store. It was created by the community to make groceries and other goods easily accessible to the farmers and their families.

The Quaker community in the Loop still occupies a portion of the area north of Winchester. The Hopewell Meeting House, built in 1734, is still there and continues to serve the Quaker community, as does the White Hall Store.

It should be pointed out that the entire Quaker Loop was originally located in Virginia territory. That changed in the midst of the Civil War when the western portion of Virginia stayed loyal to the Union while the eastern half of the state seceded with the other eleven Southern states. The result was a splitting of the Quaker community into two segments, one in West Virginia and the other in Virginia. That fact plays well into the story of the book *The Wounds of War*.

- The Amish and Quaker Groups

It is easy to confuse the Amish and Quaker religious groups. Both are denominations of conservative Christians and both are found in large numbers in Pennsylvania, Maryland, and Virginia. In earlier years, both were known to use the words *thee* and *thou* when referring to themselves and others. In those early years, both tended toward simple living and plain dress and were reluctant to adopt the conveniences of modern technology. Neither group believed in slavery or in war.

Major differences began to occur between the two groups during the mid-nineteenth century. The Amish tended to stay on their farms and to relate primarily to others within their own group, as had been their history. The Quakers, in contrast, began to open businesses and to relate to the rest of the population, whom they referred to as the English.

As the nineteenth century passed, the Quaker community remained in Northern Virginia in the Winchester and Berryville region while the Amish community migrated to the more southern and mountainous areas of Virginia. Today the Amish can be found in Halifax County and in small settlements such as the one near Pearisburg, Virginia.

- Virginia Wine Country

The area of Northern Virginia near Berryville and Winchester was known during the late 1800s as Virginia's Wine Country. The Schendler Farm is a fictional name, but it could have been home to any of a dozen or more vineyards that were active in the nineteenth century. Some of those original wineries are still productive today. For all its history, the major cash crop of the State of Virginia has been tobacco. However, in that vicinity in the 1800s, grapes were a dominant crop. The vineyard industry lagged during the first half of the twentieth century but made a comeback toward the last half of the century and into the twenty-first. In a few years, grapes may again become dominant and a key agricultural cash crop.

- The Mason Family of Virginia

Anyone who knows the history of Virginia during its early years knows of the Mason family. George Mason IV was one of the writers of the first constitution of Virginia. Most specifically, he was given credit for writing a list of guaranteed rights for the people that was included as a part of that constitution. Later, he wrote a similar document for the Constitution of the United States, which we call the Bill of Rights. George Mason University, based in Fairfax County, is named after that Mason ancestor and is the largest public university in the state.

The Mason family has spread all over Virginia. This story includes references to John Murray Mason, who was a congressman and senator to the US Congress from the 1840s until the beginning of the Civil War. He then became the Confederacy's Ambassador to England and France during the war. Isaac Mason, one of the key characters of the book, is his fictional son, and Matt Mason, the main character, is his fictional grandson. Isaac Mason spent his youth in Lexington, Virginia, living with cousins of John Murray Mason. The "why" of that living arrangement is a key aspect of the latter portion of the story.

- The Underground Railroad

A cursory look at the map of Northern Virginia will tell you why the city of Winchester and the surrounding region played such a major role in the Underground Railroad during the last twenty years before the beginning of the Civil War. Slaves served plantations in Mississippi, Alabama, Georgia, and South Carolina. The safe ground for runaway slaves was across the Mason-Dixon Line, which was the southern border of the state of Pennsylvania. The small cities of Gettysburg and Chambersburg were targets for those escapees. A line between the four listed states to the target cities in Pennsylvania runs directly through Northern Virginia. It is no coincidence that those are cities inhabited by a number of Quaker and Amish families. The Quakers and Amish did not believe in slavery and many were active in the Underground Railroad helping slaves get across the Potomac River into Pennsylvania. Thus, toward the end of their journey, runaway slaves traveled from Quaker homes in Virginia to Quaker homes in Pennsylvania.

The Schendler family, whose farm is the setting for the story, was involved directly in the Underground Railroad process by hiding runaway slaves in their winery basement and helping them move on to their destination across the Pennsylvania border. That fact played into the story when it became necessary to find workers for the fields in those years following the war.

- The Ku Klux Klan

During the period following the Civil War, the Ku Klux Klan sprang up all over the South. Law enforcement was almost nonexistent in some areas, and there was an overriding fear of the freed slaves and what their actions might be toward their former masters. Many names were applied to the Ku Klux Klan in the various areas of the south. In Northern Virginia, the Klan was called the White Knights of the Camelia.

The Ku Klux Klan was especially strong in Alabama, Georgia, and South Carolina. In some areas of the south, they exerted an inordinate amount of control and pressure on the people, the governmental units that were being reestablished, and even on the presiding military administration. In Northern Virginia, however, the White Knights flourished for a very short time and disappeared.

No one seems to be able to account for why the Klan did not last long in the Winchester area of Virginia. In truth, we don't know what happened to them, just that they appeared and, just as suddenly, disappeared in that period just after the war ended. Our story gives a plausible explanation for the disappearance of the Klan from the Northern Virginia region.

- Horses

Matt's horse, Big Billy, appears and reappears in the story from beginning to end. Matt acquired this beautiful bay horse when he spent the night on the battlefield at Brandy Station during the third year of the war as he was searching for his father. (See the chapter entitled, "Fighting the Good Fight" in *Journey to Gettysburg* for the details of this story.) When he arrived on the Schendler Farm, Mr. Schendler suggested to him that such a fine horse must have belonged to an officer. Indeed, during the Civil War, there was a big bay horse that was the property of cavalry officer Wade Hampton, who was second in command of General Lee's cavalry under the leadership General JEB Stuart. Wade Hampton was from Charleston, South Carolina, and his horse, Butler, was raised on a plantation just outside the city. Hampton was injured in the battle at Brandy Station, cut on the back of the head by a saber, and was knocked unconscious. He lost his big bay horse and did not find him again for the remainder of the war.

It is ironic that Wade Hampton might appear in Richmond, Virginia, four years after losing his horse at Brandy Station, attending

THE WOUNDS OF WAR

the same Virginia Constitutional Convention meeting that drew Isaac Mason to the city. In this book, Hampton and Isaac Mason made contact and had a conversation about Big Billy, who was being taken care of in a livery stable behind the Richmond Hotel. Hampton's comments about seeing the horse in the livery stable makes for an interesting twist in the plot late in the story.

- Collapse of the Virginia Court of Appeals Building

The collapse of the largest public building in Richmond, Virginia, was a major tragedy killing fifty-eight people and injuring more than two hundred. That tragedy occurred as a group was gathering for the opening session of a major meeting. The two-story building was constructed of wood, with the major meeting area on the second floor. It had a balcony that held approximately two hundred seats. Promptly at 11:00 a.m. on April 27, 1870, with the building almost full, the balcony collapsed and fell onto the main floor which, in turn, collapsed and fell into the smaller meeting area below. Written descriptions of the tragedy reported chaos with police and firemen, making every effort to provide aid and the injured and dead lying all over the grounds of the facility.

This is an event that is true to history and fits well into our story. However, it is necessary to point out that though all other aspects of its presentation in the story are accurate, the date is not. To fit into our story, it needed to have occurred in December of 1867. The actual date was April of 1870. This is the only historical fact in the entire book the writer took license with in order to fit it to the story.

It should be pointed out that there were many who were described as heroes of the tragedy, who risked their lives to save others who had been injured. Many of those were identified but many more were not. That fact also fits well into the story in its latter chapters.

AFTERWORD

Several issues remain unresolved as the story concludes. As is always the case, sometimes the unresolved parts of a story are as interesting as the parts that are resolved. Does Isaac Mason follow his illustrious father into politics and make his presence known in Virginia governmental circles? Will the expansion of the Schendler Winery continue to make the family a factor in the marketplace for their unique flavor of wine? Will Matt and Ami Ruth add other children to the family, thus insuring another generation of Masons in Virginia's history? Speculation on the possibilities keeps the story alive into the future. That is my intent with the story of Matt Mason and his growing family. If you enjoyed this story, I expect that you may read a sequel at some point in the not-too-distant future—a sequel of the sequel, if you please. And you may also expect to find Matt's big bay horse, Big Billy, still popular among the mares in the region.

ABOUT THE AUTHOR

Born in Missouri and a long-time resident of South Carolina, Dr. Mark L. Hopkins is a midwesterner by birth and a Southerner by choice. He holds three degrees from Missouri universities. He taught history for several years and is past president of four colleges, one each in the states of Iowa, Illinois, South Carolina, and in California. Dr. Hopkins writes a weekly column that is syndicated by GateHouse Media and is regularly published across twenty-nine states and more than five hundred newspapers. Dr. Hopkins' wife, Ruth, is a professional artist, and they have three grown children and six grandchildren that range in ages from seven to twenty-two.

The Civil War and its aftermath is a part of history that comes alive to Dr. Hopkins. Twelve of his ancestors fought in the battle of Gettysburg, four for the North and eight for the South. When one steps onto the sacred ground of that battlefield, you are stepping into the history of the Hopkins family. *The Wounds of War* begins when the Civil War ends and captures the drama for the people as they attempt to cope with the many new conflicts brought about by the five years of conflict with their neighbors to the north.

CPSIA information can be obtained
at www.ICGtesting.com
Printed in the USA
FFOW05n1847100117